A Garland Series

Foundations of the Novel

Representative Early

Eighteenth-Century Fiction

A collection of 100 rare titles
reprinted in photo-facsimile in 71 volumes

Foundations of the Novel

compiled and edited by

Michael F. Shugrue

Secretary for English for the M.L.A.

with New Introductions for each volume by

Michael Shugrue, *City College of C.U.N.Y.*
Malcolm J. Bosse, *City College of C.U.N.Y.*
William Graves, *N.Y. Institute of Technology*
Josephine Grieder, *Rutgers University, Newark*

The History
and Adventures of
Gil Blas of Santillane

by

Alain René Le Sage

in two volumes

Vol. I

with a new introduction
for the Garland Edition by
Josephine Grieder

Garland Publishing, Inc., New York & London

1972

Bibliographical note:
*This facsimile has been made from a copy in the
Houghton Library of Harvard University
(*FC7 L5633 Eg716h V.1)*

Library of Congress Cataloging in Publication Data

Le Sage, Alain René, 1668-1747
    The history and adventures of Gil Blas of Santillane.

    (Foundations of the novel)
    Reprint of the 1716 translation of the first 6 books
of L'histoire de Gil Blas de Santillane.
    I. Title. II. Title: Gil Blas of Santillane.
III. Series.
PZ3.L5635Hi3 [PQ1997]   843'.5   74-170537
ISBN 0-8240-0539-2 (v.1)

Introduction

In the history of the novel, there is no lack of authors who achieve success by imitating those who preceded them; but when an author who borrows and imitates manages to infuse his work with his own vitality and originality, the book is likely to become a classic. Such is the case with The History and Adventures of Gil Blas of Santillane *by Alain René Le Sage. The form was traditional enough: the picaresque novel, which relates the varied fortunes and misfortunes of a wandering hero, dates at least as far back as 1599 to Mateo Aleman's* Guzman de Alfarache. *Stories interpolated to enliven the principal narrative were a standard device in the multi-volume historical romances of the seventeenth century like* Astrée, Le Grand Cyrus, *and* Clélie *and in the realistic bourgeois novels of Scarron and Furetière.* Gil Blas *owes many of its incidents to the* Relaciones de la Vida del Escudero Marcos de Obregon *(1618) by Vincente Espinel; anecdotes related by other Spanish authors like Estevanillo Gonzales, Guevara, Rojas, and Antonio de Mendez are also incorporated. And yet* Gil Blas *surpasses them all: in its tableau of eighteenth-century French society at all levels; in its incisive portraits of man as a social and professional animal; and most of all, in its presentation of Gil Blas himself, who, unlike the vulgar, unchanging* pícaro, *passes from youthful naiveté to a worldly-wise and benevolent old age.*

5

INTRODUCTION

The first English edition of 1716 here presented will not demonstrate the breadth of the French novel for a very simple reason: it is not complete. Le Sage wrote the first two volumes — that is, the first six books — in 1715. In 1724 he added three more books and in 1735 still another three; and it is in these last six books that one sees Gil Blas in the highest political and social circles, as valet to the Archbishop of Granada, as secretary to the duc de Lerme and the prime minister Olivarès, and finally as an old man, happily retired, married, and surrounded by children. Nevertheless, these first six books set the stage for further development and establish Le Sage's title to accuracy of observation and pungent presentation of character.

That Le Sage was from the beginning aware of the scope of his project is evident from the two prefaces. "I make this publick Confession, That all I aim'd at was to represent the Life of Man such as it is," he declares in "The Author to the Reader." He eschews specifically personal satire for the general and admits that he has "not always exactly imitated the Manners of the Spaniards," *but "The same Vices, the same Originals are everywhere to be met with." "Gil Blas to the Reader" affirms the moral intent of the novel: "If thou readest my Adventures without having regard to the Moral Instructions that are contain'd in them, this Work will be of no Use to Thee, but if thou readest them with Attention, thou wilt meet with the Utile and the Dulce, according to the Rule of Horace."*

Books I, II, and III contained in this first volume are

structured loosely, in terms of the variety of anecdotal material in them, but they have a degree of unity which should be remarked upon. In Book I the naive scholar Gil Blas, presumably on his way to the University of Salamanca, is tricked and gulled by those he encounters and even imprisoned by robbers. At the very end of the book he meets an old friend, Fabricius, who delivers such a panegyric on the position of valet that Gil Blas definitively chooses his profession. In Book II Gil Blas exercises his new métier under various masters; old acquaintances from Book I reappear to tell their stories, and a strolling player introduces toward the end the theme of theatrical life. In Book III Gil continues as a valet for a set of employers considerably more worldly than the previous ones; servant to a rich man, then to a beau, then to an actress — the theater theme reintroduced — he is disillusioned by this sort of life and resolves to quit it.

As Gil Blas passes from milieu to milieu, his character progressively develops. Le Sage sets up his hero carefully in the first chapter; what he will become is directly related to the traits he reveals from the beginning. He is intelligent; educated by his uncle the canon and then by "the most able Pedant of Orviedo" (p. 3), he knows Greek, Latin, and "Logick." But he is also a natural knave: not only does he feign extraordinary grief at parting from his uncle, which charms the old man into giving him more money than he had intended, but he also steals a few extra reals *from his aged relative.*

A young man with such a character is, however, no

match for experienced rascality, and the naive hero is promptly gulled by innkeepers, mule dealers, and parasites. He is, for example, taken in by a stranger's extravagant praise of his reputation as a prodigy of learning and treats him to a costly meal. "Had I had ever so little Experience, 'twould have been impossible for me to be bubbled by his Hyperbole's; *I should have smelt his extravagant Flattery," the wiser narrator reflects, "But my Youth and my Vanity made me judge of him otherwise" (p. 13). Though filled with spite and shame, Gil does not immediately profit from this lesson; he continues to be cheated throughout the first book by knaves like Camilla and Raphael who play upon his inexperience and flatter his vanity. But by the end of Book I, he begins to have a better grasp of the world.*

Perhaps what makes Gil Blas such a sympathetic character throughout is the ingenuous candor with which he admits his virtues and vices — though he never thinks of them in those moralistic terms. He is totally pliable; to suit his masters, he will play up to stewards, espouse Doctor Sangrado's incompetent medical theories, even fake love letters which dishonor a virtuous woman. He is impressionable; he apes the beaux' valets and participates in the actors' revelry. "I was shock'd with their Defects," he admits, "But 'twas my Misfortune to take Delight in this Way of Living, and to plunge myself in Debauchery. How could I help it? All their Discourse was pernicious to Youth, and I saw nothing but what contributed to corrupt me" (p. 353). He has the capacity to land on his feet in difficulty, a sense of

8

self-interest which prevails over moral responsibility. When he finds his master Don Matthias killed in a duel over the false love letters, "The sight drew Tears from me, and especially when I consider'd that he had made me the Instrument of his Death. But notwithstanding my Grief, I thought of what I had to do for my own Interest on this Occasion" (p. 329). But he still retains some moral sense. The pleasures of life among the actors eventually appall him, and "in the midst of them, I often felt that Remorse which came from my Education, and imbitter'd all my Sweets: Debauchery, could not triumph over that Remorse; on the contrary, it encreas'd in proportion with it, and by an effect of my natural Disposition, I began to conceive a Horror for the Disorder of the Players Lives" (p. 355). It is this horror which leads him to quit that milieu at the very end of Book III and prepares the way for more honorable enjoyment in the next volume.

The people and the milieux which Gil frequents during these first three books are, on the whole, neither admirable nor particularly edifying. He is persuaded to become a valet by Fabricius' eloquent definition of duties: " 'Tis a fine Cure: If a Master has Vices, a good Genius will know how to humour them, and make his Advantage of them. A Valet lives at his Ease; he eats and drinks his fill, sleeps soundly, and has no Care to disturb him" (p. 120). And certainly the servants he meets fit his friend's description; they are loyal to their masters only in the hope of receiving legacies; they ape their manners, dress, and debauchery; they cheat them as

INTRODUCTION

often as they can. When, as the valet of a beau and steward of an actress, he is introduced into their strata, he becomes involved in a continual round of carousing, licentiousness, debts, insulting gossip, and foolishness.

A nice juxtaposition of social conditions occurs in the first book. Gil Blas, with his uncle's gift, is captured by robbers, who treat him courteously with the intent to make him a perpetually subterranean scullery boy. Rolando the captain urges him to consider his good fortune in having an established place and counsels that he should have no "scruple about living with Robbers. Who are there in the World that are not such? Every Man loves to take another Man's Goods from him; this Sentiment is general; the manner of doing it is only different" (p. 40). When Gil at last escapes, having providently equipped himself with booty as well as his own money, he is promptly imprisoned on a false charge. When released by the police, he has been stripped of clothes and money: "it seems the Formalities of their Office required it, and they call it doing their Duty" (p. 87). Gil in fact meets up with Captain Rolando once again and finds he has bought the post of a sergeant; but, laments the former highwayman, "I do not at all like my Profession. It requires too much Tricking and Cunning for me" (pp. 260-261).

The most sustained satirical attack in the first volume is that on the medical profession. Any sick person who confides himself to a physician is carried off immediately; if he chooses two doctors, they squabble so over methodology that he dies anyway. The epitome of the

10

INTRODUCTION

ignorant, callous physician is Gil Blas' second master Sangrado who believes that for health, "all that is necessary, is Bleeding, and Draughts of hot Water" (p. 152). His motives for such a prescription are notably ignominious: miserliness — his servants eat little and never taste wine — and personal vanity, for he has written a book defending his regime and will not renounce his principles even when Gil Blas convinces him of their harmfulness. Since he pays Gil nothing, he sends him out as his emissary to treat common patients, and Gil dutifully and lethally prescribes his master's regime. The practical Fabricius commends him on this appointment: "A Suburb-Doctor for my Money: His Faults are less in View; and his Murders make no Noise" (p. 155). During a smallpox epidemic, Gil confesses, "in less than six Weeks we made as many Widows and Orphans as the Siege of Troy" (p. 179).

By the end of the third book, Gil Blas has progressed a considerable distance from the naive youth destined for the university. By being cheated, he has been put on his guard; by frequenting cheaters, he has learned their tricks. He is not, however, corrupt; though he may put self-interest ahead of moral responsibility, his actions are motivated not by malice but by a desire to survive. He has seen enough of the unvirtuous and unscrupulous to recognize them for what they are. In the next three books, he will have an opportunity to meet more admirable characters.

Josephine Grieder

11

The History
of GIL BLAS,
of Santillan.

THE
HISTORY
AND
ADVENTURES
OF
GIL BLAS
OF
SANTILLANE.

𝕴𝖓 𝕿𝖜𝖔 𝖁𝖔𝖑𝖚𝖒𝖊𝖘.

VOL. I.

LONDON:
Printed for JACOB TONSON, at *Shake-
fpear's-Head* in the *Strand.* 1716.

THE

AUTHOR

TO THE

READER.

 HERE being some Per-
sons who cannot read a
Book without making
Vicious and Ridiculous
Applications of the Cha-
racters they find in it ; I declare to
those Malicious Readers, that they
will be in the Wrong if they apply
the Portraits in this to particular Persons. I make this publick Confession, That all I aim'd at was to represent the Life of Man such as it is.

To the READER.

God forbid I fhould have a Defign to mark out any Perfon in particular. Let no Reader therefore take that to Himfelf which fuits others as well as him : Otherwife, as *Phædra* fays, he will fhew himfelf *mal a propos, ftulte nudabit, animi confcientiam.*

There are Phyficians in *Caftile* as well as in *France,* whofe Method is to bleed their Patients too much. The fame Vices, the fame Originals are every where to be met with. I own I have not always exactly imitated the Manners of the *Spaniards,* and thofe that know what diforderly Lives the Players at *Madrid* lead, may blame me for not painting them in more lively Colours ; but I thought it proper to foften fome Parts of them, that they might be more conformable to our way of living in *France.*

GIL

GIL BLAS

TO THE

READER.

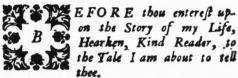

BEFORE thou enterest upon the Story of my Life, Hearken, Kind Reader, to the Tale I am about to tell thee.

Two Scholars going together from Pe-nafiel to Salamanca, and finding them-selves weary and faint, stopp'd by the side of a Fountain which they came to in their Way. As they were resting themselves there, they by chance spy'd a Stone with some Words written upon it, almost effaced by Time, and the Feet of the Flocks that came to drink at that Spring: They wash'd the Dirt off the Stone; and when they

cou'd

To the READER.

cou d read the Words *diftinctly, they found This Infcription in the* Caftilian *Tongue :* Aqui efta encerrada el alma del Licenciado Pedro Garcias : "*The Soul* " *of the Licentiate* Pedro Garcias *is* " *here enclofed. The Youngeft of the Scholars, a brisk blunt Boy, had no fooner read the Infcription, but he laugh'd and cry'd,* The Soul here enclofed,---- a Soul enclofed ? I would fain know the Author of fuch a foolifh Epitaph. *His Companion who had more Judgment, faid to himfelf, There muft be fome Myftery in it ; I'll ftay and fee whether I can find it out. Accordingly, he let the other Scholar go before him, and when he was gone, he pull'd out his Knife, and dug up the Earth about the Stone, which at laft he remov'd, and found under it a Leather Purfe which he open'd. There were a Hundred Ducats in it, with a Card, wherein was written in* Latin *to this Effect.* Be thou my Heir, Thou who haft Wit enough to find out the Meaning of this Infcription, and make a better ufe of my Money than I did. *The Scholar was overjoy'd at*
this

To the READER.

this *Discovery, cover'd the Place with the Stone again, and proceeded to* Salamanca *with the Soul of the Licenciate in his Pocket.*

Whoever thou art, Kind Reader, that art going to resemble one or t'other of these Two Scholars : If thou readest my Adventures without having regard to the Moral Instructions that are contain'd in them, this Work will be of no Use to Thee ; but if thou readest them with Attention, thou wilt meet with the Utile *and the* Dulce, *according to the Rule of* Horace.

THE

THE
CONTENTS.

BOOK I.

Chap

The CONTENTS.

BOOK II.

The CONTENTS.

BOOK III.

The CONTENTS.

THE
HISTORY
OF
GIL BLAS
OF
SANTILLANE.

BOOK I.

CHAP. I.

Of GIL BLAS's *Birth and Education.*

LAS of Santillane, my Father, having a long time born Arms for the Service of the *Spanish* Monarchy, retir'd at last to the Town he was born in, where he married a Woman that could by no means be said to be in the Flower of her Youth. At ten Months

Vol. I.   B   end

end I came into the World; and they
afterwards remov'd to *Oviedo*, where
my Mother serv'd a Gentleman in the
Quality of a Chamber-maid, and my
Father in that of Groom. As they
had nothing to live upon but their
Wages, I should have been in danger of a
very indifferent Education, if I had
not had a Canon for my Uncle. Imagine to your self a little Man of three
Foot and a half high, with a Head
sunk into his Shoulders: Such a one was
this Uncle of mine. He was a Priest
who minded nothing but good Living,
I mean good Cheer; and his Tythes,
which were pretty considerable, furnish'd him with the means of doing it,
according to his Appetite.

He took me from a Child, and had
the Care of Breeding me up. My Parts
were so promising, that he resolv'd to
cultivate them. He bought me a Horn-
book, and undertook to teach me to
read himself, which was no small Im-
provement of his own Reading also;
for by teaching me my Letters, he recovered the Knowledge of them, which
he had lost by long Dif-ufe; and thus in
a little while he could run over his
Breviary very cleverly, which he could
not

not do before. He would fain have
taught me *Latin* too; it would have
fav'd him fome Money in his Pocket;
but ah, poor *Gil Perez!* he knew not how
many Parts of Speech there were. He
was perhaps (for I would not be too
pofitive in afferting it) the moft ignorant
Canon of all the Chapter. I have been
told that he got his Benefice, not by
his Learning, but by the Favour of
fome Nuns, for whom he had
prov'd a difcreet and fuccefsful Agent;
and they had Intereft enough to get him
admitted into Orders, without pafling
thro' any Examination. His Ignorance
obliged him to put me to School; accordingly he fent me to Dr. *Sodiner*, who
had the Character of the moft able Pedant of *Oviedo*. I made fo good Ufe
of his Leffons, that in 5 or 6 Years
time I underftood fomething of the
Greek Authors, and was tolerably well
acquainted with the *Latin*. I applied my
felf alfo to *Logick*, which help'd me out
at a Pinch, when I was put to it for
want of Argument, as it often happen'd
to me, thro' an inordinate Defire of
Difputation; which I was fo fond of,
that I frequently ftopt People as they
went along the Streets, whether I knew

them

them or not, to propose Arguments to them. I sometimes met with some *Irishmen*, who lov'd disputing as well as my self, and we made rare Work of it. Lord, what Grimaces! What Gestures! What Curtericens! Fire sparkled in our Eyes, and we always foamed at the Mouth: Every one that saw us, ought to have taken us rather for Madmen than Philosophers.

By this means I acquir'd the Reputation of a learned Person, and my Uncle was overjoyed to find me so forward, hoping 'twould ease him of any farther Expence about me. So, *Gil Blas*, says he to me one Day, Thou art out of thy Childhood, 'tis time for thee to provide for thy self; thou art Eighteen, and a notable Lad: I think to send thee to the University of *Salamanca*; thou can'st not fail of getting some Employment or other there. I will give thee my Mule, which is worth ten or twelve Pistoles, and put some Ducats in thy Pocket. Thou mayest sell the Mule at *Salamanca*, and live upon the Money till thou canst get thee a Place.

He could not have made me a more agreeable Proposal; for I long'd mightily to see the Country: However I did

not

not let him fee it. I concealed my
Joy; and when we parted, I feem'd to be
fo griev'd at my leaving an Uncle who
had been fo kind to me, that the good
Man was touch'd with it, and gave me
more Money than I fhould have had
of him, had he known the bottom of
my Soul. Before I departed I took
leave of my Father and Mother, who
fail'd not to give me very good Counfel: They admonifh'd me to pray for
my Uncle, to avoid ill Company, and
above all things to beware of wronging
any body, and taking what was not my
own. After a long Harangue of this
kind, they made me a Prefent of their
Blefling, the only Gift I had of them:
I mounted my Mule, and quitted *Oviedo.*

CHAP. II.

How he was alarm'd as he was going to
Penafler; what he did when he came
thither, and with whom he fupp'd.

BEing got out of Town in the Road
to *Penafler*, Mafter of my own Actions, of a forry Mule, and forty good Ducats

cats, befides fome Reals which I had
ftolen from my moft honoured Uncle:
The firft thing I did was to give my
Mule her Head, and to go at what
Pace fhe pleas'd : I threw the Bridle on
her Neck, took the Ducats out of my
Pocket, and told them over and over
in my Hat. I had never feen fo much
Money in all my Life, and I could not
help telling it and handling it. I fuppofe it might be about the twentieth
time of telling, when my Mule prick'd
up her Ears, and ftopt in the middle
of the High-way. I imagined fhe was
frighted, and looking to fee what was
the Occafion of it, I faw a Hat on the
Ground, with a huge Rofary upon it,
and heard a lamentable Voice pronouncing
thefe Words, *Have pity*, Signior, *on a
poor Cripp'd Soldier : For the Lord's fake
throw fome of thofe Pieces into my Hat :
God will reward you for it in the other
World.* Turning my Head to the Place
from whence the Voice came, I fpy'd
a kind of a Soldier under a Hedge ten
Yards off me. He held out a Pole,
which feem'd to me to be as long as
a Pike, and rather intended for Arms
than for a Support. At fight of this
I fell into a Panick, and did not know
              what

what to do. In the firſt Place I took
care of my Ducats, put 'em in my
Pocket, and pull'd out ſome Reals.
I then approach'd the Hat, which was
diſpos'd to receive the Charity of all
frighted Believers: I threw them into
it one after another, to let the Soldier
ſee how generous I was. He was ſatisfied with my noble way of Proceed-
ing, and gave me as many Bleſſings as
I gave Strokes with my Heel into my
Mule's Sides, to get him from him as
faſt as I could; but the curs'd Jade
made not the greater Speed for it; ſhe
had been ſo long us'd to go my Uncle's
ſlow Pace, juſt one Leg before t'other,
that ſhe had forgot what a Gallop was.

I did not at all like this Omen: I
thought to my ſelf, I am not got to
Salamanca yet, and ſomething worſe
than this may befal me before I get
thither: My Uncle ſhould not have let
me go by my ſelf: but doubtleſs he did
it to ſave Charges, and not conſider'd
the Risk I run in travelling alone at my
Years. I therefore reſolved as ſoon as
I came to *Penaſter* to ſell my Mule, and
go by the Carrier to *Aſtorga*, and ſo
to *Salamanca* after the ſame manner. Tho'
I had never been out of *Oviedo*, I knew

the Names of the Towns I was to pass
thro', having inform'd my self of them
before my Departure.

Being arrived at *Penafler*, I stopt at
the Gate of an Inn, which made a
pretty good Appearance. I no sooner
alighted than the Man of the House came
and receiv'd me very civilly. He unty'd
my Portmanteau, put it upon his Shoulders, and conducted me to my Chamber: The Hostler took my Mule, and led
it into the Stable. My Landlord was
the most talkative Person of all his Fraternity; and whether there was occasion for it or no, was very free to tell
one all his private Affairs. He was no
less inquisitive about those that did not
concern him. He told me his Name
was *Andrea Corcuelo*, that he had serv'd
in the Army many Years as a Serjeant,
and had quitted the Service 15 Months
before, to marry a young Woman of
Castropol, who, tho' she was no Beauty,
did the Business of the House well e-
nough. He told me abundance of other
Things, which I was not very fond of
hearing; and in return for so great Confidence, he thought I could do no less
than satisfie his Demands who I was,
and whence I came. He would needs
                                    have

have me anfwer him Article by Article,
accompanying every Queftion with a
Paufe and a low Bow, praying me to excufe his Curiofity, and that with fo
much Refpect, that I could not help fatisfying it. This neceffarily drew me
into a long Conference with him, and
gave me an Opportunity to talk of my
defign to difpofe of my Mule, and go
the reft of my Journey by the Carrier.
He highly approved of my Reafons, and
reprefented to me the many fad Accidents I might be expofed to on the Road,
telling me feveral difmal Stories of Travellers, which he exaggerated and enlarg'd on fo much, I thought he would
never have done. At laft he came to
the Cafe, and faid, If I would fell my
Mule, he knew an honeft Jobber who
would buy it of me. I let him know
I fhould think my felf mightily oblig'd
for that piece of Service ; and he went
immediately to fetch my Chapman.

He foon returned, and brought his Man
with him, whom he recommended for
his Honefty : The Mule was led out
into the Yard, and we three went to
view it. My Chapman examin'd it
from Head to Foot, and made the
Hoftler ride him up and down the Yard,

which

which did not at all add to the Credit of the Beaſt. The Jobber found a hundred Faults with it, and truly there was not much Good to be ſaid of it; but if it had been the Pope's Mule the Fellow would have had ſomething to ſay againſt it. He ſwore mine was good for nothing; and to convince me of the Truth of what he ſaid, he obliged my Landlord to vouch for it, who doubtleſs had his Reaſons to ſay what the Jobber would have him. The latter turning to me, ſaid gruffly, You would not impoſe ſuch a Beaſt upon me for a good one, I hope; he is not worth driving home. After he and my Hoſt had paſt Judgment upon my Mule, I took it for granted that he was as bad as they made him to be. I therefore threw myſelf on the Honeſty of the Jobber, and bad him give me for it what he thought in his Conſcience it was worth. My Man pretending to be a Perſon of ſtrict Honour, reply'd, That by referring it to his Conſcience, I had taken him by the weak Side, and indeed I found it was not his ſtrongeſt; for inſtead of coming up to the Value my Uncle ſet upon it of ten or twelve Piſtoles, he had the Impudence to rate

it

it at three Ducats ; which I took with as much Joy as if I had gain'd by the Bargain.

Having difpos'd of my Mule fo advantageoufly, my Hoft carried me to a Carrier, who was to fet out next Day to *Aftorga* : The Carrier faid he fhould be going before Day-light, and that he would come and call me. We agreed for the Price, as well for the Mule he was to provide me, as for my Maintenance on the Road ; and when that was done, I return'd with *Corcuclo* to my Inn. My Landlord told me the Hiftory of the Carrier by the way, and what the People faid of him there. He deafned me with his Babbling, and I believe would have murder'd me with it, if by good luck a Man who look'd like a Gentleman had not come and interrupted him. I left 'em together, and went towards my Room, not dreaming that I was at all concern'd in their Converfation.

I called for Supper, and it being a Faft-Day, they accommodated me with fome Eggs : While they were getting them I enter'd into Difcourfe with my Landlady, whom I had not feen before. She was not over-handfome, but had

had fuch a Way with her, that if her Huf-
band had not told me, I fhould have
guefs'd that fhe knew how to do the
Bufinefs of his Houfe. When my Eggs
were ready I fat down at Table by my
felf: Before I could put a Bit into my
Mouth, in comes my Hoft, and brings
in with him the Man I fpoke of, who
took him off from his long Tale to me
about the Muletier : The Gentleman
had a Sword by his Side, and was
thirty Years of Age: He came up to
me with a very folemn Look, and accofted me thus, Mr. Scholar, I am inform'd you are Signor *Gil Blas* of *Santillane*, the Ornament of *Oviedo*, and the
Flambeau of Philofophy. Is it poffible
that your Scholarfhip fhould be fo deep,
and that you are the Perfon whofe Wit
is fo much talk'd of in this Country ?
You don't know, continues he, addreffing
himfelf to my Landlord and Landlady,
what a Man you have in your Houfe:
He is a Treafure, and the Eighth Wonder of the World. He then turn'd to
me, and taking me about the Neck,
Pardon, fays he, young Gentleman,
Pardon my Tranfports; the Sight of
you gives me fo much Joy, that I am not
my own Mafter.

I

I did not know what to fay to him, in return for his extraordinary Compliment ; and befides he held me fo faft that I could hardly fetch Breath. With much ado I got loofe of him, and reply'd, Signor, I did not think that any Body knew my Name at *Penafler*. How, fays he, not know your Name ? We keep a Regifter of all illuftrious Perfons within twenty Leagues round us : You pafs for a Prodigy, and I doubt not but one time or other *Spain* will be as proud of having produc'd you, as *Greece* was of having given Birth to the Seven Wife Men. Thefe Words were accompanied with frefh Embraces, which I was forced to undergo, tho' with the Peril of being ferv'd as *Antbeus* was. Had I had ever fo little Experience, 'twould have been impoffible for me to be bubbled by his *Hyperbole's*; I fhould have fmelt his extravagant Flattery, and have found out that he was one of thofe Parafites that are to be met with in all Cities, ready to break in upon any Stranger, and cram himfelf at his Expence : But my Youth and my Vanity made me judge of him otherwife. I took him for a Man of great Honour and Judgment, and invited him to Sup with me.

With

With all my Heart, cries he, I rejoyce too much in my good Fortune, in having met with the renowned *Gil Blas* of *Santillane,* not to take hold of so glorious an Opportunity of enjoying his Company, and having as much of it as I can. I have no great Stomach, continued he, I will however eat a Bit or two out of Complaisance. He then sat himself down over against me : A Napkin was brought him, and a fresh supply of Eggs, which he swallowed as fast as if he had not eat in three Days. That Parcel were soon dispatch'd, and then another and another ; he all the while finding leisure to overwhelm me with his Elogies, not omitting my Person ; which I took very kindly of him, tho it was not of a Size to be the Subject of Panegyrick. He drank often ; sometimes it was my Health, sometimes my Father's and Mother's, whose Happiness, in having such a Son, he could never enough admire. Every now and then he would fill up my Glass, and urge me to pledge him in a Bumper to such agreeable Toasts. I was not backward in obliging him ; and the Wine and his Flattery put me into so good a Humour, that I was not satisfied with

a

a Supper of Eggs, I muft have fome
Fifh alfo for him. Signor *Corcuelo*, who
no queftion had an Underftanding with
the Parafite, faid, he had an excellent
Trout in the Houfe, but it would come
dear, and was too nice a Difh for me.
Too nice, faid my Flatterer, raifing
his Voice ? You forget your felf, Friend,
Can any thing be too nice for Signor
Gil Blas de Santillane ? He deferves to be
treated like a Prince.

I was very glad that he took up my
Landlord fo : I was going to do it my
felf. And when he had done, cry'd,
*Bring your Trout, Sir, and don't you trouble
your felf about the Nicenefs of it.* That
was what the Hoft wanted. The Trout
was prefently got ready, and ferv'd up
to Table. At the Sight of this new Difh
I perceiv'd the Parafite's Eyes fparkled
with Joy ; and he eat of that with the
fame Complacency that he difpatch'd
the Eggs. At laft he was forc'd to give
over, for fear of an ill Accident, having
cramm'd himfelf up to the Throat ;
and to finifh the Farce, he rofe from the
Table, faying, Signor *Gil Blas*, I am
too well pleas'd with your Entertainment, to leave you without giving you
fome important Advice, which you feem

to ſtand in need of. Beware hereafter of
Flattery: Be upon your Guard againſt
Men whom you have no Knowledge
of: You may find others, who will,
like me, impoſe upon your Credulity,
and perhaps carry the Matter farther.
Be not their Cully, and do not take
their Word, if they tell you, you are
the Eighth Wonder of the World. Saying this, he laught in my Face and retired. I was as much out of Countenance at having this Trick put upon me
as ever I was at the greateſt Diſgraces
that happened to me in the Courſe of
my Life. I could not bear being ſo
groſly bubbled, or rather to have my
Pride ſo mortify'd. How, ſaid I to my
ſelf, has the Traytor made a Jeſt of me?
He was ſo cloſe with my Landlord, to
carry on his Plot againſt me: 'Twas a
Contrivance between them. Ah poor
Gil Blas, go hang thy ſelf, for Shame of
being made Sport of by ſuch Raſcals.
They'll make a fine Story of it, which
will ſoon get to *Oviedo,* and be a migh-
ty Honour to thee. Thy Parents will
doubtleſs repent that they took ſo much
Pains in inſtructing a Dunce not to cheat
any Body. They ſhould ſurely have exhorted me not to be cheated my ſelf.
                                        Thus

Thus, full of Spite and Shame, I lock'd my felf up in my Chamber, and went to Bed, but I could not fleep a Wink: The Muletier came at Break-of-Day to tell me he ftaid for me. I got up; and while I was dreffing me, *Corouclo* brought in his Bill, where the Trout was not forgotten. He not only charg'd every thing at his own Prices, but I obferv'd, when I paid him, the Rogue grinn'd at the Thought of my Adventure. My Reckoning being difcharg'd, I went with my Portmanteau to the Carrier, giving a hearty Curfe to the Parafite, my Hoft, and his Inn.

CHAP. III.

Of a Temptation that befel the Muletier on the Road : What happened thereupon: And how Gil Blas *fell out of the Frying-Pan into the Fire.*

I Was not the only Perfon that travell'd with the Muletier : There were two Lads of *Penafler*, a little Quiriftier of *Vendonedo,* who went from place to place to fing where they would hire

him

him, and a young Man of *Aſtorga*, who
was returning home with a Girl he had
lately Married at *Verco*. We were preſently acquainted, and told one another
whence we came, and whither we
were going. The Bride, tho' ſhe was
young, was ſo ugly, and ſo ſluttiſh, that
I took no great Delight in looking upon her: Nevertheleſs her Youth and her
Size, which was not of the ſmalleſt,
render'd her agreeable in the Eyes of
the Muletier, who reſolv'd to do his
utmoſt to gain her good Graces. He
ſpent the Day in contriving how to
effect it, and adjourned the Execution
of it till Night. Our Muletier reſted
at *Cacabelos*, and put up at the firſt
Inn we came to, which was more in
the Country than in the Town. The
Man of the Houſe was, it ſeems, a di-
ſcreet, complaiſant Perſon, and at the
Muletier's Requeſt he ſhew'd us to a
Room apart from the reſt of the Inn,
where we order'd Supper to be brought
us. When we had almoſt ſupp'd, the
Muletier enter'd the Room, and cry'd,
S'Death, I am robb'd; I had a hundred
Piſtoles in a Leather-Bag; I'll have 'em
again I warrant you. I am going to the
Magiſtrate of the Town, who won't
make

make it a Jesting Matter, but will put
every Man of you to the Torture, till
you confess the Crime, and restore the
Money : Saying this very seriously, he
left us all in a terrible Consternation.
We did not imagine it was a Feint of
his. We knew nothing of one another.
I suspected the Quirister had done the
Feat, and perhaps he suspected the same
of me. We were not acquainted with
the Formalities practis'd on the like Oc-
casions. We doubted not but we should
indeed be rack'd; and being also extremely terrified, we shifted every one
for himself : Some ran into the Street,
others into the Garden : All of us endeavoured to save ourselves by Flight,
and the young Man of *Astorga*, who
was in as great a Fright as any one of
us, made his Escape like another *Æneas*,
not mattering what became of his Wife.
The Muletier, as I learnt afterwards,
was overjoyed that this Stratagem succeeded so well, and went to brag of
his Artifice to the Bride, intending to
take hold of the Opportunity it had
given him. But this *Lucretia* of the *A-*
sturias, whose Virtue was fortify'd by
the Deformity of her Tempter, made a
vigorous Resistance, and cry'd out so loud,
that

that she was heard by the Watch, who by chance were coming that way ; and the Inn being a House of no good Fame, stept to hearken what pass'd there. They entred it upon hearing a Noise, and demanded what was the Matter ? The Inn-keeper was in the Kitchen, and whistled as if he knew not what was doing ; but the Watch oblig'd him to shew them to the Room where the Noise was made. They came at the nick of Time, for the Woman could hold out no longer. The Officer who commanded the Watch no sooner saw what the Muletier was about, than he fell upon him with his Staff, and rated him in Terms as impudent as the Action which was the Occasion of them. That was not all ; he seiz'd the Criminal, and carried him before the Magistrate, together with the Woman who had been assaulted, she not minding the Disorder the Carrier had put her into, so eager was she to have Justice of him. The Magistrate examin'd her, and having consider'd the Matter, thought the Offender was unworthy of a Pardon. He order'd him to be stript, and whipt in his Presence · and that if the Woman's Husband was not forth-
coming

coming the next Day, two Bayliffs, at the Cost and Charges of the Defendant, should carry the Plaintiff to *Astorga*.

For my part I was more frighted than any of my Fellow-Travellers. I ran into the Country, and travers'd I don't know how many Fields and Heaths, leaping all the Ditches I met with in my Way, till I came at last to a Forest. I entred it, and hid under the thickest Hedge: I had not been long there before two Men a Horseback came up to me: Who's there, cry'd they? And I being so afraid that I made 'em no Answer, they drew nearer me, and clapt a Pistol to my Breast, commanding me to tell them who I was, whence I came, and what I was about, and charg'd me to conceal nothing from them. They questioned me so strictly, that I thought I was bound to answer them as sincerely as if the Muletier's Threats were going to be put in Execution, and the Torture was before me. I told them I was a young Man of *Oviedo*, going to *Salamanca*: I inform'd them of the Fright I had been in, and that I had run away from the Carrier for fear of the Rack. They burst out a laughing at this Discourse, which
shew'd

ſhew'd my Simplicity; and one of them
bad me have a good heart, come along
with us, and be afraid of nothing, we'll
carry thee to a ſafe Place. Saying this, he
made me get up behind him, and rode
away with me into the thickeſt of the
Foreſt.

I could not tell what to make of this
Rencounter. However, I did not think
there was any thing ill in it. If theſe
Men were Robbers, ſaid I to my ſelf,
they would have robb'd, and perhaps
have murder'd me, They muſt be ſome
honeſt Gentlemen of theſe Parts, who
ſeeing me ſo frighted, took pity of me,
and carry'd me with them out of Charity: I was not long in an Uncertainty:
After ſeveral Turnings and Windings we
came to the Foot of an Hill, where we
alighted. We live here, ſays one of
theſe Cavaliers. I look'd about to
ſee where their Dwelling ſhould be, but
could perceive neither Houſe nor Hut,
nor the leaſt Sign of an Habitation. In
the mean time the two Men lifted up a
huge Trap-door, cover'd with Earth and
Briars, which conceal'd the Entrance of
a long Alley under Ground. Their Horſes deſcended of themſelves, as being us'd
to it. The Cavaliers oblig'd me to follow

low them. They then ty'd down the Trap-door with Ropes which were faften'd to it on purpofe: And thus was my Uncle's hopeful Nephew caught like a Moufe in a Moufe-Trap.

CHAP. IV.

A Defcription of the Habitation under Ground, and what Gil Blas *faw there.*

I Then found out what fort of Men I was got amongft ; and one may i-magine that my prefent Fear could vie of that which the Muletier had put me into. I had now more reafon to be afraid. I gave my Ducats and my Life for gone. I look'd upon myfelf as a Victim leading to Slaughter, and follow'd 'em where-ever they led me, like a Perfon who hardly knew whether he was alive or dead. After we had gone about 200 Paces in this fubterranean Labyrinth, defcending ftill as we went, we came to a Stable, where hung two great Iron Lamps fix'd to the Cieling, and always burning to light the Place.

Place. There was good Store of Hay
and Oats, and Room for 20 Horfes;
but there were then no more than the
two that we brought with us. An old
Negro, who feem'd to have quite loft
his Vigour, took them, and ty'd them
to the Manger.

We left the Stable, and by the Light
of fome other Lamps, which ferv'd, as
one would think, to fhew the Horror
of the Place, we arriv'd at a Kitchen,
where an old Woman was roafting fome
Meat, and preparing for Supper; the
Kitchen was adorn'd with all neceffary
Utenfils; and adjoyning to it was an
Office furnifhed with all forts of Provifions. The Cook, to give you her
Picture, was a Perfon upwards of Sixty.
In her Youth her Hair was of a deep
fandy Colour, as might be feen by part
which was not turn'd grey, and retain'd
ftill it's former Hue; her Chin was long
and picked; fhe was blobber-lip'd; her
Nofe of the *Roman* kind, and advancing
towards her Chin; her Eyes blood-fhed
always, and her Shape indented.

Here, Dame *Leonarda*, fays one of the
Cavaliers, prefenting me to that Angel
of Darknefs, Here's a young Man we
have brought you: He then turn'd about
to

to me, and obferving I look'd pale, and
trembled, he again bad me not to be
afraid, for they would do me no harm,
adding, We Want a Servant to affift our
Cook : We happened to light upon thee,
and thou wilt have caufe to rejoyce at
it : Thou fhalt here fupply the Place of
a Lad that dy'd 15 Days ago : He was
a fickly Youth; thou feemeft to be lufty, and wilt not die fo foon. 'Tis true,
thou wilt not fee the Sun any more;
but to make amends, thou fhalt have a
good Fire, and a full Belly : Thou
fhalt fpend thy Time with *Leouarda*,
who is a very humane Creature. Thou
wilt want for nothing; I'll fhew thee
that thou 'art not come among Beggars.
Come, follow me ; and taking a Torch
in his Hand, he led me into a Cellar,
where I faw a vaft Quantity of Bottles
and Jarrs full, as he faid, of excellent
Wine. He then carried me into feveral
Rooms, fome full of Silks, others of
Stuff, others of Linen ; in others there
were Veffels of Silver and Gold ; in o-
thers Brafs, Copper, and coarfer Me-
tals. After this I follow'd him into a
large Hall, where were three Copper
Sconces, with Candles burning. There
were other Rooms joyning to this, and

Lights In every one of them. He demanded of me, as we went along, what
my Name was, and why I left *Oviedo ?*
When I had fatisfied him, he cry'd, Well,
Gil Blas, fince you quitted your Country to get a Place, thank your Stars that
you have got fo good a one. 'Twas a
happything for thee that thou met'ft with
us : Thou wilt have Plenty of all things
here, and roll in Silver and Gold :
Befides thou canft here come to no harm.
This fubterranean Dwelling is fo fafe,
that the Officers of St. *Hermandad* may
come a hundred times into the Foreft,
and not find it out ; no body but my
felf and my Comrades know the Entrance into it. Perhaps thou wilt ask
me how we could make it, and the In-
habitants of the Neighbourhood never
difcover us : Thou muft learn therefore
that it is no Work of ours ; it was
made a long time ago. After the *Moors*
became Mafters of *Granada*, *Arragon*,
and almoft all the reft of *Spain*, the Chri-
ftians, who would not fubmit to the
Yoke of the Infidels, fled hither, and
conceal'd themfelves in *Bifcay* and the
Afturias, whither the brave *Don Pelagio*
retired. Being thus fcatter'd up and down
in fmall Companies, they liv'd in Mountains

tains and Woods, some in Caves, and
some in such subterranean Vaults as these
are. When afterwards they had the
good Fortune to drive their Enemies out
of *Spain*, they returned to the Cities;
since which Time their Retreats have
serv'd for an *Asylum* to Men of our Profession. 'Tis true, St. *Hermandad*, has discover'd and destroy'd some of them;
but, thank Heaven, there are some left
still. I have liv'd in this Place securely
these fifteen Years. My Name is Captain *Rolando*; I am the chief of a Band,
and the Man thou sawest with me is
one of them.

CHAP. V.

Of the Arrival of several other Rob-
bers in the Habitation under Ground,
and the pleasant Discourse they had
together.

AS Signor *Rolando* had done speaking,
there appear'd six new Faces in the
Hall, the Lieutenant and five Men more
of the Band laden with Plunder. They
brought with them two Baggs full of
C 2
Sugar,

Sugar, Cinnamon, Pepper, Figs, Almonds, and dry'd Raisins: The Lieutenant addreſt himſelf to the Captain, and told him he had juſt taken thoſe two Bags from a Gro-cer of *Benevento*, whoſe Mule alſo be-came his Prize. After which he gave an Account of his Expedition to the Steward; and the Booty taken from the Grocer was depoſited in the Office.

The next thing to be done was to make merry. The Cloth was laid in the Hall; I was ſent into the Kitchen, and inſtructed how I was to employ myſelf by Dame *Leonarda*. There was no help for it; I muſt do what ſhe bad me; and making a Virtue of Neceſſity, I put the beſt Face I could upon it, and went a-bout the Work ſhe ſet me upon.

I put every thing in order in the Buf-fet; I placed there the Plate that was wanted, and ſtow'd it with Bottles of that excellent Wine which *Rolando* boaſted of. I then ſerv'd up two Ra-gous, and the Cavaliers immediately ſeat-ed themſelves at the Table. They all fell to with keen Appetites, and I ſtood behind them to fill out Wine; I did it with ſo good a Grace, that I was com-plimented by them in an extraordina-ry manner. The Captain in few Words told

told them my Story, which very much
diverted them. He clos'd all with saying, I was a Lad of Merit. I could
very well have been without their Praises,
but they had never enough of it. They
said I seem'd to be born to be their
Butler, and was worth a hundred of my
Predeceffor. Dame *Leonarda* had had
the Honour of prefenting *Nectar* to thefe
Infernal Gods ever fince his Death; but
they now depriv'd her of fo glorious
an Employment, to beftow it upon me;
and I, like another *Ganimede*, fucceeded
this old *Hebe*.

The Ragous being difpatch'd, I carried in feveral Difhes of Roaft-meat:
The Robbers eating heartily of them,
as they had done of the Ragous, became at laft pretty well fatisfy'd; they
drank in Proportion to their eating, and
grew very glad, and very noifie. They
talk'd all at a time: One began a Story, another told a Jeft; one fhouted,
another fung: They knew not what
each other faid. Which made Captain
Rolando, who had in vain endeavour'd
to have the beft Part of the Talk, affume an Air of Authority, and impofe
Silence on the reft of the Company:
Gentlemen, faid he, hearken to what I

have

have to fay to you : Let us not deafen one
another by talking all together ; Wou'd
it not be better to difcourfe like reafonable Men ? A Thought is come into
my Head. Since we affociated ourfelves
together we never had the Curiofity to
enquire into each others Families, and
how we came to take upon us this Profeffion : Methinks 'tis a thing we fhould
not be ignorant of : Let us tell our Adventures to divert us. The Lieutenant
and the reft, as if they had fomething
fine to relate, accepted of the Captain's
Propofitions with great Demonftrations of Joy ; and the Captain himfelf
fpoke firft in the following Terms :

You muft know, Gentlemen, that I
was the only Son of a rich Citizen of
Madrid. There was no end of the
Rejoycings in our Family on the Day
of my Nativity. My Father, who was
ftricken in Years, was overjoyed to have
an Heir to his Eftate, and my Mother
undertook to give me Suck herfelf :
My Grandfather, by my Mother's fide,
was then living : He was an honeft old
Fellow, who minded nothing but faying his Rofary, and boafting of his mi-
litary Exploits, for he had born Arms a
                                    long

long time. I became infenfibly the I-
dol of thefe three Perfons: They always had me in their Arms: And lelt
Studying fhould fatigue me too much
in my younger Years, they fuffered
me to fpend them in the moft Childifh
Amufements. Children, faid my Father,
fhould not apply themfelves to any thing
too ferioufly; they fhould ftay till their
Judgments are riper. Waiting for this
Ripenefs, I grew up without being able
to Read or Write: But I did not however lofe my Time; my Father taught
me a thoufand little Plays; I could manage a Pack of Cards as well as any
Body; I underftood Dice too; and my
Grandfather told me Romances of the feveral Warlike Enterprizes wherein he had
been concern'd: He every day fill'd my
Head with them, and made me repeat
Verfes on fo fine a Subject, which I
did very exactly, and for which my
Parents admired my Memory: They
were as well pleafed with my Wit, when
I would break in upon their Difcourfe,
and fay any thing that came uppermoft.
What a rare Boy he is? My Father
would cry, with a Look full of Content. My Mother overwhelmed me with
her Careffes, and my Grandfather wept

for

for Joy. I did whatever I would before them; they forgave me, let it be
never so indecent. They even adored
me. I was thirteen Years of Age before they thought of getting a Master
for me: They then provided one, but
they gave him a strict Charge not to
touch me. They permitted him to
threaten me a little sometimes, to make
me afraid. This Permission was of
no great Use; for either I made a Jest
of his Threats, or with Tears in my
Eyes went to complain to my Mother
or my Grandfather of my Preceptor's ill
Usage: 'Twas to no Purpose for the poor
Devil to excuse himself. He always past
for a Brute with them, and they were
sure to take my Word before his. One
Day I scratch'd my self, and then cry'd
out as if he had done it. My Mother
ran in, and drove Him out of the
House immediately, tho' he protested,
and call'd Heaven to witness, that he
had not touch'd me.

Thus did I get rid of all my Pre-
ceptors, till I met with one of my own
liking, a Batchelor of Arts of *Alcala*,
an excellent Master for the Heir of a
Family: He lov'd Women, Gaming, and
Wine: I could not have fallen into the
Hands

Hands of a Person more to my Humour. He, in the firſt Place, endeavour'd to gain me over to him by humouring me in all things. He ſucceeded, and by that means got the Love of my Parents, who abandoned me entirely to his Conduct. He betimes inſtructed me in the Knowledge of the World. He carried me with him to all the Houſes of Pleaſure which he haunted. He inſtill'd into me the ſame love for it as he had himſelf; and excepting *Latin* he taught me every thing that he himſelf knew. Aſſoon as he ſaw I had no farther Occaſion of his Precepts, he went away, and offer'd his Service elſewhere.

Tho' I was us'd in my Infancy to a very free way of Living, 'twas nothing to what I was when I became Maſter of my own Actions. I every Moment turn'd my Father and Mother into Ridicule: They bore it all in good Part, and the more wicked I was, the more they took me to be pleaſant. There was no kind of Debauchery which I was not guilty of: My Companions were all of the ſame Make: And as our Parents did not give us Money enough to continue ſo delicious a Life, every one of us ſtole from 'em all we

C 5   could

could lay our Hands on; which not
anſwering our Occaſions, we began to
rob a Nights. The Corrigidor unhappily got Intelligence of us; he reſolv'd
to apprehend us, but we had notice of
his miſchievous Deſign. We ran for it,
and enter'd upon Exploits on the High-
way; ſince which, Gentlemen, I have
had the good Fortune to continue in
my Profeſſion many Years, in ſpite of
the Perils that attend it.

Here the Captain ended his Relation,
and the Lieutenant began his: An E-
ducation, Gentlemen, quite oppoſite to
that of Signor *Rolando*, produced the very ſame Effect: My Father was a Butcher of *Toledo*: He paſt, and with good
reaſon, for the greateſt Brute in that
City, and my Mother was ev'ry whit
as Ill-natur'd as he. They whipt me
when I was in Arms, and ſtrove who
ſhould do it to me moſt. I daily was
turn'd-up ten or twenty times: The
leaſt Fault I committed had the ſever-
eſt Puniſhment: 'Twas in vain to down
on my Knees, and beg Pardon, to pro-
miſe with Tears in my Eyes, that I
would do ſo no more: They never
would forgive me, and very often cha-
ſtis'd me tho' I did not deſerve it. When
my

my Father beat me, my Mother, as if he had not done as much as he ought to do, would be sure to have a hand in it, and set him on, instead of interceding for me. This Usage gave me such an Aversion to the House, that I left it before I was fourteen Years old: I begg'd my Way thro' *Arragon* to *Saragossa*, where I associated my self with some Beggars, who liv'd a merry Life enough. They taught me to counterfeit a Blind-man, a Cripple, a *Lazar*, and several other Parts proper to procure Alms. We every Morning acted 'em over, as Players rehearse their Comedies. Each of us knew his Post by Day, and at Night we all met again, and spent together what the Charity of pious Christians had given us. In time I grew weary of living with those Wretches, and endeavour'd to joyn my self to a Company of a higher Order, such as liv'd by their Industry. They shew'd me a hundred Tricks; but we could not stay long at *Saragossa*, having unluckily had a Quarrel with one of the Magistrates, who was of Intelligence with us, and always protected us. Each of us went his Way. As for me, I enter'd my self in a bold Troop of Adventurers.

venturers, who rais'd Contributions from Travellers; and I lik'd their way of Living so well, that I resolv'd to think of no other. I am therefore, Gentlemen, very much oblig'd to my Parents for using me so ill as they did; for if they had been kinder to me, I had doubtless been a sorry Butcher at this Time, whereas I have now the Honour to be your Lieutenant.

These Stories, Gentlemen, says a young Robber, who sat between the Captain and the Lieutenant, are not so extraordinary nor so curious as mine: I was the Son of a Peasant in the Neighbourhood of *Seville*. Three Weeks after I was born, my Mother, a young, handsome, neat Woman, had a Nursery propos'd to her, the only Son of a Man of Quality in *Seville*, of about my Age. My Mother accepted of the Proposal: She went and fetch'd the Child, which, as soon as she brought home, she observ'd to be something like me. Upon this she took a Resolution to make me pass for the Child of Quality, in hopes that I would one time or other reward her for it. My Father, whose Conscience was not more delicate than any other Peasant's, approv'd of the Cheat. Thus after she

had

had chang'd our Cloaths, she put out
the Son of Don *Rodriguez de Herrera* to
another Nurse, under my Name, and
nurs'd me herself under his.

Whatever might be said of Instinct
and the Strength of Blood, the Parents
of the Little Gentleman were easily
impos'd upon; they did not in the
least suspect the Trick that was
play'd them; and I was never out of
their Arms till I was Seventeen Years
of Age. Their Intention was to render
me a perfect Cavalier: They provided
me Masters of all kinds; but I had no
manner of Inclination to the Exercises
they taught me, nor any more Disposition to learn the Sciences in which they
would have instructed me. I had much rather play with the Footmen and Groom,
whom I every Moment followed into
the Kitchen and Stables. But Play was
not long my predominant Passion; I
learnt to Drink before I was Seventeen,
and fell upon all the Women that came
in my Way. I particularly was very
fond of a Servant Maid in the Kitchen,
who seem'd to me to be the most amiable
of them all: She was a jolly, fat Wench;
and I made Love to her so openly, that
Don *Rodriguez* took notice of it. He
reprov'd

reprov'd me sharply, upbraiding me with
the Baseness of my Inclinations; and
lest the Sight of the beloved Object
should render his Remonstrances use-
less, he turn'd my Princess out of
Doors.

I was mightily displeas'd at it, resolv'd
to be reveng'd, robb'd Don *Rodriguez*'s
Wife of all her Jewels, and ran after
my fair *Helen*, who retir'd to a Washer-
woman's House of her Acquaintance: I
took her thence at Noon-Day, that every
Body might know it; and not satisfy'd
with this, I carried her into her own
Country, where I solemnly married her,
as well to spite *Herrena* as to set a fine
Example for other Children of Quality. Three Months after I was married,
I heard that Don *Rodriguez* was dead;
which News was, I thought, the best I
ever heard in my Life: I immediately
repair'd to *Seville* to demand Possession
of his Estate. But, alas! the Case was
alter'd; my Mother was dead too, and
on her Death-bed she confess'd to the
Curate of the Parish the Trick she had
put upon Don *Rodriguez*, whose Son had
already fill'd my Place, or rather his
own; and every one was the more
pleas'd with the Discovery of his Birth,
for

for that I had given so little Hope of
coming to Good. By this means finding
my self left deftitute, and having no
great Fancy for my fat Spoufe, I took
to the Company of fome Knights of
Fortune, with whom I began my Exploits on the Road.

The young Robber having finifhed
his Story, another faid, He was the Son
of a Merchant of *Burgos*; that he rafhly took Orders in his Youth, and apo-
ftatiz'd fome Years after. In fine, the
Eight Robbers talk'd every one of his
Birth in their Turn; and when I had
heard them all fpeak, I was not furpriz'd to meet them all together: They
afterwards turn'd their Difcourfe, and
debated feveral Projects for the next
Campaign: They concluded to profecute
one of them; and it being late, went all
to fleep in their feveral Chambers. I
followed the Captain into his, where
while I help'd to undrefs him, Thou feeft,
faid he, *Gil Blas*, how we live here:
We are always merry; we have neither
Hatred nor Envy among us, nor ever
had we the leaft Quarrel; we agree
better than Monks in a Convent: Thou
art going, Child, to live a pleafant Life
of it. I don't take thee to be fuch a
Fool

Fool as to make any Scruple of living
with Robbers. Who are there in the
World that are not such ? Every Man
loves to take another Man's Goods from
him ; this Sentiment is general ; the
manner of doing it is only different .
For Example, Conquerors seize the Ter-
ritories of their Neighbours ; Persons
of Quality borrow, and never pay ;
Bankers, Brokers, and all sorts of Tradef-
men, as well great as small, are not very
scrupulous in this Point. I will not say
any thing of the Lawyers ; their Pra-
ctices are well enough known. However, it must be own'd, they are more innocent than we ; for we often take away
the Lives of the Innocent, and they sometimes save the Guilty.

CHAP. VI.

Of an Attempt of Gil Blas *to make his*
Escape, and what was the Success
of it.

AFter the Captain of the Robbers had
made this Apology for his Profes-
fion, he went to Bed, and I returned
to

to the Hall, where I clear'd the Table, and put every thing in Order. I then went into the Kitchen, where *Domingo*, so the old Negro was called, and Dame *Leonarda* were at Supper, expecting me to come to them. Tho' I had no Stomach, I sat down with them; I could eat nothing; and my Looks shewed that I was as much afflicted as I had reason to be. Those two Equivalent Figures endeavoured to comfort me. Why are you troubled, Child, says the old Woman? You ought rather to rejoyce at your being here; you are young and easy; you would soon have been ruin'd, had you liv'd in the World; you would have met with a Parcel of Libertines, who would have engaged you in all manner of Debauchery, whereas your Innocence will here be safe. Dame *Leonarda* is in the right, said the old Negro, very gravely; besides there is nothing but Trouble in the World: Come, Friend, thank Heaven that you are at once delivered from all the Perils, Cares and Afflictions of Life. I hearkned to them with seeming Attention; for it signified nothing to do otherwise. *Domingo*, after he had plentifully eaten and drank, retir'd to his Stable. *Leonarda*

took

took also a Lamp, and conducted me to a Vault which the Robbers made use of for a Burying Place, when any of their Fellows died a natural Death: I there spy'd a Pallad, which look'd more like a Tomb than a Bed. This is your Chamber, says she; the Lad, whose Place it is your good Fortune to fill, lay there as long as he liv'd, and some time after he was dead. He was such a Fool as to die in the Flower of his Age: Don't you be so silly as to follow his Example. Saying this, she gave me the Lamp, and return'd to the Kitchen. I set the Lamp upon the Ground, I flung myself on the Pallad, not so much to sleep, as to give myself up entirely to my Reflexions. O Heaven, what a terrible Fate is befallen me! cry'd I: I am not only doom'd never to see the Light of the Sun more; but as if it were not enough to be buried alive at eighteen Years old, I am also reduced to serve Thieves by Day, and to spend the Night with the Dead! These mortifying Thoughts made me burst out into Tears. I a hundred times curs'd my Uncle's Desire to send me to *Salamanca.* I repented that I ran away from the Magistrate at *Cacabelos.* I would
gladly

gladly have been rackt, to have got above
Ground again. But confidering that
bemoaning my felf thus, was all in vain;
I bent my Thoughts to contrive the
means to efcape. Is it impoffible, faid
I to my felf, to get out from hence?
The Robbers are afleep; the Cook and
the *Negro* will be the fame prefently.
While they are Sleeping, cannot I with
this Lamp find out the Alley by which
I defcended into this Hell? 'Tis true, I
don't believe I am ftrong enough to lift
up the Trap-Door, but let me try. I
will not have any Blame lie on me that
I did not what I could to efcape. Defpair will lend me Strength, and perhaps
I may accomplifh it.

Thus did I form this great Defign, and
rofe, when I thought *Leonarda* and *Domingo* were faft. I took the Lamp, and
went out of the Vault, recommending my
felf to all the Saints in Paradife. It
was not without much Difficulty that I
found out all the Turnings and Windings of this new Labyrinth. I arriv'd, in
the end, at the Gate of the Stable, and
at laft perceiv'd the Alley I was in queft
of. I march'd on, and advanced towards
the Trap-door with as much Nimble-
nefs as Joy. But alas! in the middle of
the

theAlley I met with a curfed Grate, well
faften'd, and the Bars fo clofe, a Man
could hardly put his Hand through. I
was fadly vex'd at this Obftacle, which I
had not obferv'd as we enter'd. I hand-
led the Bars, I examin'd the Lock, I
endeavour'd to break it open; when
on a fudden I felt on my Shoulders
half a dozen lufty Bangs of a Bull's-
Pifle; I cried out, fo that all the Vault
rang with it; and looking behind
me, faw the old *Negro* in his Shirt,
with a Dark Lantern in one Hand, and
the Inftrument of my Correction in the
other. So, fo, you young Rafcal! you,
cried he, you would get out, would
you? Don't think you can be too hard
for me. I heard you; you thought the
Grate was open. Believe me, Friend,
you fhall hereafter find it always fhut.
When we keep any one here againft his
Mind, he muft be cunninger than you if
he can efcape us.

In the mean time, my crying out fo,
awaken'd two or three of the Robbers,
who not knowing whether it was not the
St. *Hermandad* that was coming down upon them, got up and awoke their Comrades: They rofe all in an inftant, and
came running almoft naked to the Place
                                    where

where I was with *Domingo*. But as foon as they underftood what was the Matter, their Concern was converted into Laughter. How! *Gil Blas*, faid the Apoftate Robber, Thou haft not been here fix Hours yet, and wouldft thou be gone already? What wouldft thou do, if thou wert to be a Monk? Go, get thee to Bed, thou fhalt be forgiven this Time, in Confideration of the Blows of *Domingo*'s Bulls-Pizzle; but if thou do'ft ever make another fuch Attempt, by St. *Barholomew*, we'll flee thee alive. At thefe Words he retir'd. The other Robbers return'd alfo to their Chambers. The old *Negro* betook himfelf to his Stable again, very well pleas'd with his Expedition; and I went back to my Burying-place, where I paft the reft of the Night in Sighing and Weeping.

CHAP.

C H A P. VII.

What Gil Blas *did, when he could not
do better.*

I Thought I fhould have died of the
Grief which feiz'd me, and continu'd
feveral Days after my fruitlefs Attempt
to efcape; I could hardly hold up my
Head, or ftand on my Feet; but at laft
my good Genius infpir'd me with a Refolution to diffemble. I affeƈted to feem
lefs Melancholy, I began to laugh and
fing, though I had no manner of mind
to it. In a Word, I put fuch a Con-
ftraint upon my Self, that *Leonárda* and
Domingo were deceiv'd by it. They believ'd that Ufe had made the Cage familiar to the Bird. The Robbers were
of the fame Opinion. I affum'd a gay
Air when I fill'd out their Wine for
'em, and put in a Word now and then
among them, when I could do it to divert them. They were pleas'd with the
Freedom I took. *Gil Blas,* faid the Captain, one Evening when I had been very
pleafant, thou didft well to banifh Melancholy; I am charm'd with thy Humour

mour and thy Wit : One don't know People at firſt ; I did not take thee to have ſo much Wit, and ſo much good Humour.

The reſt of them ſpoke mightily in Praiſe of me. They appeared ſo well diſpos'd towards me, that I reſolved to take hold of that Occaſion, and ſaid, Gentlemen, Let me ſpeak my Mind to you : Since my being here, I find I'm quite another Creature ; you have cured me of the Prejudices of Education ; I have inſenſibly acquir'd your Sentiments and a Liking to your Profeſſion. I long to have the Honour of being one of your Brethren, and to ſhare with you in the Perils of your Expeditions. All the Company applauded this Diſcourſe ; they extoll'd my Good-will, and reſolv'd unanimouſly that I ſhould ſerve a-while to to make Tryal of my Vocation, and afterwards be admitted into the Band. In hopes of ſo honourable a Preferment, I continued to put a Force upon my Inclinations, and to exerciſe my Employment of Butler. It was an extreme Mortification to me to ſtay where I was; for I had no Ambition to become a Robber, only to have an Opportunity by it to get out of the Vault where I was

confin'd

confin'd, in hopes to make my Efcape from them. Thefe Hopes kept me alive: I was often tir'd with waiting; and more than once endeavour'd to furprize *Domingo's* Vigilance, but there was no way of doing it, he was too much upon his Guard: I would have defy'd a hundred *Orpheus's* to charm this *Cerberus*. Indeed I was fo afraid of rendring my felf fufpected, that I did not do what I could to deceive him. He watch'd me, and I was obliged to act very warily, that I might not betray my felf. I adjourn'd therefore all Thoughts of getting out, till the appointed Time for my Reception into the Troop; and I waited for it as impatiently, as if I was then to be admitted among the Knights of the Order.

The Time, thank Heaven, came, fix Months after, when Signor *Rolando* addreft himfelf thus to his Comrades: We muft keep our Words, Gentlemen, with *Gil Blas*; I have no ill Opinion of that Lad: I believe we fhall make fomething of him; I think we had beft let him go with us to morrow to gather Laurels on the High-way. We'll take it upon ourfelves to breed him up in the Way to Glory. The Robbers join'd
all

all in with him ; and to fhew me that they already look'd upon me as one of their Companions, they difpens'd with my waiting upon them. They reftor'd to Dame *Leonarda* the Poft they had taken from her in my Favour. They made me throw afide my Habit, which was' only a Thread-bare Frock, and e-quipt me out with the Spoils of a Gentleman whom they had lately robb'd. After which I prepar'd myfelf for my firft Campaign.

CHAP. VIII.

Gil Blas *accompanies the Robbers. An Exploit of his on the High-way.*

'TWas about Day-break, in the Month of *September,* that I fallied out of our Subterranean Dwelling with the Robbers. I was arm'd like them, with a Carabine, two Piftols, a Sword and Bayonet, and mounted on a pretty good Horfe, which they took from the fame Gentleman whofe Cloaths I wore : I had fo long liv'd in Darknefs that the Light dazled my Eyes ; but by degrees I could bear it.

Vol. I.　　　　D　　　　We

We paſt by *Ponferrada*, and poſted
ourſelves in Ambuſh in a little Wood
near the High-road to *Leon*. We were
there waiting for ſome good Booty,
when we ſpy'd a Monk of the ·Order
of St. *Dominique*, mounted, contrary to
the Rules of that Order, on a ſorry
Mule. Heaven be prais'd, cry'd the Captain, ſmiling ; This is a Maſter-piece for
Gil Blas ; he muſt diſmount the Monk ;
Let's ſee how he'll do it. All the Robbers agreed I was very fit for that
Commiſſion ; and they exhorted me to
behave my ſelf well in the Execution of
it. I will pleaſe you, Gentlemen, ſaid I
to them, I will ſtrip the Prieſt to his
Skin, and bring you his Mule hither.
No, no, reply'd *Rolando*, 'tis not worth
while ; bring us only his Reverence's
Purſe ; that's all we require of you. Upon which I rode out of the Wood : I
came up with the Monk, praying Heaven
to forgive the wicked Action I was about.
I would gladly have made my Eſcape
then ; but the greateſt part of the
Thieves were better mounted than I ;
if they had perceived that I fled, they
would quickly have been at my Heels,
and have either carried me back with
them, or have diſcharg'd their Carabines
at

at me, which I did not care to hazard,
the Step was too delicate. I demanded
the Prieſt's Purſe as ſoon as I drew near
him : I held my Piſtol to his Breaſt to
ſhew I was in earneſt. He ſtopt ſhort
to take a View of me, and did not
ſeem at' all afraid. Child, ſays he, you
are very young ; you begin this Rogues
Trade betimes. Father, ſaid I, as bad
as 'tis, I wiſh I had begun it ſooner. Ah
Son, reply'd the good Man, who did
not underſtand my Meaning, What doſt
thou ſay ? How blind art thou! Suffer
me to lay before thee thy wretched Condition. Father, ſaid I, interrupting him,
No Preaching, I beſeech you ; I don't uſe
the High-way to hear Sermons ; I want
Money. Money cry'd the Monk ! in a
Surprize: You have an ill Opinion of
the Charity of the *Spaniards*, if you i-
magine that Perſons of my Character
have occaſion of Money when they travel in *Spain*. Be not deceiv'd, we are entertain'd where-ever we come, we are
lodg'd, we are fed ; and all that is required of us in return, is our Prayers.
In ſhort, we never carry Money on the
Road with us; We give our ſelves up to
Providence. No, no, reply'd I, you do
not always give your ſelves up to it ;

you have sometimes good Piftoles about
you to make you the more fure of Providence : Father, let us have done ; my
Comrades who are in this Wood expect
my Return with Impatience. Fling your
Purfe on the Ground this Minute, or I'll
kill you.

I pronounc'd thefe Words with fo
threatning an Air, that the Prieft began
to be afraid of his Life. Stay, fays
he, I'll do as you would have
me, fince it muft be fo; I perceive that
Rhetorical Figúres have no Force with
fuch Men as you are. Saying this, he
pull'd a great Shammy Purfe out from
under his Gown, and threw it upon the
Ground. I then bad him go on, which
he did not give me the Trouble to repeat. He prick'd his Mule's Sides ; and
the Beaft doing much better than I
thought fhe could, for I took her to be
fuch another as my Uncle's, anfwer'd very well the Hafte he was in to get out
of my Sight. When he was at fome
diftance, I alighted, and took up the
Purfe, which was weighty ; I mounted
my Horfe again, and made as faft as I
could to the Robbers, who were impatient to felicitate me on my Victory :
They would fcarce give me time to a-
                              light,

light, fo hafty were they to embrace me.
Courage, *Gil Blas*, fays *Rolando*, thou
haft done Wonders ; I had my Eye upon thee all the while ; I obferv'd thy
Countenance: I foretel that thou wilt
make an excellent Man for the Road.
The Lieutenant and the reft of them applauded the Prediction, and affur'd me
that I could not fail of accomplifhing it.
I thank'd them for the high Idea they
had of me, and promis'd them to do my
utmoft to deferve it.

After they had prais'd me fo much
more than belong'd to me, they wanted to examine the Booty I had brought
them. Let's fee, cry'd they, what the
Monk had in his Purfe. It muft be
well ftor'd, faid one of them, for thofe
Reverend Fathers do not generally travel
like Pilgrims. The Captain unty'd the
Purfe, open'd it, and took out of it
three or four Handfuls of little Copper
Medals, intermix'd with *Agnus Dei's*,
and fome Crucifixes. At the Sight of
fuch an uncommon Prize, all the Thieves
fell into an immoderate Fit of Laughter. We are mightily oblig'd to *Gil
Blas*, faid the Lieutenant ; his firft Booty is a very falutary one. This Jeft was
the Occafion of many others: Thofe

Rogues

Rogues, particularly he who had apofta-
tiz'd, were very merry upon it; they
faid a thoufand things that fhew'd the
Wickednefs of their Morals: I was the
only Perfon who did not make a laughing Matter of it. The Rallery was all
at my Expence, which was enough to
fpoil my Mirth, had I been fo inclin'd :
Every one had a Fling at me ; and the
Captain faid, Faith, *Gil Blas*, I advife
thee to have no more to do with Monks;
they will be too cunning, and too hard
for thee.

CHAP. IX.

*Of a ferious Adventure which follow'd
that pleafant one.*

WE ftaid almoft all Day in the
Wood, but met with no Prize to
make amends for our Baulk in the Prieft.
In the Evening we return'd towards our
Dwelling under Ground : The Robbers
diverted themfelves all the Way with my
Booty. At laft we fpy'd at a Diftance
a Coach and four Mules. They drew
nearer to us upon a full Trot ; and by the
Coach

Coach rode three Men, who seem'd
to be very well arm'd. *Rolando* bid his
Band halt, to consult what was to be
done. The Robbers resolv'd to attack
them; so we march'd up to the Coach
in Rank and File, prepared for a Battle.
Tho' I had been so highly compli mented
in the Wood, I fell a trembling, and was
seiz'd with a cold Sweat all over me.
My Post happened to be unluckily in the
Front between the Captain and the
Lieutenant; I suppos'd they contriv'd it
so, to see how I would stand Fire. *Rolando*
observing in what a Panick I was, cast
a sour Look at me, and said surlily,
Mind me, *Gil Blas*, I give thee fair War-
ning, If thou dost flinch, I'll shoot thee
thro' the Head. I was too well satisfied
that he would do as he said, not to take
care of my Behaviour; so I took a Resolution to dare my Fate, and recommended my Soul to Heaven. By this
time the Coach was got up with us;
they perceived what sort of Men we
were, and what our Design was: They
stopt at 20 Paces distance; they had Carabines and Pistols as well as we; and
while they were preparing to receive us,
there leapt out of the Coach a Gentleman richly drest. He mounted a led
Horse,

Horfe, and put himfelf at the Head of
thofe that attended him. He had no
Arms but a Sword and two Piftols:
There were nine of us, and but four
of them, the Coachman fitting neuter
in his Box. They advanc'd towards us
fo daringly, that my Fright redoubled
upon it; however, tho' I fhook hand
and foot, I made ready to do as the
reft did: To fpeak the Truth, I was
fo afraid that I wink'd when I fir'd my
Carabine, and fhot it off in fuch a manner, that I believe I have nothing to
repent of on that fcore.

I will not enter into the Particulars
of the Action: Tho' I was by I faw
nothing; and my Fear was fo ftrong,
that I did not fee the Horror of the
Sight that terrified me: All that I know
is, that after great Firing on both fides,
I heard my Companions fhout, and cry
Victory! Victory! Upon which I took
Heart, and looking up, faw the four
Men who defended the Coach dead on
the Spot. On our fide we loft only
one Man, the Apoftate, who met with a
juft Punifhment for his Apoftacy, and
ridiculing Religion in the Prieft's Crucifixes: The Lieutenant was wounded
in the Arm, but very flightly, the Ball
only

only razing the Skin. Signor *Rolando* ran immediately to the Coach-door: There was a Lady in it of 24 or 25 Years of Age, who look'd very lovely, notwithftanding the fad Condition fhe was in: She fwoon'd away during the Combat, and was not recovered out of her Swoon when the Captain came up to her. While he ftood gazing upon her, we fell upon the Plunder: The firft thing we did was to fecure the Horfes of the dead Cavaliers; thofe Animals, frighted at the Noife of the Carabines and Piftols, broke loofe, and ran about without their Riders, who were kill'd in the Combat: The Mules ftood ftill all the time of the Action, tho' the Coachman quitted his Box to fave himfelf. We alighted off our Horfes, took the Mules from the Coach, and loaded them with feveral Bundles and Parcels which we found before and behind the Coach. That done, the Captain ordered us to take the Lady, who was ftill in a fort of Fit, and put her on Horfeback. Accordingly one of the Robbers, who was beft mounted, took her in his Arms, and feated her before him. We ftript the dead Men, and

D 5   left

left em with the Coach in the High-
way, taking with us the Lady, the
Mules, and the Horses.

CHAP. X.

*How the Robbers treated the Lady.
Of a great Design form'd by* Gil
Blas, *and what was the Consequence
of it.*

ABout an Hour after Night we arriv'd
at our subterranean Habitation : We
put the Horses and Mules up in our
Stable, and were forc'd to look after them
our selves; for the old Negro had been
a-bed three Hours ; besides a violent Fit
of the Gout which he had upon him,
he was seiz'd all over with a Fit of the
Rheumatism. We left that Wretch cur-
ling and swearing, and went into the
Kitchen, where we carried the Lady,
and was every one of us very busy a-
bout her : We manag'd it so well, that
we recover'd her out of her Swoon ;
but when she had her Senses restor'd to
her, and saw herself in the Arms of several Men who were Strangers to her,
she

she imagined how miserable she was, and fell a trembling. Whatever Grief and Despair could represent to her, appear'd before her Eyes, which she lifted to Heaven, as if to upbraid it for the the Injury she was threatned with : These terrible Idea's threw her into a second Swoon; her Eyes shut; and the Robbers were afraid that Death had depriv'd them of their Prey. The Captain thinking it more proper to leave her to herself, than to plague her with new Relief from them, order'd her to be put upon *Leonarda*'s Bed, where she lay by herself, expos'd to the Insults of the most wicked of Mortals.

We went thence into the Hall, where one of the Robbers, who had been a Surgeon, drest the Lieutenant's Wound. We then examin'd our Parcels and Bundles, which we found full of all sorts of Cloaths, Linen, Woollen, and Silk, and among the rest a Bag of Pistoles, which was very welcome to the Gentlemen concern'd. After this the Cook laid the Cloth, and brought in Supper. All our Discourse was of the great Victory we had gain'd. Upon which *Rolando* addres'd himself to me, and said, Thou must own, *Gil Blas*, thou wast in a dreadful Fright.

Fright. I cannot deny it, reply'd I ; but
when have ferv'd two or three Cam-
paigns, you fhall fee what Feats I'll do,
All the Company took my Part, and
faid, that for that Time I fhould be excus'd ; that it was a brisk Action, and
confidering I was a young Man, who had
never ftood Fire before, I had come off
pretty well. We then talk'd of the
Mules and Horfes we had taken ; and it
was refolv'd that we fhould all go the next
Day, before 'twas light, to *Manfilla* to fell
them ; for probably our Expedition would
not be heard of there by that time. When
we had fupp'd, we return'd to the Lady, whom we found as we left her :
Tho' fhe was in that Condition, and
feem'd rather dead than alive, fome of
the Robbers caft a prophane Eye upon
her, and fhew'd their Brutal Luft, which
they would have fatisfied, if *Rolando*
had not hinder'd them, by reprefenting
that they ought at leaft to ftay till the
Lady was recovered out of her Fit, which
her Grief had thrown her into, and
taken from her the Ufe of her Senfes :
The Refpect they bore for their Captain,
was a Reftraint upon their Incontinence.
Nothing elfe could have fav'd the Lady ;
perhaps Death itfelf had not been a
Defence

Defence for her Honour. We again left
that unfortunate Woman in the fame
Condition ; *Rolando* charging *Leonarda*
to take care of her, and retir'd all to
our Chambers. As for me, as foon as
I lay down, inftead of fleeping I could
not help thinking on the Misfortune of
the Lady, I trembled to confider the
Horrors that furrounded her, and was
as much concern'd for her as if fhe had
been my Relation or Friend. In fine,
after having pity'd her heartily, I contriv'd how to deliver her from the Danger fhe was in, and carry her out of our
Under-ground Habitation. I confider'd
that the old Negro could not ftir ; and that
fince his Indifpofition the Cook kept
the Key of the Grate : This made me
form a Project, which I immediately
put in Execution in the following Manner.

I pretended to have the Colick, and
cry'd out as if I was in terrible Pain.
The Robbers awoke, and prefently came
to me : They ask'd me why I made fuch
a Noife ? I anfwer'd I was rack'd with
a Fit of the Colick ; and to fhew them
that I was fincere, I made a hundred
ugly Faces, like a Man in violent Pain.
I then lay ftill, as if the Fit was over, and

I

I somewhat easier. Presently after I roll'd on my Pallad, and twisted my Arms as if the Fit came upon me again: In a Word, I act.d my Part so well, that, as cunning as they were, I impos'd upon all of 'em, and they took me to be terribly tortur'd by my Distemper. They were all very officious to assist me ; one brought me a Bottle of Brandy, and made me drink half of it ; another, whether I would or not, anointed me with Oil of sweet Almonds ; a third warm'd a Napkin, and clapt it burning hot to my Belly. I in vain cry'd out, Hold : They imputed my Cries to my Colick, and made me continually endure Real Pain to ease me of a Counterfeit one. At last, not being able to bear it any longer, I told them I was pretty well again, and begg'd them to have Mercy upon me. They then gave over applying their Remedies ; and I took care how I complain'd again, for fear they should again torture me with their Relief.

This Scene lasted above three Hours: After which the Robbers supposing it was about the Time they had resolv'd to go to *Mansilla*, prepar'd for that Expedition. I made as if I would fain go with them,

them, and was getting up, but they would not let me : No, no, says Signor *Rolando*, stay here, Child, thou shalt go with us when thou art better in Health; the Colick may now take thee again; thou can't not yet bear travelling. I did not think fit to insist farther upon going, lest they should have comply'd with my Request; I only seem'd to be very sorry I could not be one amongst them on that Occasion: And this I did so well, that they all went out of our subterranean Dwelling, without the least Suspicion of my Design. When they were gone, as I heartily wish'd them, said I to myself, Now, *Gil Blas*, is the time for thee to pluck up all thy Resolution ; take courage to finish what thou hast so happily begun: *Domingo* is not in a Condition to oppose thy Enterprize, and *Leonarda* cannot hinder thy executing it: Take hold of this Opportunity to escape, thou wilt never have a more favourable one. These Reflexions embolden'd me ; I rose, took my Sword and my Pistols, and went first into the Kitchen : But before I enter'd, I heard *Leonarda* talk, and stepp'd to listen, where she was endeavouring to comfort the strange Lady, who being come to herself, and considering

fidering her Misfortune, wept bitterly.
Ay, ay, fays *Leonarda*, weep on, figh as
much as you can, 'twill be fome Eafe to
you ; the Fit you were in was dangerous ; but now 'tis over, there's nothing
to fear : While you weep there's no Danger : Your Grief will wear away by degrees ; and you'll like living with our
Gentlemen here, who are Men of Honour : They'll treat you like a Princefs ;
they'll be extremely fond of you, and
doubtlefs you will grow as fond of them
alfo : There's many a Woman that would
be glad to be in your Place.

I did not give *Leonarda* time to pro-
ceed ; I enter'd, and clapping a Piftol to
her Breaft, bad her give me the Key of
the Grate. She was in a dreadful Surprize ; and tho' well advanc'd in Years,
fhe was too much in love with Life to
refufe my Demand. When I had got
the Key, I addreft myfelf thus to the
Lady : Madam, Heaven has fent you a
Deliverer : Rife, and follow me, I will
conduct you whither you pleafe to command me. The Lady was not deaf to
this Offer. It made fuch an Impreffion
on her Mind, that recollecting all her
Strength, fhe arofe, threw herfelf at my
Feet, and implor'd me to fave her Honour :

nour. I rais'd her up, and affured her, she might depend upon me. I then took some Cords, which I fpy'd in the Kitchen, and with the Lady's help ty'd *Leonorda* to the Leg of a Table, protefting that I would kill her if fhe made the leaft Noife: I lighted a Lamp, and went with the Lady to the Room, where was the Robbers Treafure of Gold and Silver: I put as many fingle and double Piftoles in my Pockets as they would hold, and oblig'd the Lady to take what fhe could carry, reprefenting to her that fhe only took what was her own. Having thus made a good Provifion for ourfelves, we went to the Stable, which I entred by myfelf, with my Piftols cock'd. I fuppos'd that the old Negro, as ill as he was of the Gout and Rheumatifm, would not tamely let me faddle my bridle my Horfe, and refolved, if he refifted, to cure him of all his Ails for ever. But as good Luck would have it, his Pains were at that time fo violent that I took the Horfe out of the Stable without his perceiving it. The Lady waited for me at the Door: We foon paft thro' the Alley that led to the Grate, which we open'd, and coming to the Trap-door, with much ado lifted it up.

Had

Had we not been ſtrengthen'd by our
great deſire to eſcape, we ſhould never
have been able to have done it. Day
began to break when we ſaw ourſelves
out of that Abyſs, from whence we endeavoured to get away as faſt as we could.
I mounted my Horſe, and took the Lady behind me: We gallop'd along the
firſt Path we met with, and ſoon got
out of the Foreſt: We came to a Plain,
where were ſeveral Roads; we took
the firſt; and I was in mortal Dread
leſt it ſhould lead to *Manſilla*, and ſo
meet *Rolando* and his Comrades: But it
happened that I was afraid without a
Cauſe; and about two a Clock in the
Afternoon we arriv'd at *Aſtorga*. I obſerv'd the People gaz'd at us, as at a
Novelty, to ſee a Woman a Horſeback
behind a Man. We alighted at the firſt
Inn we came to; and I immediately ordered a Partridge and Pheaſant to be laid
down to the Fire. While my Orders
were executing, I conducted the Lady to
a Chamber, where we entred into Converſation, which we could not do on
the Road, becauſe of the Haſte we made.
She expreſs'd her ſelf to be extremely
ſenſible of the Obligation I had lain upon her, ſaying, She could not think that

a Person capable of so generous an Action, was a Companion of the Rogues, out of whose Hands I had deliver'd her. I told her my Story, to confirm the good Opinion she had conceiv'd of me. By which she put Confidence in me, and inform'd me of her Misfortunes, as I am about to relate them in the following Chapter.

CHAP. XI.

The Story of Donna Mencia de Mosquera.

I Was born at *Valladolid*, my Name is Donna *Mencia de Mosquera*; my Father Don *Martin*, after having spent almost all his Patrimony, was kill'd in *Portugal* at the Head of a Regiment which he commanded there. He left me so little Fortune, that I was an indifferent Match for any one, though I was an only Daughter. However, as little as I had, I did not want Lovers, for several of the most considerable Gentlemen of *Spain* courted me, but I preferr'd Don *Alvar de Mello* to all of them. Indeed he was the handsomest Man of them all, tho' that only

only would not have gain'd him the Preference. He had Wit, Difcretion, Courage, and Probity ; befides, he had the Character of the moft gallant Man of his Time. If he made an Entertainment, nothing could be more Elegant : If he appear'd at the Jufts, his Strength and his Dexterity were admir'd by all; For thefe Reafons I lov'd and marry'd him.

A few Days after our Marriage, he met Don *Andrea de Baefa*, his Rival, in a Bye Place; they quarrell'd and drew. Don *Andrea* was kill'd, and he being the Nephew of the Corregidor of *Valladolid*, a violent and mortal Enemy of the Family of *Mello*, Don *Alvar* did not think himfelf fafe in that City. He came Home immediately, where, while his Houfe was getting ready, He told me what had happen'd : My dear *Mencia*, faid he, we muft part. You know the Corregidor. Don't let us flatter our felves. He'll profecute me to the utmoft. You are not ignorant of his Power. I fhall not be fafe in the Kingdom. He was fo troubled at our Parting, and fo griev'd at my Grief, that he could fay no more. I made him take
fome

fome Jewels, and as much Gold as he
could carry with him. We then embraced, and for a Quarter of an Hour
did nothing but mingle Sighs and Tears.
Having notice that his Horfe was ready,
he broke from my Arms, and departed,
leaving me in a Condition which 'tis
impoflible to reprefent. Happy had I
been, if my Affliction had kill'd me at
the Inftant. How much Grief and Pain
had Death then fpar'd me. Some Hours
after Don *Alvar*'s Flight, the Corregidor
was inform'd of it, and order'd him
to be purfu'd. He did his utmoft to get
him into his Cuftody. My Husband
was too hard for him, and got into a
Place of Security. Thus the Magiftrate
was forc'd to content himfelf with the
poor Satisfaction of feizing the Goods
of a Man whofe Blood he thirfted after,
and he did that effectually. He left me
nothing to live upon. Poor and pitiful
was my Condition. I had but one Wo-
man-Servant to wait upon me. I fpent
all my Days in Weeping, not for my
Poverty, which I bore patiently, but for
the Abfence of my Husband, whom I
lov'd, but could hear no Tidings of. I
had no News of him for Seven Years together, and not knowing what was become

come of him, liv'd in continual Sorrow.
At laſt I underſtood that he was kill'd
in a Battle, fighting for the King of *Por-*
tugal, in the Kingdom of *Fez*: A Man
who came from *Africa* gave me an Account of it, aſſuring me that he was perfectly well acquainted with Don *Alvar*
de Mello ; that he had ſerv'd with him in
the *Portugueſe* Army, and ſaw him fall
in the Action: To this he added ſome
Circumſtances which made me believe
that my Husband was dead.

About that time Don *Ambroſio Meſia*
Carillo, Marquis *de la Puerdia*, came to
Villadolid. He was one of thoſe old Lords
who, by their polite and gallant Behaviour, make Women forget their Age, and
think 'em as taking as if they were in
their Youth ſtill. One Day ſome body
told him the Story of Don *Alvar* ;
and deſcribed me to him ſo favou-
rably, that he had a mind to ſee
me. He came to my Lodgings, gave me
a Viſit, and, tho' I was in ſo much Grief,
took ſuch a Liking to me, that it turn'd
to a tender Paſſion. Perhaps indeed he
pitied my ſad and diſmal Condition ;
and Pity very often converts itſelf into
Love : My mournful State touch'd him,
and he told me more than once, he look'd
upon

upon me as a Prodigy of Conftancy, and ev'n envy'd the Fate of my Husband in having fuch a faithful Wife, tho' his End was fo deplorable. In fhort, from the very firft Vifit he made me, he refolved to marry me, if I would have him. He broke his Mind to a Relation of mine, who came to me, and reprefented to me, that my Husband being kill'd in *Fez*, it was by no means reafonable that I fhould bury my felf alive, and make my Charms ufelefs to my Youth ; that I had mourn'd long enough for a Man with whom I had liv'd fo little a while, and ought to take hold of the Opportunity that was offer'd me to be the happieft Woman in the World. She then fet forth the Marquis's Nobility, Riches, and Charaƈter. But all fhe faid was loft upon me : I would not hearken to her : Not that I made a Doubt of Don *Alvar*'s Death, or was afraid of feeing him return on a fudden, when I leaft expeƈted him. I had fo little Inclination to a fecond Marriage, or rather fo much Repugnance to it, after I had been fo unfortunate in my firft, that I could not think of complying with my Kinfwoman's Counfel. However, fhe did not give over perfuading me : On the contrary

trary, she grew daily a more zealous Advocate for Don *Ambrosio* : She engaged all my Relations in that old Lord's Interests ; They all importuned me to accept of so advantageous a Match. I was every Minute teaz'd by them ; and my Poverty, which encreas'd upon me more and more, pleaded with them also, insomuch that I could resist no longer.

I gave way to their Importunity, and at their pressing Instances married the the Marquis *de la Guardia*, who, the next Day after we were married, carried me to a fine Seat of his near *Burgos*, between *Grajal* and *Rodillas*. His Love became more violent than ever ; he studied to please me in every thing he did ; he prevented my Desires, and never did Husband do more to gain the Heart of a Wife ; never was Lover more complaisant to a Mistress. I should passionately have lov'd Don *Ambrosio*, notwithstanding the Difference of our Ages, if I could have lov'd any one but Don *Alvar*. But a constant Heart can have but one Passion. The Remembrance of my first Husband, render'd all the Pains my second took to please me, ineffectual. All the Returns I made for his Tenderness, were Respect and Gratitude.

In

In this Difpofition was I, when looking out of my Window one Day to take the Air, I perceiv'd a kind of Peafant in the Garden, who look'd at me very attentively. I took him for an Afliftant to the Gardner, and did not much mind him; but the next Day looking out of the fame Window, I fpied him in the fame Place again, and he feemed to look at me with more Attention than before; which had fuch an Effect upon me, that I examin'd his Face too more curioufly, and fancied I faw the Features of the unhappy Don *Alvar*. This Thought put me into a terrible Apprehenfion of the Truth of it. I cry'd out; by good Fortune no body was then near me, but *Ines* my favourite Woman. I told her what my thought was; fhe laugh'd at me, fuppofing fome fmall Likenefs had impos'd upon my Sight. Don't think it, Madam, faid fhe; What likelihood is there that your firft Husband fhould be in the Garden, in the Form of a Peafant? Can you believe him to be ftill in the Land of the Living? I'll go down, added fhe, and talk to this Countryman. I will know who he is, and bring you an Account of it in an Inftant. Accordingly fhe did fo, and when fhe came

Vol. I.   E   back,

back, I obſerved her to be in great Diſorder. Madam, ſays ſhe, your Suſpicion
was but too well grounded. It is Don
Alvar himſelf, whom you ſaw. He
made the Diſcovery immediately, and
deſires to have ſome Diſcourſe with
you.

The Marquis was then gone to *Burgos*,
by which means I had an Opportunity
to receive Don *Alvar*, and ordered my
Woman to conduct him into my Cloſet.
You may imagine I was in the utmoſt
Confuſion, I could not bear the Sight
of a Man who had ſo much Reaſon to
upbraid me with Inconſtancy, I fell into a
Swoon when he enter'd the Cloſet. *Ines*
and he gave me all their Aſſiſtance, and
as I came a little to my ſelf, Don *Alvar*
ſaid, I beg you, Madam, to recover your
ſelf: Do not let my Preſence incommode
you. It is not my Intention to give
you the leaſt Trouble. I am not come like
an enraged Husband to demand an Account of the Faith you vow'd to me,
and to charge you with the Crime of a
ſecond Engagement contracted by you.
I am not ignorant that it was your Relations doing. I know how they per-
ſecuted you to conſent to it: That it
was reported and believ'd at *Valladolid*
that

that I was dead, and that you yourfelf had good reafon to think fo, having receiv'd no Letter from me to inform you of the contrary. In fine, I know what manner of Life you led after our cruel Separation ; and that Neceffity rather than Love threw you into the Arms of —— Ah, my Lord, faid I, interrupting him, Why will you excufe me ? I am guilty, fince you are alive. Oh, that I was now in the fame miferable Condition that Don *Ambrofio* found me. Oh wretched Marriage ! I fhould otherwife, as miferable as I was, have had the Comfort to meet you without Blufhing.

Dear *Mencia*, reply'd he, with an Air which fhew'd how much he was concern'd at my Grief, I do not complain of you, and am very far from upbraiding you with the flourifhing Condition I find you in ; I rejoyce at it. Ever fince I left *Valladolid* Fortune has been againft me ; My Life has been a continual Series of Mifery ; and nothing made me more miferable than the want of an Opportunity to fend you News of me, and to hear from you. I knew how you lov'd me, and had always in my Mind the fad State to which that Love had reduc'd

E 2   duc'd

duc'd you. I reprefented you to my Eyes always in Tears; and my Concern for you was ever my greateft Trouble : Sometimes I blam'd myfelf for having been the occafion of making you fo wretched; and even wifhed that you had given yourfelf to one of my Rivals, fince your preferring me to them had coft you fo dear. However, after feven Years Suffering, and doating on you ftill as much as ever, I could not help defiring to fee you; and having finifh'd a long Slavery, I went in this Difguife to *Valladolid*, where I was like to be difcover'd. I there learnt every thing: Thence I came to this Caftle, found a Way to come at the Gard'ner, and enter'd myfelf in his Service, in hopes, that as I wrought in the Garden, I might have an Opportunity to fee you; but don't think that by my Abode here I have the leaft Defign to interrupt your Happinefs. I love you more than I love my felf. I am pleas'd to fee you fo happy, and the Pleafure I fhall take to reflect on the Condition I leave you in, will be the only Comfort of a Life which I fhall now fpend far off from you, and return no more to trouble your Repofe. No, no, Don *Alvar*, cry'd I, at thefe Words, I
will

will not suffer you to leave me a second
Time : I will go with you : Nothing
but Death shall now part us. Hearken
to me, reply'd he, Live still with Don
Ambrosio : Let me be wretched by my
self. A great many other things he said
of the same nature ; but the more ready
he was to sacrifice himself for me, the less
willing was I to let him. When he found
that I was determin'd to go away with
him, he on a sudden alter'd his Tone, and
looking very well pleas'd upon me, said,
Madam, since you still love Don *Alvar*
so well, as to prefer his Misery to the
Prosperity you enjoy here, we'll go to
Belancos, at the farther end of the Kingdom of *Galicia*, where I have a secure
Retreat prepared for us. If my Misfortunes have depriv'd me of all my Estate,
they have not also depriv'd me of all my
Friends : I have some left who have e-
nabled me to carry you off with me.
I have, by their Assistance, got a Coach
ready at *Zamora :* I have bought Mules,
and am attended with three stout *Galicians*, arm'd with Carbines and Pistols :
They wait my Orders in the Village of
Rodillas : Let's take hold of this Occasion, the Absence of Don *Ambrosio :* I'll
fetch the Coach, and we will be gone

this

this Moment. I confented to his Propofal. Don *Alvar* flew to *Rodillas*, and in a little while return'd with his three *Galicians*. I was with my Women when he came with the Coach : He took me in his Arms, and put me into it. My Women ran away in a Fright, *Ines* only ſtaying near me ; but ſhe would not go along with us, becaufe ſhe was in Love with one of Don *Ambrofio*'s Valets.

I carried off only my Cloaths, and what Jewels I had before my ſecond Marriage. I took nothing that belong'd to the Marquis, or that he had given me. We travell'd towards *Galicia*, under Apprehenſions of being purfued by Don *Ambrofio*. We continued our Journey two Days together without any Oppoſition : We were in hopes to do the ſame the third ; and were difcourſing very agreeably of this Adventure, and of what happen'd to Don *Alvar* in his Abfence: How he had been a Slave five Years ; and what it was that occaſion'd the Report of his Death, when yeſterday, on the Road to *Leon*, we met the Robbers who were with you. It was He you kill'd, and the three Men were his *Galicians* : It is for him that thefe Tears

flow

flow from mine Eyes. Saying this, she
burst out a weeping ; and *Gil Blas* could
not help bearing her Company.

CHAP. XII.

How disagreeably Gil Blas *and the Lady were interrupted.*

WHEN her Grief permitted her to
hear what I had to offer, I ask'd
her what she intended to do in the present Conjuncture ? And as she was a-
bout to answer me, we were interrupted
by a great Noise in the Inn. The Corregidor was come thither with several
Serjeants, and other Officers : They enter'd our Chamber ; a young Gentleman that was with them coming up
to me, look'd very curiously upon me ;
and examining my Dress, cry'd out, By
St. *James*, he has my Coat on : 'Tis
he himself ; take hold of him ; he has
my Horse too ; he is one of the Thieves
that lurk in this Country. By this I understood that the young Cavalier was the
Gentleman who had been robb'd by
them, and whose Spoils I had unluckily
equipt

equipt my felf with. The Corregidor,
who, by my Looks, Imagin'd that I was
the Perfon the Gentleman took me for,
and that the Lady was an Accomplice,
fent us to feparate Prifons. This Magiftrate was not one of thofe whofe
frightful Looks are Death to a Criminal:
He had a foft fmiling Air, God knows
if he was the better Man for't. Affoon as
I was lodg'd in Prifon, he came thither
attended by his Officers; the firft thing
they did was to plunder me, according
to Cuftom. I was a fine Booty for
them; they never had a better: As often as they div'd into my Pockets, I
perceiv'd their Eyes fparkled with Joy;
the Corregidor could hardly contain him
felf. Child, fays he, fear nothing; we
only do our Duty: If you are innocent
no Harm will come to you. They were
all the while emptying my Pockets, and
took from me even what the Robbers
paid more refpect to, the Forty Ducats
given me by my Uncle. This did not
fatisfie them. They ftript me to my
Shirt, to fee whether I had hid any thing
between that and my Skin. When they
had thus done their Duty, as they faid,
the Corregidor examin'd me. I told him
ingenuoufly all that had happen'd to me.
He

He took my Examination in Writing·
He then departed with his Crew a-
bout him, and my Money and Goods
in their Cuſtody, leaving me naked on
ſome foul Straw in the Priſon.

What is human Life! cry'd I to my
ſelf, when I reflected on my forlorn
State: How full of Croſſes and Loſſes!
I have met with nothing elſe ſince I
left *Oviedo*: I am ſcarce got out of one
Peril, but another befals me. I little
thought when I arriv'd in this City that
I ſhould ſo ſoon become acquainted with
the Corregidor. I curs'd the fatal Coat
as I put it on again, and the reſt of the
Equipage that was left me, which I
brought from the Robbers ſubterranean
Dwellings. At laſt I encouraged my
ſelf with other Reflexions. Have a good
Heart, *Gil Blas*, ſaid I, Does it becom :
thee to deſpair in a common Jail, after
thou hadſt Patience in thy dark Confinement among the Thieves. But alas,
what ſignifies it to take Courage? How
can I get hence? they have depriv'd me
of all Means of procuring my Liberty,
by taking my Money from me, without which a Priſoner is like a Bird whoſe
Wings are clipp'd.

Inftead of the Fowl I had ordered to the Fire, they brought me fome Bread and Water. I was fifteen Days in my Hole without feeing any body but the Jailor, who gave me my Allowance of that thin Diet. I did what I could to have fome Difcourfe with him, but he would not fpeak a Word with me. He came in and out, and would not often fo much as look upon me. The fixteenth Day the Corregidor appear'd, and faid, Rejoyce, young Man, I bring thee glad Tidings: I have caus'd the Lady that was with thee to be conducted to *Burgos* : I examin'd her before fhe went, and her Anfwer will difcharge thee. Thou fhalt to day have thy Liberty, provided the Muletier, who, as thou faidft, brought thee from *Penafler* to *Cacabelos*, confirms thy Depofition; he is now in *Afterga*, I'll fend for him. If he agrees in the Article of the Torture, I'll difcharge thee immediately. I was overjoy'd to hear him talk thus. I did not doubt of my Liberty, and thank'd him for his Readinefs to do me fpeedy Juftice. I had hardly finifh'd my Compliment when the Muletier entred to us, attended by two Sergeants. I prefently knew him again ; but the Rogue having fold my

Port-

Portmanteau, and all that was in it, and fearing he should be oblig'd to make me satisfaction, if he own'd that he knew me, said very impudently he had never seen me in his Life before. Ah Traitor, said I ; confess rather that thou hast sold my Cloaths, and bear witness to the Truth: Look on me; I am one of the young Men whom thou threatnedst with the Torture at *Cacabelos*, and whom thou puttest in such a Fright. The Muletier replied very gravely, he knew nothing of the Matter, and persisting in disowning any knowledge off me, my Deliverance was put of to some other time. Patience was to be my Cure again ; the Jailor's Bread and Water my Diet. It was an intolerable thing to be there without having committed the least Crime. But what Help was there for't: I wish'd I had staid under-ground still : I was more at ease there, said I to my self, than in this Prison: I far'd well with the Robbers : We liv'd merrily ; and I comforted my self still with Hopes of escaping, whereas, innocent as I am, perhaps the best of my Fortune will be to be let out hence, to go to the Galleys.

CHAP.

CHAP. XIII.

By what Chance Gil Blas *was delivered out of Prison, and whither he went.*

WHile I was ſpending my time upon upon theſe Reflexions, the Story of my Adventures, as it was contain'd in my Depoſition, was reported about the Town, ſeveral Perſons came out of Curioſity to ſee me : They ſtood one after another at a little Window, by which the Light came into my Priſon ; and when they had gaz'd at me ſome time they march'd their Way. I was ſurpriz'd at this Novelty: I had not till then ſeen a Mortal at the Window ſince my Confinement. I imagined that I was talk'd of in the City ; and could not tell whether it was for the better or the worſe.

One of thoſe that came to ſee me happen'd to be the little Quiriſter of *Mondonedo*, who, as well as I, had been afraid of the Rack, and taken to his Heels to avoid it. I knew him, and he
knew

knew me : We faluted one another, and enter'd afterwards into a long Converfation. I was obliged to give him a full Account of all my Adventures ; and he told me what paft in the Inn at *Cacabelos* between the Muletier, and the young Woman: In fhort, he inform'd me of every thing I have faid concerning it ; and promis'd when he took leave of me, that he would that Minute go and labour for my Deliverance. Then every Body who came to my Window out of Curiofity, as well as he, exprelt themfelves to have Pity on my Sufferings, and affur'd me they would joyn with him in endeavouring to procure my Liberty.

They were as good as their Word : They fpoke to the Corregidor on my Behalf. That Magiftrate made no more doubt of my Innocence, efpecially after he had heard what the Quirilter had to fay. Three Weeks after his firft Vifit he appear'd in my Prifon again, and faid, *Gil Blas*, not to keep thee in pain, thou may'ft go whither thou wilt. But tell me, doft thou think, if we fent fome *Sergeants* and others with thee to the Forelt, thou couldft find out that Habitation Under-ground. No, my Lord,

Lord, replied I; 'twas Night always
when I enter'd it, and never came out
but before Day: 'Tis impoffible for
me to difcover it. Then the Corregidor
left me, faying, he would order the Jaylor
to open the PrifonDoors for me. The Jaylor and his Turnkey enter'd my Hole foon
after; and having taken from me the little I had left, which they lik'd better
than their own, they exchange Cloaths
with me, and turn'd me out of the Prifon by the Head and Shoulders. I was
afham'd to be feen in the Rags they
had given me inftead of my Cloaths; and
my Confufion leffen'd the Joy Prifoners
have ufually when they are fet at Liberty.

I would fain have gone out of Town,
and avoided being gaz'd at by the People ; but my Gratitude would not let
me go, without taking leave of the Quirifter, to whom I was fo much oblig'd,
I went and returned him my Thanks:
He could not help laughing at feeing
me. You have far'd very indifferently,
fays he, in the Hands of Juftice. I don't
complain of it, replied I; Juftice is always right ; I wifh only that the Officers that belong to it were honeft Men.
I think they fhould at leaft have let me
have

have my Cloaths: They would have
been well enough paid by my Money.
Very true, faid he; but it feems the
Formalities of their Office required it,
and they call it doing their Duty. How,
I pray, do they do this Duty of theirs?
Is the Horfe you had reftored to the right
Owner? No furely, he is now in the Serjeant's Stable that took him from you,
to be a Proof of the Robbery there: The
poor Gentleman that owns it will not
I believe, have fo much as the Crupper reftor'd to him. But to fay no more of this;
What do you intend to do? I have a
mind, replied I, to go to *Burgos*, and
find out the Lady whom I deliver'd out
of the Hand of the Robbers: She will
give me fome Piftoles; I will buy me a
new Gown, and go to *Salamanca*, where
I hope to make fomething of my *Latin*:
The worft of it is, 'tis a great way to
Burgos, and I have nothing to maintain
me on the Road. I underftand you,
faid my Companion, my Purfe is at
your Service; it is a little low indeed,
but we will do as well as we can with
it. Saying this, he pull'd it out of his
Pocket, and gave it me with fo good a
Grace, that I could not refufe accepting
of it, fuch as it was; and gave him a
thoufand

thousand Thanks, and promis'd to be
always ready to do as much for him,
when it lay in my way, which it never
did.   I took my leave of him, and departed from the City without visiting
the other Persons who had contributed
to my Deliverance.   I contented myself
with heartily wishing them well.   My
Friend's Purse was, as he said, at the bottom.   'Twas well for me that I had
lately been us'd to a very frugal way
of Living, I could not have made it
hold out else.   I was so good a Husband
that I had some Reals left when I arriv'd at *Ponte de Mula*, which is not far
from *Burgos* : I went into an Inn, and
was accosted by the Hostess.   She was an
ugly scolding Dame ; and I perceiv'd
she did not like me, by my Appearance.
I matter'd it not, sat down, and called
for some Bread and Cheese.   The Wine
they brought me was detestable.   While
I was eating, I would fain have entred
into Conversation with my Landlady :
I defir'd her to tell me if she knew
the Marquis *de la Guardia* ; if his Seat
was near ; and what she heard of
the Marchionefs his Wife ?   You ask me
abundance of Questions, reply'd she, with
an Air of Contempt : However, after a
                                        rude

rude manner, fhe told me Don *Ambro-fio's* Houfe was but a League from *Ponte Mula.*

Having fupp'd as well as my Purfe afforded, I bad them fhew me a Chamber. You a Chamber, faid the Hoftefs very fcornfully : I can't fpare a Room for fuch as fup on a Bit of Bread. All my Beds are taken up ; I expect feveral Gentlemen of Fafhion to Night : You may lie in the Barn if you will : I fuppofe 'tis not the firft Time. She was in the Right of it. I made her no Anfwer, but went to the Barn, laid my felf down on fome Straw, and flept as foundly as a Man that was heartily tir'd.

CHAP.

CHAP. XIV.

Of the Reception Donna Mencia *gave him at* Burgos.

I Did not lie long next Morning. I went to my Landlady to let her know I was up; and she was in a better Humour than I left her in over-night. I imputed it to the Company of three of St. *Hermandad's* Bayliffs, who were very familiar with her: They had lain in our Inn that Night; and I doubt not but it was for these Gentlemen that all the Beds were taken up. I ask'd the way, when I came into the Village, for Don *Ambrosio's* Castle. By chance I met with a Man of the same Character as my Landlord at *Penafler :* He did not only tell me the Way to the Castle, but that Don *Ambrosio* had been dead three Weeks, and the Marchioness his Wife was retir'd into a Convent at *Burgos.* I directed my Steps towards that City, instead of taking the Road to the Castle, as I at first design'd ; and

made

made what Hafte I could to the Mo-
naftery where Donna *Mencia* liv'd. I
pray'd the Door-Keeper to tell the Lady
that a young Man newly come out of
the Prifon at *Aftorga* defir'd to fee her.
The Door-keeper told her immediately,
and when fhe came back conducted me
into a Hall, where I was not long before Don *Ambrofio's* Widow appear'd at
the Grate in very deep Mourning. You
are welcome, faid the Lady : Four Days
ago I wrote to a Perfon at *Aftorga* to
go to you, and acquaint you that affoon
as you got out of Prifon, I defir'd you
to come hither. I doubted not you
would not be long detain'd there. I
faid enough to the Corregidor in your
Behalf to difcharge you. The Anfwer
I receiv'd was, That you had had your
Liberty, but they did not know what
was become of you. I was afraid I
fhould never fee you more, nor ever have
the Satisfaction to make you a Return
for the Obligations I have to you. Don't
be caft down, faid fhe, perceiving I was
out of Countenance, at appearing before
her in fo forry a Garb : Don't be concern'd at your Drefs. After the Service
you have done me, I fhould be the moft
ungrateful of Women if I did nothing
'for

for you : I'll deliver you out of the miferable State you are now in : . I ought to do it, and I can do it. I have Wealth enough to difcharge my felf towards you, as obliged by Gratitude, without ftreightning my felf.

You know, continued fhe, my Adventures till the Time that we were both imprifon'd : I will now acquaint you with what hapned afterwards, when the Corregidor's People had conducted me to *Burgos* from *Aftorga*. After I had told him my whole Story, I went to Don *Ambrofio's* Caftle. My Return occafioned a great Surprize ; but they inform'd me there that I came too late ; that the Marquis was fo troubled at my Flight, that he was fallen fick, and the Phyficians defpair'd of his Life. I had now a frefh Occafion to complain of my Stars ; however I bad them to acquaint him with my Arrival. They did fo : I went to his Chamber with my Eyes full of Tears, and my Heart full of Grief. What brought you here ? faid he as foon as he faw me : Are you come to glory in the Sight of a Work of your own making ? Are you not fatisfy'd with having taken my Life from me ? Muft your Eyes too be the Witneffes of my Death ?
My

My Lord, reply'd I, *Ines* ought to have inform'd you that I fled with my firſt
Husband; and had it not been for a very dreadful Accident which befel us,
you ſhould never have ſeen me more.
I then told him how Don *Alvar* was
kill'd by the Robbers, and how I was
carried afterwards to an Habitation Under-ground; how I was deliver'd thence,
and what happen'd to me ſince. When
I had done ſpeaking, Don *Ambroſio* held
out his Hand to me, and ſaid with a
tender Air, 'Tis enough; I ceaſe to complain of you: Indeed what reaſon have
I to reproach you? You met with a
Husband whom you dearly lov'd: You
left me to go with him: Can I blame
you for that? No, Madam, I ſhould
be in the wrong to complain: I would
not ſuffer you to be purſued: I conſider'd
the ſacred Rights of your Raviſher, and
your Inclination for him. In fine, I did
you Juſtice; and by your Return hither
you recover all my Affections. Yes, my
dear *Mencia*, the Sight of you fills me
with Joy; but alas! I cannot long enjoy it; I find my Laſt Hour approaches: You are no ſooner reſtor'd to me,
than I muſt bid you an eternal Adieu.
Theſe Words were ſo moving, that
they

they made my Tears flow afresh, and
my Soul to diffolve with immoderate
Sorrow. I could not help weeping a-
loud ; and queftion whether I wept
more for the Death of Don *Alvar* whom
I ador'd. Don *Ambrofia* had not a falfe
Alarm of his Death : He died next Day,
and I became Miftrefs of the confiderable
Eftate he fettled upon me at our Marriage. I fhall not make an ill Ufe of it.
And tho' I am ftill young, no body fhall
ever fee me in the Arms of a third
Husband. Befides that, in my Opinion,
it looks indecent and immodeft to be
thrice married. I am refolv'd to end
my Days in a Convent, and become a
Benefactrefs.

Having finifh'd her Difcourfe thus, fhe
pull'd a Purfe from under her Gown,
which fhe gave me, faying, There's a
hundred Ducats which I give you to
equip yourfelf ; only when you have done
it, come and fee me again. I don't intend to confine my Gratitude to fo nar-
row a compafs. I gave the Lady a thoufand Thanks, and fwore to her I would
not leave *Burgos* without waiting on
her. After this Oath, which I had no
Inclination to break, I went and look'd
out for an Inn ; I enter'd the firft I came
to,

to, ask'd for a Room, and that the Landlord might not have an ill Opinion of
me by the Figure I made, I let him know
I had wherewithal to pay my Reckoning. At thefe Words *Majuelo* my Hoft
furveyed me from Head to Foot; and
being a Wag, made Anfwer, that he had
no need of fuch an Affurance from me,
to let him know that I fhould be a good
Gueft to his Houfe; that he faw fomething noble in me, thro' the Difadvan-
tage of my Drefs, and doubted not but
I was a Gentleman of Subftance. I found
the Rogue banter'd me; and to put an
end to his Rallery, I fhew'd him my
Purfe, told out the Hundred Ducats,
and perceived that the Sight of the Gold
difpos'd him to a more favourable Judgment of me. I defir'd him to fend a
Tailor to me: He faid it would be better
to have a Broker, who would bring all
forts of Cloaths, and equip me immediately. I approv'd of his Counfel, and
refolv'd to follow it; but it growing towards Night, I put off doing it till Morning, and order'd Supper to be got ready
as foon as poffible, refolving to make a-
mends for my bad Living ever fince I
came out of my Subterranean Dwelling.

CHAP.

CHAP. XV.

How Gil Blas *dreft himfelf. Of another Prefent the Lady made him, and in what Equipage he departed from* Burgos.

THE Waiters ferv'd me a Fricaffy of Sheeps Trotters, which I almoft de-vour'd whole. I drank in Proportion to what I eat, and then went to bed, and it being a pretty good one, I was in hopes that I fhould have flept all Night and made but one Nap of it. Inftead of which, I could not fleep a Wink for thinking of my new Cloaths, and what I fhould do afterwards. I could not tell what Garb to wear ; fometimes I was for buy-ing a Gown, and equipping my felf for *Salamanca* ; fometimes for taking Orders. But at laft I found the World prevail'd, and I refolv'd to make my Fortune in it. In order to which, my purpofe was to put on a Sword, and fet my felf out like a Gentleman. I was impatient for Day-light, and as foon as it appear'd I got up. I made fuch a Noife in the Inn,

that

that I wak'd all about me. I knock'd up
the Waiters, who curs'd me for my
Pains; but they could not help rising,
and I would not let them be at reft till
they had brought me a Broker, which was
done in a Minute; he came, attended with
Two Boys, who brought each a Green
Bundle. Their Mafter faluted me very
civilly, faying, *Signior*, it was your very
good Luck to light of me: however,
I would not run down my Brethren; I
would, by no means injure their Reputation, but between you and I, there's
not one of them who has a Confcience:
They are all as hard as *Jews*: I am the
only Broker who has a Grain of Honefty. I am contented with a reafonable
Profit: A Penny in the Pound is all I
defire; thanks my Stars, I love fair Deal-
ing.

After this Preamble, which I took all
for Gofpel, like a Fool as I was, he bad
his Boys to open their Bundles. He
fhew'd me Suits of all forts of Colours,
and fome that were Plain, but I rejected
the latter with Difdain. They were
too modeft for me. He at laft made me
try one on, which fitted me exactly
every way, the Coat was of Blue-Vel-
vet embroider'd with Gold, and the

F   Cloak

Cloak of the same. I liked it mightily, tho it had been worn, and ask'd the Price of it. The Broker perceiving I had taken a Fancy to it, said, I had a very good Choice. By my Faith, cry'd he, you understand these things. This Suit was made for one of the greatest Lords in the Kingdom; he never had it on but thrice. Examine the Velvet, nothing can be finer; and as for the Embroidery, never was any thing better wrought. How much will it cost? reply'd I. Sixty Ducats, said he. I have refus'd it, as I'm an honest Man. I offer'd him Five and Forty, which was as much again as the Suit was worth. Signor, reply'd the Broker, I'll make but one Word with you. See some of these Suits, continu'd he, pointing to those I had rejected, I'll sell them to you much cheaper. This made me the more eager for that I had pitch'd upon, and imagining that he would not bate any thing, I told him out Sixty Ducats. When he saw I was so easy, as honest a Man as he was, I perceiv'd he was sorry he had not demanded more for't. However, contenting himself with his Peny in the Pound, he took my Money, and departed with his Two Boys, whom I shall never forget.

I had

I had now got a handfome Suit and Cloak; the next thing was to buy Linnen, Hat, Shoes, Stockins, and a Sword; which done, I put 'em all on, and was wonderfully delighted to fee my felf fo equipp'd: I was never fatisfy'd with furveying my felf; never was Peacock prouder of his Feathers. I went the fame Day and paid a fecond Vifit to *Donna Mencia*, who receiv'd me as gracioufly as fhe had done at the firft: She thank'd me again for the Service I had done her, and abundance of Compliments paft on both fides. She then wifh'd me all Happinefs, and bad me farewell, giving me only a Ring worth about Thirty Piftoles, when fhe left me, praying me to keep it for her fake. I was very much baulk'd at this Prefent, expecting fomething better than a Ring; and not at all contented with the Lady's Generofity, I return'd to my Inn very thoughtful. But, as I enter'd it, a Man follow'd me, and throwing open his Cloak, fhew'd a huge Bag which had the Appearance of a Money-Bag; and at the fight of it, I ftar'd greedily upon it, as did all prefent. As for me, I thought I heard the Voice of a Seraphim, who laying the Bag upon a Table, faid to me, Signor *Gil Blas*, this

F 2   is

is what, Madam the Marchioness has
sent you. I bow'd very reverently to
the Bearer, I confounded him with my
Civilities, and as soon as he was got out
of the Inn, threw my self on the Money-Bag, like a Hawk on his Prey. I
carry'd it to my Chamber, open'd it,
and found therein a Thousand Ducats:
I had just done counting them, when
my Host, who heard what the Bearer
had said to me, enter'd my Chamber to
fee what was in the Bag. He was surpriz'd at the Sight of so many Ducats
lying on the Table. What a Duce, says
he, is all this Money yours? You must
know how to please the Women, sure;
you have not been 24 Hours in *Burgos*,
an' have already Marchionesses under
Contribution.

This Discourse did not displease me:
I was tempted to leave *Majuelo* in his
Mistake. It flatter'd my Vanity. I don't
wonder Young Men love to be thought
in the good Graces of the Ladies. But I
was more Innocent than Vain. I unde-
ceiv'd my Landlord. I told him the
Story of *Donna Mencia*; to which he listen'd very attentively. I consulted him
what was best for me to do in my present Circumstances, the Man seeming to
be

be in my Intereſt. He ſtood ſilent ſome
time, and then anſwer'd ſeriouſly, Signor *Gil Blas*, I have a love for you, and
ſince you put ſo much Truſt in me,
as to open your ſelf ſo frankly, I will
tell you plainly what I think you had
beſt do. You ſeem to be made for a
Court. I adviſe you to endeavour to
get into the Service of ſome great Lord,
and either to gain his Confidence, by ſerving him in his Intereſts, or in his
Pleaſures. If you don't do that, you
loſe your Time. I know ſome Perſons
of Quality, they do not care a Farthing
for the Zeal of an honeſt Man; they
mind no Body that is not neceſſary to
them. You have another way left ſtill.
You are Young, Handſome; and if you
had no Wit, that would be enough to
gain you ſome rich Widow, or ſome
pretty Woman unhappily married. If
Love Ruins Men who have Eſtates, it
often Makes thoſe that want them. I
think you will therefore do well to go
to *Madrid*; but I would not adviſe you
to go alone. People judge by Appearances,
and you will be look'd upon according to
the Figure you make. I'll help you
to a Valet, an honeſt Fellow, and as
handy a one as any in *Spain*. Buy Two
F 3 Mules,

Mules, one for your felf, and another
for him, and depart as foon as you
can.

This Counfel was too agreeable to my
Humour for me to neglect it. I bought
Two Mules the next Day, and hir'd
the Valet he fpoke of: He was about
Thirty Years old, and appear'd to be
a plain downright Fellow. He faid he
was a Native of *Galicia,* and his Name
Ambrofe de Lamela. Whereas other
Servants haggle about their Wages, he
was contented with any thing, and I
thought he would take it as a Favour
if I would let him ferve me for nothing.
I bought alfo fome Boots, and a Portmanteau, paid my Reckoning, and on
the Morrow departed before Sun-rifing
from *Burgos* to *Madrid.*

C H A P.

_____

CHAP. XVI.

*Shewing that one ought not to make too
sure of Prosperity.*

WE lay the firſt Night at *Duenas*, and arriv'd the ſecond at *Villado-lid*, about Four a Clock in the Afternon. We alighted at an Inn which look'd to be one of the beſt in the Town. I left the care of the Mules to my Valet, and went to a Room, which was ſhewn me by one of the Servants of the Houſe, who carried my Portmanteau. Finding my ſelf tired, I threw my ſelf down on the Bed without pulling my Boots off, I fell aſleep, and did not awake till almoſt Night, when I call'd for *Ambroſe*, but he was not in the Inn. He came ſoon after: I aſk'd him where he had been, and he anſwered, with a holy Grimace, At Church, to return Thanks to Heaven, for having preſerv'd us from all ill Accidents in our Journey from *Burgos* to *Valladolid*. I approv'd of what he had been doing, and then bad him get me a Pullet for my Supper. While I was

giving

giving him this Order, my Landlord
enter'd the Chamber with a Taper in his
Hand, lighting a Lady, who appear'd to
be more Fair than Young, and very
richly Drefs'd, a *Negro* holding up her
Tail. I was not a little furpriz'd, when
after having made me a low Courtſy, ſhe
ask'd me, as if by chance, Whether I
was not Signor *Gil Blas* of *Santillane ?*. I
no ſooner replied Yes, than ſhe let go
the Hand of her Gentleman Uſher, to
embrace me with a Tranſport of Joy,
which added the more to my ſurprize.
Heaven, cry'd ſhe, what a happy Adventure is this ; 'tis you that I am ſeek-
ing. I then called to mind the Paraſite
of *Penaſler*, and was about to conclude
that this Lady was much ſuch another
ſort of Creature. But what ſhe ſaid afterwards, gave me a more favourable
Opinion of her. I am, continu'd ſhe,
Couſin-German to *Donna Mencia de Moſ-*
quera, who is ſo much oblig'd to you.
I this Morning receiv'd a Letter from
her, informing me, that underſtanding
you were going to *Madrid*, ſhe deſired
me to entertain you, if you paſt this
Way. I have been running up and
down the City theſe Two Hours in
queſt of you, I went from Inn to Inn

to enquire of all the Strangers I faw, and
by this Hoft's Defcription of you, I
imagin'd at laft that you might be the
Deliverer of my Coufin. And now that
I have met you, I will let you fee how
fenfible I am of the Service you did my
Family, and my dear Kinfwoman in particular. Pray, go with me to my Houfe,
you will be more commodioufly lodg'd
there than here. I would have excufed
my felf, and reprefented to the Lady
that I fhould be too troublefome to her,
but fhe would not be put off. There
waited a Coach at the Gate of the Inn ;
fhe took Care her felf to fee my Portmanteau put into it, becaufe, faid fhe,
there are Rogues at *Valladolid* ; which I
found too true. In fhort, I went into
the Coach with her and her Gentleman-
Ufher, and was in this manner carry'd
away from the Inn, to the great diflike
of my Landlord, who loft the taking of
fo much Money as he fuppos'd I fhould
have fpent there. After our Coach had
paft through feveral Streets, it ftop'd.
We alighted at a pretty large Houfe ,
and came to an Apartment well furnifh'd,
and illuminated with Twenty or Thirty
Sconces. There were feveral Servants
waiting, of whom the Lady demanded

F 5   whether

whether Don *Raphael* was arrived? They answer'd, No. Then she addrest herself thus to me, Signor *Gil Blas*, I expect my Brother to night from a Country Seat which we have two Leagues off: How agreeably will he be surpriz'd, to find a Man in his House, to whom all our Family is so much obliged. In the Moment she was talking we heard a Noise, and understood it was occasion'd by the Arrival of Don *Raphael.* That Gentleman presently made his Appearance. He was a young, handsome, brisk Man. I am overjoyed to see you, Brother, says the Lady to him; You will help me to entertain Signor *Gil Blas* of *Santillane* ; we can never do enough in return for his Services to our Cousin Donna *Mencia.* Here, added she, offering him a Letter; read what she has written me. Don *Raphael* opened the Billet, and read these Words out aloud:

Dear *Camilla*,

S*Ignor* Gil Blas *of* Santillane, *who saved my Honour and Life, is now going to Court ; he will doubtless pass by* Valladolid. *I conjure you, by our Relation, and, what is*
                                                more,

*more, by our Friendſhip, to entertain him,
and keep him ſome time at your Houſe. I
flatter my ſelf that you will give me this
Satisfaction; and that my Deliverer will
receive of you and my Couſin Don* Raphael
all manner of kind Treatment at Burgos.
  Your Affeſtionate Couſin,
    Donna Mencia.

How! ſaid Don *Raphael,* when he had
read the Letter, Is this the Gentleman
to whom my Couſin owes both Honour
and Life? Heaven be prais'd for ſo happy a Meeting. Saying this, he caught
me in his Arms; How do I rejoyce, continued he, in ſeeing here Signor *Gil Blas*
of *Santillane.* My Couſin the Marchio-
neſs had no need of deſiring us to entertain you: Had ſhe only hinted to us that
you were to paſs thro' *Valladolid,* my
Siſter *Camilla* and I know our Duty too
well, not to make much of a Perſon who
has ſo highly obliged a Lady ſo dear to
our whole Family. I made the beſt Anſwer I could to theſe Diſcourſes, which
were followed by others of the ſame nature, intermix'd with a thouſand Ca-
reſſes. After which, obſerving that I
had ſtill my Boots on, they order'd
their Servants to take 'em off.

       We

We then went into another Room,
where there was a Table fpread : We
fat down ; and all their Talk at Supper
was as obliging as that before : I could not
fay a Word, but they were taken with
it, and were both of 'em very officious
to help me out of every Difh. Don *Ra-*
phael often drank Donna *Mencia*'s Health:
I follow'd his Example ; and obferv'd
fometimes that *Camilla*, who would have
her Glafs too, caft a Look upon me, which
had a Signification in it. I took notice
that fhe would watch her Opportunities
to do it, as if fhe was afraid her Brother
would perceive it. I needed no more to
be perfuaded that I was in her Favour,
and Imagin'd I might make my Advantage of it, if I ftaid ever fo little while
at *Valladolid.* The Hopes of this made
me eafily comply with their Requeft
to pafs a few Days with them. They
thank'd me for my Complacency ; and
Camilla was fo glad, that I doubted
not of her having found out fomething
amiable in me.

Don *Raphael* finding that I had determin'd to ftay there fome time, propos'd
to carry me to his Caftle. He made a
magnificent Defcription of it to me, and
enlarg'd upon the Diverfions we fhould
                                        meet

meet with there. Sometimes, fays he,
we'll Hunt, fometimes Fifh, fometimes
take the Air; we have fine Woods and
delicious Gardens; befides, we fhall have
rare Company; I hope you will not be
tir'd there. I accepted of his Propofal; and
the next Day was appointed for our
going to that fine Caftle of his. Having
form'd fo agreeable a Defign, we rofe
from the Table. Don *Raphael* feem'd
to be tranfported; Signor *Gil Blas*, faid
he, embracing me, I leave you with my
Sifter; I am going this Minute to give
the neceffary Orders, and invite the Perfon that fhall be of our Company. At thefe
Words he went out. I continued the
Converfation with the Lady, whofe
Difcourfe was of a-piece with her Looks;
fhe took me by the Hand, and caft her
Eyes upon my Ring: That's a fine Diamond, fays fhe: Do you underftand
Stones? I reply'd, No. I am forry, faid
the Lady; for you might then have told
me what this is worth. She then fhew'd
me a large Ruby fhe had on her Finger;
and while I was looking on, added, An
Uncle of mine, Governor of the *Phillippine* Iflands belonging to the *Spaniards*,
gave it to me. The Jewellers of *Valladolid*

dolid value it at about Three hundred
Piſtoles. I believe they hit it, ſaid I:
'Tis extremely fine. Since you like it,
reply'd ſhe, I'll truck with you. She
then took my Ring, and put her own on
my little Finger. I thought this way
of making a Preſent very gallant. She
after this ſqueezed me by the Hand, and
giving me a tender Glance, broke off the
Converſation on a ſudden, bad me Good-
night, and retir'd in Confuſion, as if
ſhe had been aſham'd to have diſcover'd
her Sentiments to me in that manner.

Tho' I was a Novice in Gallantry, I
imagin'd that her going away ſo haſtily,
boded well for me; and that I ſhould
not ſpend my Time ill in the Country,
Full of theſe pleaſing Fancies, and the
happy State of my Affairs, I ſhut my
ſelf up in the Chamber where I was to
lie, having bid my Valet call me early
in the Morning. Inſtead of ſleeping, I
ſweetly meditated on the Portmanteau
that lay on the Table, and the Ruby that
I had on my Finger. Thank Heaven,
ſaid I to my ſelf, I was once unfortunate; I am not ſo now: Here's a Ring
worth Three hundred Piſtoles; there
a Thouſand Ducats in Gold; theſe will
laſt me a long while. *Majuelo*, I find,

did

did not flatter me: The Ladies of *Madrid* will receive me very kindly, since
Camilla is already so gracious to me. I
was charm'd by the Bounty of that generous Lady, and my Head full of the
Diverfions I was to have with Don
Raphael at his Caftle. However, as de-
lightful as thefe *Idea's* were to me, Sleep
at laft overtook me ; and when I awoke
next Morning, I found, that the Day was
pretty well fpent. I was furpriz'd that
my Servant had not call'd me, according
to my Order. My faithful *Ambrofe,* faid
I to my felf, is either at Church, or he
is very lazy to day: But I had not fo
good an Opinion of him long ; for
getting up, and miffing my Portmanteau, I
fufpected he had robb'd me of it in the
Night. To fatisfie my felf in the matter, I opened my Chamber - Door, and
call'd the Hypocrite feveral times. Upon
which an old Man came to me, and askt
what I wanted? adding, All your People went away this Morning before day;
there's not one of them in my Houfe.
How! your Houfe! cry'd I; Is not this Don
Raphael's? I know no fuch Man, faid he ;
you are in a Lodging-houfe : The Lady
who fupp'd with you laft Night came to
us yefterday in the Evening, and hir'd
this

this Apartment for a great Lord who travelled *incognito*, and paid me before-
hand.

This was enough for me. I prefently
perceived what fort of People *Camilla*
and Don *Raphael* were ; and that my
Valet having fully inform'd himfelf of
my Affairs, had fold me to thofe Cheats.
Inftead of blaming my felf for this fad
Accident, and thinking that it would not
have happened to me, if I had not had
the Indifcretion of opening my felf to
Majuelo without any manner of neceffity.
I laid all the Fault on innocent Fortune,
and a hundred times curs'd my Stars.
The Landlord of the Lodgings, to whom
I told the Adventure, appear'd to be
very fenfible of the Concern I was in.
He pity'd me, and faid he was forry fuch
a thing fhould happen in his Houfe: But
notwithftanding all his Pretences, I doubt
not but he had as great fhare of the Vil-
lany and Booty as my Landlord at *Burgos*, to whom I imputed the Honour of
the Contrivance.

CHAP.

CHAP. XVII.

What Gil Blas *did after the Adven-*
ture of the Lodging-houfe.

WHEN I had enough deplor'd my
Misfortune, I confider'd that I
ought rather to bear up againft it, than
fuffer myfelf to be deprefs'd by it. I took
heart, and faid to my felf, as I was
putting on my Cloaths, 'Tis well the
Rogues have not taken them too. I
have fome Ducats ftill in my Pockets.
They had been fo merciful to me as
that came to, and had alfo left my Boots,
which I gave to my Landlord for a third
part of what they coft me. I then left
his Houfe, without bidding adieu to
any one in it, having occafion for
no body to carry my Luggage for me.
The firft thing I did, was, to fee whether
my Mules were at the Inn, where I
left them the Day before. I guefs'd that
Ambrofe had taken them with him, and
I wifh I had always made fo right a
Judgment of him. I learnt that he carried 'em off the Evening before. So,
never

never thinking to fee them or my Portmanteau again, I walk'd up and down
the Streets, pondering in my Mind what
I fhould do next.

I was tempted to return to Burgos,
to have a fecond Recourfe to Donna
Mencia; but I thought again that would
be to impofe upon that Lady's Bounty,
and fhe would look upon me as a Sot:
So I gave over that Defign. I fwore
alfo that I would for the future be upon
my Guard againft Women, and would
not truft even the Chaft Sufannah. I e-
very now and then caft my Eyes upon
my Ring, and reflecting that it was a
Prefent of Camilla's, I figh'd, and faid
to my felf, 'tis certainly no Ruby, and
fail'd not to go to a Jeweller to be inform'd that I am a Bubble. Neverthelefs I was willing to know whether
it was fo or not, and fhew'd my Ring
to an Artift, who faid 'twas worth three
Ducats. At this Eftimation, which I
expected, I gave the Governour of the
Phillippine Iflands Niece to the Devil.
As I was going out of the Jeweller's Shop,
I met with a young Man who ftopp'd
to take a View of me. I did not call
him to mind prefently, tho' I knew him
very well. How! Gil Blas! fays he; Do
you

you make as if you did not know me?
Can you in two Years time forget the
Barber *Nunez*'s Son? Am I so much al-
tered? Do you not remember your old
Playfellow *Fabricio*, your Countryman,
and School-fellow, after we have so often disputed together at Doctor *Godman*'s
of Universals, and Metaphysical Degrees?
I call'd him to mind before he had
done speaking, and embrac'd him with
a great deal of Joy. I am glad to see
you, my dear Friend, cry'd I : I cannot express my Transport. But said
he, with a Look of Surprize, How comes
it that you are as fine as a Prince? a Sword,
Silk Stockins, an embroider'd Coat, and
Velvet Cloak? On my Word you must
have had very good Luck, some old
Woman or other has been so bountiful
to you. Thou art mistaken, replied I ;
things do not go with me so swimming-
ly as you imagine. That Sham won't
take, says he ; you affect to be discreet.
Where had you that fine Ring upon your
Finger? tell me that, Monsieur *Gil Blas*.
From an errant Cheat, dear *Fabricio*,
a Jade, that, instead of enriching me
with her Favours, has ruin'd me by her
Deceit.

I spoke

I fpoke this fo forrowfully, that *Fa-bricio* perceiv'd I had been bubbled ; and preft me to tell him the Matter ; which I was ready enough to do. But the Story being long, and I being not willing to part with him foon, we went into a Tavern, to be the more at Eafe. I there told him all that had happened to me ever fince I left *Oviedo.* My Adventures feem'd very odd to him ; and after he had fympathiz'd with me in my prefent fad Eftate, he faid, Come, Child; one fhould never be caft down in Misfortune : When a Man of Senfe is in Trouble, he waits with Patience for better Times. A Man, as *Cicero* fays, fhould never be fo depreft in his Mind, as to forget he is a Man. For my part, that's my Temper. My Misfortunes have not funk me ; I am ftill above ill Fate : For Inftance, I lov'd a Girl of a good Family in *Oviedo,* and I was beloved by her ; I askt her Parents Confent : They refus'd me. Another Man would have hang'd or drowned himfelf. What do you think I did ? I ftole her, and carried her off with me. She was brisk, blunt, and a Coquet. Her Humour wore off my Paffion : I travell'd up and down in the Kingdom of *Galicia* fix Months with her.

her. Thence I would have gone a Voyage to Sea; but fhe would needs go to *Portugal*, and take with her another Companion. This would alfo have made made fome Men defperate. I bore up under it, and, wifer than *Menelaus*, inftead of taking Arms againft the *Paris* who had robb'd me of my *Helen*, I was glad he took a Plague from me, which I was willing enough to get rid of. After this, not caring to return to the *Afturias*; and having a Controverfy with the Judges, I proceeded to the Kingdom of *Leon*, fpending in every Town I came to the Money I had left, part of what I brought off with my Damfel; for we took as much both of us as we could get at our coming from *Oviedo*. When I arriv'd at *Palencia* I had but one Ducat, which I was oblig'd to change for a Pair of Shoes, and a few Reals, that were not like to laft me long. I therefore refolv'd to go to Service, and hir'd myfelf to a Linen-Draper, who had a Rake to his Son. I far'd well enough here; but had a difficult Task how to carry my felf. The Father order'd me to watch his Son; the Son defired me to help cheat his Father. Which fhould I do? Why truly I prefer'd the one's Defire to the other's Order,

Order, and was turn'd out of doors for so
doing. I then got into the Service of an
old Painter, who out of kindness would
teach me his Art ; but then he starv'd
me into the Bargain, which gave me a
Disgust of Painting and *Palencia* ; whence
I came to *Valladolid*, where, by the greatest Luck in the World, I was hir'd by
the Steward of an Hospital. I live with
him still, and have a rare Place of it.
Signor *Manuel Ordonnez*, my Master, is
a Man of profound Piety : 'Tis said that
from his Youth he has minded nothing
else but relieving the Poor : The Pains
he has taken has met with their Reward :
Every thing prospers with him ; and by
looking after the Poor, he is himself
grown Rich.

   Fabricio having finish'd his Discourse,
I said to him, I am glad you like your
Condition so well; but, between you
and I, methinks you may do better in
the World. Thou art mistaken, *Gil Blas*,
replied he : A Man of my Humour can
never do better than I do. To be a
Lackey, is not grateful to some Men ;
but a Lad of Wit will find it full of
Charms. A Man of a superior Genius
never does his Business in Service so
well as one of us merry Fellows. We
                 rather

rather command, than obey: We begin with studying our Master well; we get his blind Side, and then lead him where we lift. Thus have I behav'd myself with my Steward; I found him out immediately, that he would fain pass for a Saint, and I pretended to take him for such a one, carrying myself towards him accordingly. I copied after him, acted the same Part, deceived the Deceiver, and am his *Fac-totum*. I hope one time or other to acquire, under his *Auspices*, the Care of the Poor also, and then I doubt not but to make my Fortune as well as he has done, for I find I have the same Itch after Riches.

: Fine Hopes these, dear *Fabricio*, reply'd I; and I felicitate you upon them. As for me, I'll resume my first Design: I'll turn my embroider'd Coat into a Gown, go into *Salamanca*, list my self under the Banner of the University, and take on me the Office of a Preceptor. A hopeful Project, cries *Fabricio*; a pleasant Fancy! Wou'dst thou be so mad as to turn Pedant at this Age? Dost thou know what thou art about to undertake? As soon as thou art plac'd there, all the College will observe thee, they will have a watchful Eye on thy

b   least

leaſt Actions: Thou muſt inceſſantly put
a Conſtraint on thy ſelf: Thy Exterior
muſt be all hypocritical ; and thou muſt,
in appearance, be poſſeſt of 'all the Virtues. Eternally muſt thou be chiding
thy Scholar, and ſpend thy time in
teaching him *Latin*, and reproving him
when he ſays or does any thing againſt
Decency. After all this Toil and Trouble, what will be the Fruit of thy Care ?
If the young Gentleman takes ill Courſes,
they'll ſay thou ſpoil'ſt him ; and thou
ſhalt have nothing for thy Pains; not
perhaps ſo much as the poor Salary they
were to give thee. Prithee talk no more
of the Office of a Preceptor : A Lackey's
Place is worth ten of it : 'Tis a *ſine Cure:*
If a Maſter has, Vices, a good Genius
will know how to humour them, and
make his Advantage of them. A Valet
lives at his Eaſe ; he eats and drinks his
fill, ſleeps ſoundly, and has no Care to diſturb him.

I ſhould never have done, Child, purſued he, if I ſhould go about to tell
thee all the Advantages of a Valet.
Truſt me, *Gil Blas*, do as I do. Ah *Fabricio*, replied I, one can't meet with
a Steward of an Hoſpital every Day ; and
when I accept of a Valet's Place, I'm
resolv'd

resolv'd it shall be a good one. You say right, said he, and leave that to me. I'll answer for it; and if I hinder a gallant Man's throwing himself away at the University, I shall have done a meritorious Act.

The Poverty with which I was threatned, and *Fabricio's* contented Look prevailing upon me more than his Reasons, I determin'd to enter into some Service. We then left the Tavern, and my Countryman said, I will this Minute carry thee to a Man to whom most of the Valets that want Places apply themselves. There are Intelligence Offices where one can at any time hear of a Place : This Man keeps one : He has Informers that acquaint him with whatever is done in a Family : He knows who wants Valets, and keeps an exact Register not only of vacant Places, but also of the good and the bad Qualities of the Master : He has a Brother in some Convent ; and, in a word, 'twas he who help'd me to my Place.

We were entertaining our selves with this Intelligence Office, when the Barber *Nunes's* Son brought me to a little House, where we found a Man of about fifty writing at a Table. We saluted him with a great deal of Refpect; but whether or not he was furly in his Nature, or being us'd to fee no body but Valets, had accuftom'd himfelf to that rude manner, he did not rife off from his Seat, he nodded his Head, and that was all: However, he look'd upon me very attentively. I faw he was furpriz'd that a young Man in an embroider'd Velvet Coat fhould turn Lackey: He had more reafon to think I came to look out for one; but he was not long in Sufpence: *Fabricio* faying to him, Signor *Arias de Londona*, I have brought one of my beft Friends to you; he is a Lad who was well born, but Misfortunes have reduc'd him to the Neceffity of Serving: Help him to a good Place; and depend upon't he'll be very grateful to you. So you all cry, Gentlemen. Before you have a Place you make the faireft Promifes in the World; but when you have got it you think no more of them. I hope, replied *Fabricio*, you have no reafon to complain of me: Have not I done handfomely by you? You might have done better, faid *Arias*, your Place is as good as a Clerk's in the Treafury, and you paid me as if I had put you with an Author. I thought it was now time for me to

                                   fpeak,

speak, and gave Signor *Arias* to understand, that to shew I was not ungrateful,
I would give him a Gratulty before-hand.
Accordingly I put my Hand in my Pocket, and took out two Ducats, with a
Promise not to stop there if I was well
plac'd.

He seem'd very well pleas'd with my
Proceedings, and cry'd, Ay, this is something like ; I love every one should deal
so with me ; there are some excellent Places vacant, continued he ; I'll name 'em to
you, and do you chuse for yourself. Saying this, he put on his Spectacles, open'd
a Regiſter which lay on his Table, turn'd
over some Leaves, and read as follows:
Captain *Torbellino*, a paſſionate, whim-
fical Man, wants a Valet : He is always
fwearing, and beats his Servants fo, that
he cripples them. That will not do,
cry'd I, go on to another ; I don't like
this Captain. *Arias* ſmil'd at my Quick-
ness, and read on again : Donna *Manuela
de Sondeval*, a ſuperannuated Lady, a Woman of peeviſh, odd Temper, has no Valet : She generally keeps but one, and
hardly that for a Day together. There
is a Livery Coat in the Houſe which
ferves for all the Valets that come thither, let them be of what Size they
will.

will. It may be faid that they have only try'd it on ; for it is as good as new,
tho' two thoufand Valets have had it on.
Dr. *Alvar Fanez* wants a Valet : He is a
Chymift ; he keeps his Servants well,
and allows them good Wages ; but then
he tries his Medicines upon them. There
are often Vacancies in this Man's Houfe.
You have fhewn us a fine Parcel of
Places, faid *Fabricio*, interrupting him.
Have a little Patience, fays *Arias de Londona*, we have not done yet; we fhall
come to fome by and by that will content you. He then read in his Regifter :
Donna *Alfonfa de Solis*, an old Bigot, who
fpends two thirds of her time at Church,
and will always have her Valet with her;
fhe has been without one thefe three
Weeks. The Licentiate *Sedillo*, an old
Canon of the Chapter of this City, turn'd
away his Valet yefterday. Stop there,
Signor *Arias de Londona*, cry'd *Fabricio*,
we will go no farther; this Place will do.
Sedillo is a Friend of my Mafter's, and I
know him perfectly well : He has an
old Houfe-keeper, call'd Dame *Jacinta*,
who manages every thing ; and they
live as well as any People in *Valladolid*.
There's Plenty of all things : Befides,
the Canon is an infirm Man, an old,
gouty,

gouty Creature; he can't live long, and
his Valet is fure of a Legacy when he
dies. A charming Profpect for a Lackey,
Gil Blas, added he, turning to me: Let's
lofe no Time, Friend; we'll go to the
Licentiate's this Minute: I'll prefent
thee to him my felf, and be refponfible
for thee. For fear of lofing fo fair an
Opportunity, we took our leaves abruptly of Signor *Arias*, who affured me
for my Money, that if I mifs'd this Place,
he would help me to as good a one.

The End of the Firſt Book.

G 3   T H E

THE
HISTORY
OF
GIL BLAS
OF
SANTILLANE.

BÓOK II.

CHAP. I.

Fabricio *carries* Gil Blas *to the Licen-*
tiate Sedillo's *Houſe. In what State*
they found the Canon. The Portrait
of his Houſe-keeper.

WE were ſo afraid of coming too
late to the old Licentiate's,
that we ran all the way. The
Doorwas ſhut when we came to hisHouſe:
We knock'd ; a Girl of ten Years of Age,
whom

whom the House-keeper made pass for
her Niece, in spite of Scandal, open'd
the Door; and we demanding to speak
with the Canon, Dame *Jacinta* appear'd:
She was certainly arriv'd at Years of
Discretion; but she was still Handsome,
and had particularly a very fresh Complexion. She had an ordinary Stuff
Morning Gown on, with a Leather Gir-
dle, to which hung on one side a Bunch
of Keys, and on the other a String of
large Beads. We saluted her very respectfully; she did the same by us, looking very modest and courteous.

I understand, says my Comrade, that
the Licentiate Signor *Sedillo* wants an honest Lad to serve him; and I have brought
him one that, I doubt not, will content
him. At these Words the House-keeper
fix'd her Eyes upon me; and thinking
my Embroidery did not very well suit
with *Fabricio*'s Discourse, demanded if
'twas I who wanted the vacant Place?
Yes, this young Man, said the Son of
Nunez: As fine as he appears, some Misfortunes oblige him to look out for a
Service: He will soon forget them, added he, with a genteel Air, if he's so
happy as to get into this House, and
live with the virtuous *Jacinta*, who de-

serves

ferves to be Houfe-keeper to the Pa-
triarch of the *Indies.* At thefe Words
the old Jade gave over looking on me,
to take a Survey of the civil Perfon that
fpoke to her ; and, thinking that fhe
had fome Knowledge of him ; I had a
confus'd Notion of having feen you before, faid fhe, ; pray, where was it ?
Chaft *Jacinta,* replied *Fabricio,* I am
very proud that you are pleas'd to take
notice of me : I have been here twice
with my Mafter Signor *Manuel Ordonnez*
Steward of the Hofpital. 'Tis fo, fays
the Houfe-keeper ; I remember it, and
call you to mind. And fince you belong
to Signor *Ordonnez,* you muft doubtlefs
be a fober, honeft young Man : ! Your
Place fpeaks in Praife of you ; and this
Lad can't have a better Man' to be refponfible for him ; Come in, continued
fhe, I'll introduce you to Signor *Sedillo* ;
I believe he'll be glad to have a Youth
of your Recommendation. We followed Dame *Jacinta* to the Canon's Apartment, which was below Stairs, and confifted of four little Rooms. *Jacinta* defired us to ftay in the outermoft, while
fhe went into the next, where was the
Licentiate. When they had talk'd the
Matter over between themfelves, fhe
                                        came

came out, and faid, we might go in. We found the old Dotard in a large Eafy Chair, with a Pillow under his Head, and Cufhions under his Arms and Legs, the latter on a Stool. We approached him without ftanding much upon Ceremony. *Fabricio* was ftill the Spokefman; and not content with repeating what he had faid to the Houfe-keeper, he highly extoll'd my Merit; and enlarg'd particularly on the Honour, I had acquir'd at Dr. *Godinoz's* in my Philofophical Difputations, as if one had need to be a great Philofopher, to qualifie one to be a Canon's Valet. However his Panegyrick had fo good an effect on the Licentiate, who befides had obferv'd that Dame *Jacinta* was not a-gainft taking me, that he anfwer'd, the Son of *Nuncz*, Friend, I take the Lad thou haft brought into my Service. I like him well, and have a good Opinion of his Manners, being recommended to me by a Servant of Signor *Ordonnez*.

Fabricio perceiving that I was hired, made a low Bow to the Canon, and a lower ftill to the Houfe-keeper. After which he retired, well fatisfied with what he had done, whifpering me in the Ear, We fhall fee one another again;

keep

keep where you are. Affoon as he was
gone, the Licentiate ask'd me what my
Name was? Why I left my Country?
And by fuch Queftions engag'd me to tell
my whole Story before Dame *Jacinta.*
I diverted them both, efpecially by the
Relation of my laft Adventure. The Old
Man almoft kill'd himfelf with laughing at the Civility of *Camella* and Don
Raphael. It threw him into fuch a Fit
of Coughing, that I thought he never
would have come to himfelf again. He
had not made his Will yet; and one
may by that imagine what a Fright his
Houfe-keeper was in: She ran trembling
to his Afliftance, and did every thing
that's done to Infants when they cough,
rubb'd his Forehead, and clapt him on
the Back, which recover'd him. The old
Man gave over Coughing, and his Houfe-
keeper ceas'd to torment him. I was
going to finifh my Story; but Dame
Jacinta, fearing a fecond Cough, was a-
gainft it. She then took me with her
to the Canon's Wardrobe, where hung
up a Livery-Suit, which had ferv'd my
Predeceffor. She gave it to me, and
put mine in its Place; which I was willing to keep, hoping ftill that I might have
occafion

occafion to make ufe of it. After this we
went both of us to get Dinner ready.

She found that I was no Stranger to
what belong'd to a Kitchen ; I had ferv'd
an Apprenticefhip to it under Dame *Leonarda*, who was a tolerable Cook, but not
comparable to Dame *Jacinta*, who perhaps out-did the Archbifhop of *Toledo's*.
She excell'd in every thing : Her Jellies
were exquifite ; her Sauces the fame ;
her Fricaffees and Hafhes the beft feafoned
in the World. When Dinner was ready
we return'd to the Canon's Room, where
while I laid the Cloth near his eafy
Chair, the Houfe-keeper tuck'd a Napkin under his Chin, and ty'd it about his
Shoulders.

This done, I brought him fome Soop,
which might have been ferv'd up to the
famous Director of *Madrid* ; and two
Ragous's that might have fatisfied the
Senfuality of a Vice-Roy, had not Dame
Jacinta been fparing of her Spices, for
fear of enraging the Licentiate's Gout.
At the Sight of thefe two Difhes, my
old Mafter, who feem'd before debili-
tated in all his Members, fhew'd me that
he had not entirely loft the Ufe of his
Arms. He help'd himfelf to put away
his Pillow and Cufhions, and prepar'd

to

to fall to very briskly. Tho' his Hand
shook, he did not refuse its Service: It
came and went freely, but so that he
spilt half of what he would have carried to his Mouth, on the Table-cloth,
and his Napkin. When he had done with
the Soup and Ragous, I serv'd him up a
Partridge, and two Quails roasted. Dame
Jacinta was very officious to supply him
with Wine, a little temper'd, in a large,
deep Silver Cup, which she held to his
Mouth as if he had been a Child of fifteen Months old.

He devoured the Ragous, and made
the same Dispatch with the Trotters.
When he had stuff'd himself up to the
Chin, his Handmaid took off his Napkin, put his Pillows and his Cushions
in their Places again; and left him in
his easie Chair to take that Repose which
generally attends a full Stomach : We
clear d his Table, and went ourselves to
Dinner at another.

Thus did the Canon regale himself e-
very Day, being perhaps the greatest
Eater of the whole Chapter. Indeed,
somewhat less satisfied him for a Supper than for Dinner. A Pullet and a
Desert would do at Night. I far'd very
well in this House. I liv'd at my Ease.
There

There was but one thing that I could complain of, which was, my being obliged to watch a-nights with my Master, as if I had had a sick Body to tend, besides a Retention of Urine, which made him call for his Chamber-pot ten times an Hour. He was very apt to sweat ; and when he did so, I must change his Shirt for him. *Gil Blas,* said he to me the second Night, thou art a dexterous, active Youth : I foresee I shall like thee well : I only recommend to thee to carry it towards Dame *Jacinta* with Complacency. She has serv'd me very zealously these fifteen Years. She has always taken particular Care of my Person. I cannot be too grateful to her. I must own to thee freely I love her better than all my Family. I turn'd a Relation of mine, my own Sister's Son, out of Doors on her Account. He paid no manner of Respect to her ; and instead of doing Justice to her sincere Attachment for me, the Rascal treated her as an Hypocrite. Virtue now-a-days is nothing but Hypocrisy with such young Fellows : Thank Heaven I got rid of him. He who has a Kindness for me is my best Relation, and I will own Kindred to no body but those that do me good Offices. You
are

are in the right, Sir, said I to the Licentiate. Gratitude ought to have more Force upon us than the Laws of Nature. Most certainly, replied he; and my Will makes it appear how little I value my Relations. My Governante comes in for a good Share; and I shall not forget thee, if thou goeft on as thou doft begin. The Valet I difmifs'd yeferday loft a good Legacy by it. If the Wretch had not forc'd me by his ill Carriage to turn him off, I should have enrich'd him; but he was a proud Rogue, and did not pay due Refpect to Dame *Jacinta*; and fo lazy, he car'd not to be at the leaft Trouble. He did not love to wake with me; and 'twas a moft tirefome thing to him to, pafs the Nights in Attendance upon me. A Rafcal, cry'd I, as if infpir'd by the Genius of *Fabricio*, he deferv'd not to wait upon fo honeft a Gentleman as you are. A Lad that has the good Fortune to belong to you ought to be indefatigable in his Endeavours to pleafe you. He should delight in his Duty; and tho' he fweat Blood and Water for you, not think he did too much.

I per-

I perceiv'd these Words were very acceptable to the Canon; nor was he less delighted to hear me assure him how respectfully I would behave my self towards Dame *Jacinta*. Resolving therefore to pass for a Valet, I strove to be easie, and then I went thro' my Service with the best Grace in the World. I made no Complaint of being kept up a-nights; but I must confess I did not very well like it; and had not the Legacy ran in my Mind, I should soon have been weary of my Place. 'Tis true, I slept some Hours in the Day-time. I must do the Governantee the Justice to own she was very civil to me, which I attributed to the Pains I took to get into her good Graces by my obliging and respectful Carriage. If I was at Table with her and her Niece *Inesille*, I chang'd their Plates for them, fill'd out their Wine, and was very officious to serve them in all things. By these Methods I made 'em my Friends. One Day when Dame *Jacinta* was gone to Market, I began to discourse *Inesille* about her Parentage: I ask'd her if her Father and Mother were living? No, reply'd she, they have been dead a long long Time; so my good Aunt tells me,
for

for I never faw them. I took what the
Girl faid for truth, tho' her Difcourfe
did not feem to be fo plain as it fhould
be, and drew the Girl into Talk fo freely
at laft, that fhe told me more than I
would have had her: She inform'd me,
or rather I apprehended by what fhe
faid (feveral Words efcaping her which
fhe did not intend) that this good Aunt
of hers had a good Friend who liv'd
alfo with an old Canon, whofe Tem-
poralities he had the Care of ; and that
thefe two happy Domefticks were in
hopes to join together the Spoils of their
Mafters by a Marriage, the Pleafures of
which they enjoyed before-hand. I have
obferv'd already, that Dame *Jacinta*, tho'
a little fuperannuated, had ftill a pretty
good Complexion. 'Tis true, fhe fpar'd
for no Pains to preferve it : She took a
Clyfter every Morning ; and all the Day
long, and at Night too, till fhe fell a-
fleep, fhe fwallowed excellent Pills, prepared for that Purpofe : She alfo had her
full Sleep, while I was waking with my
Mafter : But what contributed perhaps
more than any thing to preferve her Complexion fo frefh, were two Iffues, which
Inefille faid fhe had, one in each Leg.

C H A P

CHAP. II.

How the Canon was treated when he fell sick: What happen'd upon it. The Legacy he left Gil Blas *by his Last Will.*

I Serv'd the Licentiate *Sedillo* three Months without complaining of the bad Nights he made me pass with him. At the end of that time he fell sick. He was taken with a Fever; and the Pain it gave him inflam'd his Gout. Then it was that he sent for a Doctor, the first Time he had made use of one all his Life, tho' it had been pretty long. He order'd Dr. *Sangrado* to be call'd, a Physician whom all *Valladolid* took to be another *Hippocrates.* Dame *Jacinta* wish'd that the Canon would have, in the first Place, settled his Last Will and Codicil. She hinted it to him; but he did not think himself so near his End, and was besides very obstinate in certain Matters. I went for Dr. *Sangrado,* and brought him to our House. He was a meagre, pale Man, and had been a Practitioner forty

forty Years. He affected a grave Look.
He weighed his Words, and would be
thought to talk eloquently. His Arguments feem'd to be Geometrical, and
his Opinions extremely fingular.

Having look'd upon my Mafter, he faid,
with a Doctoral Air, we muft fupply the
want of Perfpiration, which is ftope:
Others in my Place would, without
doubt, make ufe of Salts and vola-
tile Medicaments, which are, for the
moft part, made up of Sulphur and Mercury; but Purgatives and Sudorificks
are pernicious Drugs. All Chymical
Preparations are prejudicial. I ufe nothing but what's fimple and fafe. What
Diet have you us'd yourfelf to? continued he to the Canon. I eat generally Soups and Jellies, replied he.
Soupes and Jellies! cry'd the Doctor: I
don't wonder you are ill: All fuch delicious Meats are poifon'd Pleasures;
Snares laid for Men by Voluptuoufnefs,
to deftroy them more furely. You muft
renounce fuch high Food. The plain-
eft is the moft healthy. As the Blood
is infipid, fo it requires Meats that come
neareft to Nature. Do you drink Wine?
added he. Yes, faid the Licentiate,
Wine mingled with Water. As much
Water

Water as you thought proper, replied
the Phylician. How irregular you are!
What a frightful Regimen is this! I wonder you have liv'd fo long as you have.
How old are you? Sixty-nine, fays the
Canon. Juft as I thought, replied the
Doctor: Old Age is anticipated by In-
temperance. If you liv'd on a plain Diet, as roafted Apples, and drank Water
only, you would not now have had the
Gout. All your Members would eafily
have perform'd their Functions. However, I don't defpair of fetting you upon your Feet again, provided you do as
I fhall direct. The Licentiate promis'd
to obey him in all things. Then *San-*
grado fent me for a Surgeon of his Acquaintance, and took away fix good
Difhes of Blood from my Mafter, to begin to fupply the want of Perfpiration.
Mafter *Onez,* fays he to the Surgeon,
Come three Hours hence, and take a-
way as much more; Do the fame to
morrow. 'Tis an Error to think Blood
is neceffary for the Prefervation of Life.
One can't bleed a fick Man too much.
He is not obliged to any Motion or confiderable Exercife. He has nothing to
do but to fave himfelf from Dying;
and wants no more Blood to fupport
                                    Life

Life than a Man that's afleep does: Life
in both confifts only in the Pulfe and
Perfpiration. Thus did the Doctor order frequent and plentiful Bleedings;
and that the Canon fhould have hot Water given him every Moment, affuring
him that Water drank in abundance was
a certain Specifick againft all forts of Difeafes. When he went out, he look'd
on Dame *Jacinta* and I with an Air of
Content, and faid, he would anfwer for
the Sick Man's doing well, if he be manag'd in the manner he prefcrib'd. The
Governantee, who perhaps had another
Opinion of his Method, protefted that
his Prefcriptions fhould be exactly followed. Accordingly, we immediately
fet Water a heating; and the Doctor having recommended to us, above all things,
not to be fparing of it to him, we made
my Mafter take two or three Pints at
a Draught. An Hour after we repeated
the Dofe; and fo every Hour, till we
had poured into his Stomach a Deluge
of Water. The Surgeon feconded us by
the Quantity of Blood he drew from
him; and all of us in two Days time
reduc'd the old Canon to Extremity. The
good Man not being able to fwallow
any more of the Specifick, faid to me,
with

with a faint Voice, Hold, *Gil Blas*, do
not give me any more, Friend. I fee I
fhall die, notwithftanding the Virtue of
the Water; and tho' they have hardly
left me a Drop of Blood, I am not a
bit the better for't, which is a Proof
that the moft skilful Phyfician cannot
prolong a Man's Life, when his Hour is
come. Go, fetch me a Notary; I will
add a Codicil to my Will. Tho' I was
far from being afflicted to hear him talk
of his Will, yet I affected to feem very
forry; and concealing the Pleafure I
took in executing the Commiffion he
gave me, Ah Sir, cry'd I, 'Tis not fo
bad with you yet: With Heaven's help
you may recover. No, no, Child, replied he, I find the Gout returns upon
me, approaches nearer to my Vitals, and
my Time is come; be quick, hafte, and
do as I bid you. Indeed I could perceive
that he alter'd, and was drawing near his
End; fo I made hafte to obey his Commands with refpect to the Notary, leaving with him Dame *Jacinta*, who was
more afraid than I that he fhould die
without adding his Codicil to his Teftament. I went to the firft Notary I
could get; and finding him at home, Sir,
faid I, my Mafter the Licentiate *Sedillo*,

is

is a dying. He wants a Codicil to be
added to his Will : Pray difpatch ; we
muft not lofe a Moment. The Notary
was a little old Man who lov'd Rallery. He ask'd me who was the Canon's
Phyfician ? I anfwer'd, Dr. *Sangrado.* At
the Name of him he took his Cloak
and Hat, and cry'd, Let's be gone, for that
Doctor is very expeditious ; he hardly
gives his Patients time to fend for No-
taries : That Man has hinder'd me of
many a good Teftament. Saying this,
he made what Hafte he could ; and we
went together to my Mafter, not letting
the Grafs grow under us, to prevent his
going out of the World before he had
fettled his Affairs. As we were on the
Way, I faid to the Notary, You know,
Sir, that a Dying Man often lofes his
Memory : If by chance my Mafter fhould
forget me, I beg you to put him in
mind of my Induftry. That I will,
Child, replied the little Notary, depend upon it. I'll exhort him to give
thee fomething confiderable, if he is
ever fo little difpos'd to reward thee
for thy Services. When we came to
my Mafter, he had his Senfes ftill a-
bout him. Dame *Jacinta* was with
him; and her Tears, which fhe had at
Will,

Will, flow'd from her in abundance : She had play'd her part, and prepar'd the good Man to do very handfomely for her. We left the Notary with our Matter, and fhe and I ftaid without in the Anti-chamber, where the Surgeon came to us, to give the Canon a new and his laft Bleeding. But we would not let him enter the Room. Stay, Mr. *Martin*, fays the Governantee to him, you fhall not go into Signor *Sedillo's* Chamber now he's bufy. There's the Notary with him; and you fhall not bleed him any more till his Teftament is finifh'd. My Dame and I were afraid the Licentiate fhould die before 'twas done : But by good Luck the Act for which we were in fo much Pain was executed. The Notary coming out of the Chamber, clapt me on the Shoulder, and faid, fmiling, Thou art not forgotten, *Gil Blas*. I was overjoy'd to hear it, and fo well pleas'd with my Matter for remembring me, that I promis'd to pray for him after he was dead, which was not long firft ; for the Surgeon having blooded him once more, the poor old Man, who was before but too weak, expir'd almoft in the Moment. As he was at his laft Gafp, the Doctor came in, and
feem'd

seem'd a little startled, as quick as he
us'd to be in dispatching his Patients.
However, instead of imputing the Death
of the Canon to his Bleedings, and repeated Draughts of hot Water, he only
said as he went away, There was not
Blood enough taken from him; neither
has he drank hot Water enough. The
Doctor's Executioner, I mean the Surgeon, seeing there was no more Business
for him, follow'd Signor *Sangrado*.

No sooner was our Master dead, but
Dame *Jacinta*, *Inesilla*, and I set up a
howling, which was heard by all the
Neighbourhood. *Jacinta*, who had the
greatest reason to rejoyce, so bewail'd his
Death, that one would have thought she
was the most afflicted Woman in the
World. The Room in an instant was
full of People, who came out of Curiosity more than Compassion. The
Relations of the Defunct hearing he was
dead, ran to our House, and seal'd up
every thing. They saw the Governantee
in such Affliction, that they imagin'd
at first the Canon had not made his
Will: But they soon understood that
it was done in all the Forms, and had
a Codicil annex'd to it. Upon opening
it, they found the Testator had bequeath'd
his

his beft Effects to Dame *Jacinta* and her Daughter: And the Relations of the Deceafed made a Funeral Oration on him, in Terms which were by no means honourable to his Memory. They alfo fell upon the Governantee, and beftow'd fome Eulogies upon me too. It muft be own'd that in appearance I deferv'd them: The Licentiate, reft the Soul of him, to engage me to remember him as long as I liv'd, order'd this Article to be inferted in the Codicil: *Item, Since* Gil Blas *is a Lad who already has fome Literature, I leave him my Library, all my Books and Manufcripts, without Exception.*

I could not imagine where this pretended Library was. I had not feen any fuch thing in the Houfe. I knew there were a few Papers, and five or fix Books on a Shelf in my Mafter's Clofet; and that was all my Legacy. The Books were befides of no Ufe to me. One was intitl'd, *The Compleat Cook:* Another a Treatife of *Indigeftion, and the Method of Curing it.* The others were the four Parts of the *Breviary*, half eaten away by the Moth. As for the Manufcripts, the moft curious was fome Briefs and Bills relating to a Law-Suit the Canon had formerly had about his

Vol. I. H Bene-

Benefice. When I had examin'd my
Legacy with more Attention than it
deferv'd, I left it for his Relations who
had envy'd it me fo much. I reftored
alfo to them the Coat I had of the
Licentiate, and took my own again, receiving my Wages only for the Fruit
of my Services. I left them as foon as
I was paid off, and look'd out for another Place. Dame *Jacinta*, befides the
Money which was bequeathed her, by
the Help of her good Friend, found
means, while the Licentiate was ill, to
plunder him of his moft valuable Effects.

CHAP. III.

Gil Blas *hires himfelf to Doctor* Sangrado; *and becomes a famous Phy-*
ficIan.

I Refolv'd to go to Signor *Arias de Lon-*
dona, and fearch his Regifter for a-
nother Service : But as I was juft entring his Houfe, I met Dr. *Sangrado,*
whom I had not feen fince my Mafter's
Death. I took the liberty to falute
him,

him, and he knew me again prefently, notwithftanding I had chang'd my Habit. Child, fays he, I was thinking of thee this Minute. I want an honeft Lad to ferve me; and I believe thou would'ft do my Bufinefs, if thou can't Read and Write. If that's all, Sir, replied I, I am for your Purpofe. Say'ft thou fo, cry'd he? Thou art my Man then. Come along with me: Thou fhalt live pleafantly, and I'll treat thee with Diftinction: I will give thee no Wages; but thou fhalt want for nothing. I'll keep thee handfomely, and teach thee the great Art of Curing Difeafes. In a word, thou fhalt rather be my Pupil than my Valet.

I accepted of the Doctor's Propofal, hoping that under fo learned a Mafter I fhould become an eminent Phyfician. He took me home with him immediately: He fhew'd me what I was to do there; which was, to write down the Names and Dwellings of the Patients that fent for him when he was Abroad. He kept a Regifter for that Purpofe, wherein an old Maid-Servant of his us'd to fet down who came for him; and whither he was to go; but her Orthography was unintelligible; and fhe wrote

H 2 fo

fo ill, that the Doctor could not decipher it. He gave this Book in charge to me ; and it might be well call'd *The Register of the Dead* ; for hardly a Man whofe Name was enter'd there, lived after it.

I wrote down, as I may fay, the Names of the Perfons who were bound for the other World, as the Porter to an Inn writes down the Names of the Perfons that take Places in a Stage-Coach. My Pen was often in my Hand ; for there was not at that time a Phyfician in *Valladolid* of more Repute than Dr. *Sangrado.* He impos'd on the Publick by a fpecious way of Talking, and fome lucky Cures, which had done him more Honour than he deferv'd. He had as much Practice as he could go thro' with, and confequently got Money a-pace. He did not fpend it too profufely : We liv'd very frugally : Our Food was generally Peafe, Apples, and Cheefe. He faid thofe Aliments agreed beft with the Stomach, and were moft healthy. However, as light as they were of Digeftion, he would not fuffer us to have our Fill of them. He took Care we fhould not furfeit ourfelves : But tho' he forbad the Maid and I to eat much, to make

amends

amends, he permitted us to drink as
much Water as we would. Inſtead of
ſetting us Bounds in that, he ſometimes
cry'd, Drink, Children, Health conſiſts
in the Suppleneſs and Humectation of
Parts. Drink Water abundantly: Water breaks all the Salts: If the Blood is
too thick, Water thins it; if too thin,
it thickens it. Our Doctor was ſo honeſt in that himſelf, that he drank nothing
but Water, tho' he was pretty well in
Years. He defin'd Old Age to be a natural Ptiſick, which dry'd up and con-
ſum'd us; and purſuant to this Definition, he deplor'd the Ignorance of thoſe
that call'd Wine the Old Man's Milk.
He maintained that Wine wore them
out and deſtroy'd them; and ſaid very
eloquently, that that Liquor is to them,
as well as to all the World, a Friend that
betrays, and a Pleaſure that deceives
them.

Notwithſtanding all his fine Arguments, I had not been eight Days in
his Houſe before I was taken ill of a
Flux, and a violent Pain in the Stomach, which I was ſo bold as to attri-
bute to the abundance of the Liquid,
and the ill Diet I liv'd upon. I com-
plained to my Maſter, hoping he would

relieve

relieve me, and allow me a little Wine
at Meals; but he was too great an Enemy to that Liquor to confent to it. If
Water offends thy Stomach, fays he,
there are innocent Helps againft the A-
quatick Qualities: Sage, for Example,
or Balm infus'd in it, renders it moft
delectable to the Tafte. Mint, Rofemary,
and many other excellent Herbs are not
only falutary, but gives an admirable
Flavour to the Liquid Element. Whatever he could fay in Praife of Water,
and whatever Recipe's he would have
given me to improve my Beverages, I
drank it with fo much Moderation,
that he obferving, faid, I don't wonder,
Gil Blas, you do not enjoy your Health
well; you don't drink enough, Friend.
Water, unlefs it is taken in large Quantities,
quickens the Parts of the Choler which
ought to be drown'd in it. Don't be
afraid of weakning or chilling thy Stomach by abundance of Water: I'll anfwer for what fhall come of it, drink
as much as thou wilt: *Celfus* will be
my Second: That Oracle of the *Latins*
has written an admirable Panegyrick
upon Water: He tells us in exprefs
Words, That thofe who excufe their
drinking Wine, on account of a weak
Stomach,

Stomach, do a manifeſt Injuſtice to the Stomachick Powers, and make it only a Cover for their Senſuality.

That I might not appear indocile when I was entring into the Career of Phyſick, I ſeem'd to be convinc'd that he was in the right. I even confeſs'd that I was of his Opinion; and on his and *Celſus's* Guaranty, continued to take large Draughts of Water to drown my Choler in it: And tho' I found my ſelf worſe and worſe every Day, yet Prejudice was too hard for Experience. I had, as may be ſeen, a happy Diſpoſition to become a Phyſician; but I could not always reſiſt the Violence of my Ails, which grew upon me to ſuch a Point that I reſolv'd to quit Dr. *Sangrado's* Ser-vice; but he beſtowed a new Employ-ment on me, which made me change my Mind. Child, ſays he to me one Day, hearken to me, hearken to me: I am not one of thoſe hard, ungrateful Maſters who let their Domeſticks be paſt their Labour before they reward them. I am ſatisfied with thy Conduct. I love thee, and will make a Man of thee. I will diſcover to thee the whole Myſtery of the Salutary Art, which I have ſo many Years profeſt. Other Doctors

H 4 make

make it confift in a thoufand difficult
Sciences; but I'll fhorten the Way, and will
fpare thee the Pains of ftudying Phyfick,
Pharmacy, Botany, and Anatomy. Know,
Friend, that all that is neceffary, is Bleeding and Draughts of hot Water: This
is the whole Secret of Curing all the
Diftempers in the World: A wonderful Secret which I reveal to thee; and
which Nature, impenetrable to my Brethren, has not been able to keep from
my Obfervations. 'Tis all included in
thefe two Points, much Bleeding, and
much Drinking of Water: I have nothing more to teach thee: Thou know-
eft the very Bottom of Phyfick. Make
thy Advantage of my long Experience,
and thou wilt at once become as skilful as I am. Thou may'ft alfo be Affi-
ftant to me: Thou fhalt keep the Regifter in the Morning, and in the Afternoon fhall vifit fome of my Patients,
while I take care of the Nobility and
Clergy, thou fhalt attend the third Order for me; and when thou haft done
fo fome time, I will get thee admitted
into the Faculty. Thou fhalt be Learned, *Gil Blas*, before thou art a Phyfician; whereas others are a long time,
and

and most of them all their Lives, Phyſi-
cians before they are Learned.

I thank'd the Doctor for having ſo
ſpeedily render'd me capable of becoming his Subſtitute ; and to teſtiſie how
ſenſible I was of his Goodneſs to me,
I aſſur'd him I would follow all his O-
pinions as long as I liv'd, even tho' they
were contrary to *Hippocrates*. This Aſ-
ſurance of mine was nevertheleſs a little
inſincere : I did not at all approve of his
Bleeding and Water-drinking Preſcriptions, and reſolv'd to drink Wine as
often as I viſited my Patients. I hung
my Coat upon a Peg the ſecond time,
put on one of my Maſter's, and aſſum'd
the Air of a Phyſician, whoſe Profeſſion I enter'd upon at the Expence
of all thoſe that ſent for me. I began
with an Alquazil who was taken ill of
a Pleuriſie. I order'd him to be Blooded
without Mercy, and that he ſhould have
an immoderate portion of Water. I,
in the next place, was ſent for by a Paſtry-Cook, who was roaring out with
the Gout. I was no more ſparing of
his Blood than I had been of the Alquazil's, and preſcrib'd him a Deluge of
Water alſo. I receiv'd twelve Reals for
my Preſcriptions ; which gave me ſuch

a

a liking to my Profeſſion, that I reſolv'd to ſpend the reſt of my Days
in taking People's Blood from them,
and filling them up with Water. As I
was coming out of the Paſtry-Cook's
Houſe, I met with *Fabricio*, whom I had
not ſeen ſince *Sedillo* the Licentiate's Death.
He gaz'd upon me ſome Moments in a
Surprize, and then burſt out into a Fit
of Laughter, till he was ready to ſplit
his Sides. Truly he had good reaſon to
laugh ; for I had a Cloak that trail'd on
the Ground ; my Coat and Breeches
were four times as long and as wide as
they needed to have been. I might
very well paſs for an Original. I let
him have his Laugh out, and could hardly forbear keeping him Company ; but
I put a Conſtraint on my ſelf for De-
corum's. ſake, it being in the Street,
and the beter to counterfeit the Phyſician, who is no riſible Animal. *Fabricio*, who laught ſo heartily at my ridiculous Air, laught ſtill more at my ſerious one ; and when his Fit was a little
over, For Heaven's ſake, *Gil · Blas*, ſays
he, who has equipp'd thee ſo plea-
ſantly ? What Devil has diſguis'd thee
ſo ? Not ſo faſt, Friend, ſaid I ! Shew
reſpect to a new *Hippocrates*. Know
that

that I am Subſtitute to Dr. *Sangrado* the moſt famous Phyſician in *Valladolid*. I have liv'd with him theſe three Weeks. He has ſhewn me the Bottom of Medicine; and not being able to attend all the ſick Men that ſend for him, I am employ'd to aſſiſt him. He looks after the great Folks, and I after the little Ones. Very well, replies *Fabricio*, that is to ſay, he abandons to thee the Blood of the Common People, and reſerves that of the Quality to himſelf. I congratulate thee upon thy Diviſion. 'Tis better to have to do with the Populace than with the Nobility. A Suburb-Doctor for my Money: His Faults are leſs in View; and his Murders make no Noiſe. Yes, Child, added he, thy Condition is to be envy'd; and to talk like *Alexander*, If I were not *Fabricio*, I would be *Gil Blas*.

To let the Son of the Barber *Nunez* ſee that he was not in the Wrong when he extoll'd the Happineſs of my Circumſtances, I ſhew'd him the Reals given me by the Alquazil, and the Paſtry-Cook. Then we entred a Tavern to ſpend part of them. The Drawer brought us ſome pretty good Wine, which

which I thought to be much better than
it was, having tafted none a long time.
I drank large Draughts ; and with all
due Refpect to the *Latin* Oracle, I found
that the Stomachick Powers were mightily refrefh'd by them. We did not
foon part ; but made our felves merry
at the Expence of our Mafters, according to the ufual Way of Valets. Night
coming on, we parted, after having
promis'd to meet again the next Day
in the Afternoon at the fame Place.

CHAP. IV.

Gil Blas *continues the Practice of a
Phyfician with as much Succefs as
Capacity. The Adventure of the
Ring recover'd.*

I got home juft about the time that Sangrado did. I told him what Patients
I had vifited ; and gave him eight Reals, which were all I had left of the
Twelve that were given me for my Prefcriptions. Eight Reals, cry'd he, when
he had told them : 'Tis a fmall Matter
for two Vifits ; but we muft take what
we can get. He kept fix, and gave me
the other two : There, *Gil Blas,* continued

tinued he, there's fomething for thee to lay·by. Thou fhalt have a Quarter-part of what thou takeft. Come, Friend, this will make a rich Man of thee ; for, God willing, we fhall have a fickly time of it this Year.

I was contented with my Proportion; for refolving to keep back every Day a Quarter-part ; and having another Quarter of the Remainder from him, that was a half of the whole, according to my Arithmetick. The next Day, as foon as I had din'd, I put on my Subftitute's Habit, and went about my Bufi‑nefs. I vifited feveral Patients of our Regifter, and treated them all after the fame manner, tho' they had different Diftempers. Hitherto Matters had pafs'd without making any Noife; and no body as yet, thank Heaven, had any thing to fay againft my Prefcriptions: But let a Phyfician be ever fo excellent, there will be thofe that cenfure him. I came at laft to a Grocer's, whofe Son had a Dropfy. I found there a little Blade of a Doctor call'd *Cuchillo*, who was brought thither by a Relation of the Grocer's. I made very low Bows to all that were prefent, efpecially to the Perfon whom I took to be fent for to confult

confult with me on the Patient's Dif-
eafe. He faluted me with a grave Air;
and having examined my Features and
Figure fome time with Attention, Signor Doctor, fays he, I pray you to excufe my Curiofity. I thought I had
known all the Phyficians my Brethren in
Valladolid, but I muft own to you that I
have no manner of Knowledge of you.
You cannot have been long fettled in this
City. I replied, I was a young Practitioner, and as yet did only prefcribe under the Aufpices of Dr. *Sangrado*. I congratulate you, fays he very civilly, upon
your embracing the Method of fo great
a Man. I make no queftion you have
already profited very much by his Leffons, tho' you appear to be very young.
He faid this fo naturally, that I could
not tell whether he fpoke ferioufly or
banter'd me. I was ftudying what to
anfwer him, when the Grocer interrupted our Converfation, by putting us
in mind of that Bufinefs we came a-
bout, faying, I'm fatisfied, Gentlemen,
that both of you are perfect Mafters of
the Art of Medicine. Pray look upon
my Son, and prefcribe what you think
proper for his Cure. Upon this my Brother Doctor made his Obfervations on
the

the Sick Man; and having mark'd the
Symptoms which difcover'd the Nature
of the Diftemper; he demanded of me
after what manner I thought we fhould
manage him? I am of Opinion, replied
I, that he fhould be blooded every Day,
and take hot Water abundantly. At
this the other Phyfician, fmiling on me
with a malicious Air, faid, And you are
of Opinion that thofe Remedies will
fave his Life? No doubt of it, replied
I, with great Confidence, they will
have that Effect, being Specificks againft
all forts of Difeafes: Ask Dr. *Sangrado*.
Then *Celfus* was very much out, anfwer'd
he, when to cure a Dropfy he enjoin'd
the Patient to abftain from Eating or
Drinking. *Celfus*, cry'd I, is not my O-
racle. He is out as well as others; and
fometimes I affect to go to quite contrary to his Sentiments. I perceive by
your Difcourfe, fays *Cucbillo*, that Dr.
Sangrado would infinuate a fure and fa-
tisfactory Method to young Practition-
ers. Bleeding and Water-drinking are
his Univerfal Medicine. I am not at
all furpriz'd that fo many honeft
Gentlemen have perifhed under his
Hands. No Invectives, replied I haftily; It does not become a Man of your
Profeffion

Profeffion to talk fo. I muft tell you,
Monfieur Doctor, that for want of
Bleeding and Drinking hot Water, many fick Men have been fent into the o-
ther World. If you have any thing to
object againft Signor *Sangrado*, put it
into Writing; I'll anfwer you; and we
fhall fee on whofe fide the Laughers
will be. By St. *James* and St. *Denis*,
cry'd *Cuchillo*, in as great a Paffion as I
was, you don't know me, Sir; I can
bite and fcra'ch as well as another. I
am not afraid of *Sangrado*, who with
all his Prefumption and Vanity is an O-
riginal. Here I bid him hold. I de-
fpis'd his mean Figure, and he did the
fame by my ridiculous one. We gave
one another hard Words, and made
Faces at each other. We in the end
came to pulling and fcratching, and
loft fome Hair on each fide, before the
Grocer and his Kinfman could come
in and part us. When they had done,
the Mafter of the Houfe paid me for
my Vifit, and difmifs'd me, keeping
my Antagonift, who feem'd to him to
have the more Skill of the two.

I had like to have met with another
fuch ill Adventure at a fat Quirifter's
Houfe who had a Fever. I no fooner
began

began to make mention of hot Water,
than he fell a railing at my Specifick,
and cursing me for my Prescription.
He call'd me a thousand Names, and
threatned to have me thrown out at
Window. I went out of his House
much faster than I came in; and made
what haste I could to meet *Fabricio* at
the Place we had appointed for our
Meeting. I found him there. We were
both in a drinking Humour, and got
very merry; in which Condition we
return'd home to our Masters. Signor
Sangrado did not perceive I was fuddled,
because I told him the Story of my
Quarrel with the Doctor, with a great
deal of the Action; and he took it
for an Effect of the Emotion our Combat had put me into. Besides, he found
himself concern'd in the Report I made;
and was himself piqu'd against *Cuchillo.*
You did well, *Gil Blas*, said he, to defend the Honour of our Remedies a-
gainst a Dwarf of the Faculty. Does
he pretend that Aquatick Beverages are
not to be given in Cases of Dropsy?
A Blockhead! I'll maintain the Use of
them is very proper. Yes, continued
he, Water will cure all sorts of Drop-
sies, as it is good for Rheumatisms and
Jaun-

Jaundice. 'Tis also excellent in those Fevers, when the Sick burn and freeze at the same time. 'Tis marvellous ev'n in those Diseases that arise from cold Phlegmatick Humours. This Opinion may seem strange to young Physicians, such as *Cuchillo* ; but it is very supportable in good Medicine : And if those Men were capable of arguing like Philosophers, instead of railing at me, they would become my most zealous Defenders.

He did not suspect my being disorder'd with Wine, *Cuchillo's* Censures had put him into such a Passion : For to inflame him the more, I had added some Circumstances of my own Head to my Story. However, as full as he was of the Matter, he perceiv'd that I drank more Water that Evening than usually. The Wine heated me ; I was very dry, and took large Draughts of Water: But he thought I began to take a liking to his Aquaticks. I find, *Gil Blas*, says he, smiling, Thou hast not now such an Aversion to Water; 'twill go down like *Nectar* in a little while. I knew thou would'st bring thy self to love it. Sir, replied I, every thing has its time. I would at this instant give a Gallon of Wine for

for a Pint of Water. This Anfwer charm'd the Doctor, who would not lofe fo fair an Occafion to enlarge upon the Excellence of Water : He undertook to make a new Eulogy on it ; not like a cold Orator, but like an Enthufiaft. A thoufand and a thoufand times, cries he, more eftimable and more innocent were the Houfes of Meeting of old than our modern Taverns. The Antients did not meet to confume their Eftates and deftroy their Healths, but to have harmlefs Converfation, and refrefh them felves with hot Water. We cannot fufficiently admire the Forefight of the earlieft Mafters of Civil Life, who erected Publick - Houfes, where hot Water was given to all Comers. Wine was then lock'd up in the Apothecaries Shops, that none might ufe it without the Prefcription of the Phyfician. Oh, what Wifdom was that ! A Remainder of that ancient Frugality is ftill to be met with in thee and me who drink nothing but Water which has never been boil'd ; for I have obferv'd, that Water, when it has been boil'd, is heavier and more offenfive to the Stomach.

I could

I could hardly forbear laughing, to hear him talk thus. I kept my Countenance as well as I could. Nay, I agreed with him as to the Virtues of hot Water. I condemn'd the Use of Wine, and pitied those Men who unhappily took Pleasure in so pernicious a Beverage. The Wine continuing to heat me still, I fill'd a huge Cup with Water, and after having taken a good Draught, Come Sir, said I to my Master, Let us drink this agreeable Liquor. Let us revive in your House the Wisdom and Frugality of the Antients. He applauded me for saying so, and held out an Hour longer in the Praise of Water, exhorting me never to drink any thing else. I promis'd him to take a large Quantity every Night, to use myself to it; and that I might keep my Promise the more easily, I went to Bed with a Resolution to go every Day to the Tavern. As ill as it far'd with me at the Grocer's, it did not hinder my prescribing next Day fresh Bleedings and fresh Doses of hot Water. As I was coming out of a House, where I had been to visit a Poet who had a Frenzy, I met an Old Woman in the Street, who ask'd me if I was a Physician? I told her, Yes.
I then

I then moſt humbly entreat you, replied
ſhe, to go along with me. My Niece
was taken ill yeſterdy, and I can't find
out her Diſtemper. I followed the Old
Woman, who conducted me to a Houſe,
where I enter'd a Room pretty well
furniſh'd, and ſaw a Woman a-bed. I
immediately thought I had ſeen her
ſomewhere before ; and after having a-
while examin'd her Face a little better,
I knew her again to be *Camilla*, who
had acted her Part ſo well with me before. As for her, ſhe did not know
me, either thro' the Diſorder her Diſtemper put her into, or thro' the Alteration of my Dreſs, being now in the
Garb of a Doctor. I took her by the
Hand, to feel her Pulſe, and perceived
my Ring was upon her Finger. I was
overjoyed to light upon a Treaſure I
had ſo much Right to ſeize, and I had
a great mind to do it at the inſtant ; but
conſidering that thoſe Women might
cry out, and Don *Raphael*, or ſome o-
ther Defender of the Fair Sex, run to
their Help, I took care not to give way
to the Temptation. I thought it was
better diſſemble and conſult *Fabricio*
thereupon ; which I did as ſoon as I
ſaw him. In the mean time the Old
Woman

Woman was very earnest with me to
tell her what Diftemper her Niece had.
I was not fuch a Fool as to own that
I could not tell. On the contrary, I
pretended to be Mafter of it; and faid
gravely, in Imitation of Signor *Sangrado*, that her Illnefs was occafion'd for
want of Perfpiration: That fhe muft be
let Blood immediately, Bleeding being
the Natural Subftitue of Perfpiring. I
alfo order'd her hot Water, that all
things might be done according to our
Rules.

I fhortned my Vifit as much as I
could, and hafted away to the Son of
Nunez, whom I met juft as he was coming out of his Mafter's Houfe, who
had fent him on an Errand. I inform'd
him of my new Adventure, and afk'd
his Advice, whether I had beft have
Camilla apprehended by the Magiftrates?
No, replied he, by no means; that is not
the way to have your Ring again. Thofe
fort of Men don't love to make Reftitu-
tions. Rember thy being imprifon'd at
Aftorga, what became of thy Horfe, thy
Money, and thy Cloaths. Did not they
keep all? The beft Way will be to make
ufe of our own Induftry to recover thy
Diamond. I ll contrive how to do it.

I'll

I'll think upon it as I go to the Hospital, where I have two or three Words to tell the Purveyor from my Master. Meet me at our Tavern, and do not be impatient ; I'll be with thee in a very little time.

Nevertheless, it was three Hours before he came to me : I did not know who he was at first : Besides that, he had chang'd his Habit, and ty'd his Hair up in Ribbans ; he had plac'd a Mustachio on his Beard which cover'd half his Face. He had a Sword on, the Hilt of which was at least three Foot in circumference. He march'd at the head of five Men, who, like him, had their huge Mustachio's, and their long Rapiers, looking all like Persons of Resolution. Your Servant, Signor *Gil Blas*, says he, in accosting me : Behold an Alquazil of a new Make, and Sergeants of the same Turn attending him ; Carry us to that Woman that has robb'd you of the Diamond, and take my Word for't we'll make her restore it. I embraced *Fabricio* at these Words, which let me into the Secret of his Stratagem, and gave him to understand that I highly approv'd of his Expedient. I also saluted the counterfeit Sergeants, who were three Footmen

men and two Journeymen Barbers of
his Acquaintance, whom he had engaged
in this Bufinefs. I made the Brigade
drink, and we went ftreight to *Camilla's,*
where we arriv'd juft as 'twas dusk.
We knock'd at the Door, which was
fhut. The Old Woman open'd it, and
taking the Perfons that were with me for
Officers who did not come thither
without Reafon, fhe was terribly af-
frighted. Don't be afraid, Mother, faid
Fabricio ; we came hither only about a
fmall Affair, which will be foon over.
At thefe Words we went forward, and
entred the Sick Body's Chamber, conducted by the Old Woman, who lighted
us along with a Candle in a Silver Candle-ftick. I took the Candle of her,
went to the Bed-fide, and look'd in
Camilla's Face very fully, that fhe might
know me. Behold, cry'd I, thou Cheat,
the Credulous *Gil Blas,* whom thou haft
fo wrong'd : Have I met with thee at
laft ? The Corregidor has my Petition
againft thee, and this Alquazil is order'd to apprehend thee. Mr. Officer,
added I, do your Duty. I need not
be put in mind of that, reply'd he,
heightning his Voice ; I fhall take hold
of that Creature ; I have had a Note
of

of her Name along while in my Regifter.
Come, get you up, Madam, continu'd
he ; Drefs immediately, I will be your
Gentleman-Ufher, and lead you to one
of the beft Jails in *Vailadolid*. At thefe
Words, *Camilla*, as ill as fhe was, perceiving the two Sergeants with huge
Muftachio's were about to take her out
of Bed by Force, held up her Hands,
and with a Look which fhew'd the
Fright fhe was in, cry'd out to me,
Signor *Gil Blas*, have Pity on me, I conjure you, by the Chaft Mother to whom
you owe your Birth : Tho' I am very
guilty, I am yet more miferable : I will
give you your Diamond, therefore don't
ruine me. Saying this, fhe pull'd the
Ring off her Finger, and gave it to
me. But I anfwer'd , That my Diamond alone wou'd not fatisfie me ;
I muft have my Thoufand Ducats alfo
which I had been robb'd of in the
Lodging-houfe. As for the Ducats,
Signor, do not demand them of me,
reply'd *Camilla* ; the Traytor *Raphael*,
whom I have not feen from that time
to this, ran away with them that very
Night. Poor Soul, fays *Fabricio* ; do'ft
thou think 'tis fufficient to clear thee,
to pretend thou haft none of the Spoil ?

Thou ſhalt not come off ſo. Thou wer't
one of *Raphael*'s Accomplices, and muſt
give an Account of thy ſelf before thy
Betters : A fine Account thou haſt to
give, I'll warrant you : Be pleas'd to
go to Priſon with me, and there thou
may'ſt make thy general Confeſſion.
This good Woman ſhall bear thee
Company : I doubt not ſhe can tell
Monſieur the Corregidor a hundred
pretty Stories, which will be very entertaining to him. Upon this the two
Women did what they could to ſweeten
us. They cry'd, they ſued, the Old one
fell on her Knees before the Alquazil ; and
when he was deaf to her, ſhe turn'd to e-
very one of his Serjeants. *Camilla* begg'd
me, in the moſt moving manner, to ſave
her out of the Hands of the Magiſtrates.
I made as if her Prayers had prevailed
on me. Mr. Officer, ſaid I to the Son
of *Nunez*, ſince I have my Diamond, I
am ſatisfied ; I would not be the Death
of this Woman. Don't tell me of your
Humanity, replied he ; I have ſomething
elſe to mind. I muſt diſcharge my Office. I have expreſs Orders to appre-
hènd theſe Wretches : Monſieur the
Corregidor will make Examples of
them. For Heaven's ſake, ſaid I, don't be
ſo

so cruel, but have mercy upon them,
and accept of the Present these Ladies
will make you for your Trouble. That's
another thing, replied he; that's a Figure of Rhetorick which is well plac'd.
Come, what is it they will give me ? I
have a Pearl Necklace, cry'd *Camilla*, and
two Pendants, of a confiderable Price.
If they came from the *Philippine* Ifles,
faid he, interrupting her, I will not med-
dle with them. You may be affured
they are right, replied fhe, While they
were talking, the Old Woman brought
a little Box, out of which fhe took the
Necklace and the Pendants. She gave
them both to Monfieur the Alquazil.
'Tho'' he knew no more of Pearl than I
did, yet he did not queftion their being
right. He look'd upon them attentively,
and faid, They appear to be what they
fhould be ; and if the Silver Candleftick
which Signor *Gil Blas* has in his Hand
be added to them, I will not anfwer for
my Fidelity. I don't believe, cry'd I to
Camilla, you'll break off an Accommo-
dation fo much to your Advantage for
a Trifle. Pronouncing thefe Words, I
took the Candle out, and gave the Candleftick to *Fabricio*, who contenting him
felt with what was offer'd, perhaps be-

I 2   caufe

caufe he faw nothing in the Room befides that could be conveniently carried
off, faid, Farewel, my Princefs, be at
reft, I will fpeak for you to Monfieur
the Corregidor, and reprefent you to
him as white as Snow. We know how
to give things what Turn we pleafe,
and never make true Reports, but when
we are not oblig'd to make falfe ones.

C H A P. V.

*The Sequel of the Adventure of the
Recover'd Ring.* Gil Blas *quits the
Practice of Phyfick, and the City of*
Valladolid.

AFTER we had thus executed *Fabricio's* Project, we left *Camilla's* Houfe,
rejoycing in the Succefs of our Enterprize. We expected nothing but the
Ring: We took the reft as we could get
it. We were fo far from making any
fcruple of robbing the Courtezans, that
we thought we had done a meritorious
Act. Gentlemen, fays *Fabricio* to us, when
we were got into the Street : I think the
beft thing we can do, is to return to our
Tavern,

Tavern, and make merry all Night. To morrow we'll fell the Candleſtick, the Necklace and the Pendants, and divide the Money among'ſt us, like Brethren: This done, each of us ſhall return home, and make the beſt Excuſe he can to his Maſter. The Opinion of Monſieur the Alquazil ſeem'd to us to be moſt judicious: We return'd to our Tavern, ſome of us imagining they could eaſily invent an Excuſe for lying abroad, and others not caring whether their Matters turn'd them off or not.

We order'd a good Supper to be got ready, and ſat down to it with as much Gaiety as Appetite. We were very pleaſant all the while, and eſpecially *Fabricio*, who knew how to keep up Converſation, diverted the whole Company. There eſcap'd him I can't tell how many Strokes of *Caſtilian* Wit, as good as the *Attick* of old. When we were in the midſt of our Mirth, an unforeſeen Event diſturb'd all our Joy. A Man enter'd the Room where we were at Supper, with a very grave Mien, attended by two others of moſt unpromiſing Aſpect. After theſe came three more, and after them three and three, till they made a Dozen. They were arm'd with Ca-

I 3   rabines

rabines, Swords, and Bayonets. We foon
perceived they were the Watch, and,
'twas not hard for us to guefs their Bufinefs. We at firft made a Shew of Re-
fiftance ; but they furrounded us in an
inftant, and kept us quiet, as well on account of their Number as their Fire-Arms.
Gentlemen, fays the Captain of them,
with a bantring-Air, I underftand by
what Artifice you have lately taken a
Ring from a certain She-Adventurer ;
'Twas dexteroufly done ; and you deferve a publick Reward, which without
queftion you'll meet with. The Law,
that has provided a Lodging for you,
will be fure to provide alfo a Recom-
pence for fo notable an Exploit. All
thofe to whom this Difcourfe was addreft were in terrible Confufion. We
chang'd Colour, and in our turn were
poffefs'd with the fame Fear as we had
occafion'd in *Camilla.* However, *Fabricio,* tho' he look'd pale and confounded, offer'd to juftifie us. Signor, faid he,
we had no ill Defign, and therefore
ought to be forgiven this Device. What
a Duce, replied the Captain in a Heat,
do you call this a Device ? Don't you
know that 'tis a Hanging Matter ? Befides that, no Man is permitted to do
Juftice

Juftice for himfelf: You took a Candleftick, a Necklace, and Diamond-Earings; and which is ftill worfe, to accomplifh this Robbery, you ' turn'd yourfelves into Serjeants. Rogues difguife themfelves like honeft Men to do ill. You will be very happy if you efcape without a Halter. When he had given us to underftand that the Matter was more ferious than we at firft took it to be, we fell at his Feet, and pray'd him to have Pity on our Youth; but our Prayers were to no no purpofe. He rejected the Propofition we made him to deliver up the Candleftick, the Necklace, and the Pendants. He refus'd even my Ring, perhaps becaufe it was offer'd in Company. In fine, he was inexorable. He caus'd my Companions to be difarm'd, and carried us all to Prifon. As we were carrying along, one of his Serjeants told me that the Old Woman who liv'd with *Camilla*, fufpecting us not to be really what we were in appearance, Officers belonging to the Courts of Juftice, dogg'd us to the Tavern; and finding her Sufpicions to be well grounded, fhe gave Information of us to the Captain of the Watch, to be reveng'd of us.

L 4   The

The firſt thing the Officers did, was
to ſearch us. The Necklace, the Pendants, and the Silver Candleſtick were
immediately taken from us. They took
from me alſo my Ring, and the *Philippine* Iſle Rubies, which I had unfortu-
nately in my Pockets. Nay, they did
not leave me ſo much as the Reals I had
got that Day by my Preſcriptions : By
which I perceiv'd that the Officers belonging to the Courts of Juſtice at *Valladolid* underſtood their Offices as well
as thoſe at *Aſtorga*, and that the Manners
of thoſe Gentlemen were every - where
alike. While they were taking my Jewels and Money from me, the Captain
of the Watch reported our Adventure
to the Magiſtrates. The Matter was ſo
extraordinary, that the greateſt part of
them thought we deſerv'd to be truſs'd
up for it : Others, leſs ſevere, ſaid we
might come off for Two hundred good
Laſhes, and ſome Years Service at Sea.
We were ſhut up in a Dungeon, to wait
for the Sentence of Monſieur the Corregidor. We lay on Straw, which was
by no means as clean and as fine as that
in a Stable with which Horſes are lit-
ter'd. We had ſtaid there longer, and
not been let out but to go to the Galleys,

leys, if Signor *Manuel Ordonnez* had not heard of our Affair, and refolved to get *Fabricio* difchar'd ; which he could not do, without delivering us alfo. He was a Man in great Efteem in the City. He fpar'd for no Solicitations ; and what by his own Credit, and that of his Friends, in three Days time he procur'd our Difcharge. But we did not go out of that Place as we got in. The Candle-ftick, the Necklace, the Pendants, my Ring, and the Rubies all remain'd there ; which put me in mind of thofe Verfes in *Virgil*, which begin with thefe Words, *Sic vos non vobis.*

Affoon as we were fet free, we return'd to our Mafters. Dr. *Sangrado* receiv'd me kindly. Poor *Gil Blas*, fays he, I did not hear of thy Misfortune till this Morning. I was preparing to folicit for thee vigoroufly. Thou muft comfort thy felf up for this Accident, my Friend, and apply more than ever to Phyfick. I anfwer'd, 'Twas my Defign, and I did fo accordingly. I was fo far from wanting Bufinefs, that it happening, as my Mafter faid, to be a fickly Time, I had my Hands full of Patients. The Small Pox and malignant Fevers reign'd in the City and Suburbs. All the

I 5   Dœctors

Doctors in *Valladolid* were full of. Practice, and we in particular. There did not a Day go over our Heads, but we each of us visited eight or ten Patients. Of Consequence there was a great deal of Water drank, and much Blood let. But I can't tell how it happen'd, they all dy'd. Either we manag'd them very ill, or their Distempers were incurable. We rarely visited the same Sick Man thrice. At the second we found him either bury'd or in the Agony. Being a young Physician, my Heart was not sufficiently hardned for Murders. I was griev'd at so many sad Events, which might be imputed to me. Sir, said I one Evening to Dr. *Sangrado,* I call Heaven to witness I follow your Method exactly, yet all my Patients go to the other World. One would think they died on purpose to bring our Practice into Discredit : I met two carrying to the Grave this Afternoon. Child, says he, I might tell thee the same of my self : I have not often the Satisfaction to cure the Persons that fall into my Hands ; and if I was not as certain as I am of the Principles of my Practice, I should take my Remedies to be contrary to almost all the Diseases I have in hand. If you will be
rul'd

rul'd by me, Sir, replied I, we'll change
our Method, and out of Curiosity give
our Patients some Chymical Preparations. The worst that can happen is, that
they'll have the same Effect as our hot
Water and Bleeding. I would willingly make the Experiment, says he, if it
would not have an ill Consequence, and
be against my own Writing; for I have
publish'd a Book in Vindication of frequent Bleeding, and Hot-Water-drink-
ing. Would'st thou have me decry my
own Work? You are in the right, Sir,
replied I, you must not give an Occasion to your Enemies to triumph over
you. They'll say you have suffer'd your
self to be abus'd. You'll lose your Reputation; Rather let the People, the Nobility, and the Clergy perish. Let's continue our wonted Practice. Our Brethren, after all, notwithstanding the A-
version they have for Bleeding, do no
greater Wonders than we; and our Specificks are as good as their Drugs.

We proceeded in our old Course, and
in such a manner, that in less than six
Weeks we made as many Widows and
Orphans as the Siege of *Troy*. One would
have thought the Plague was in *Valladolid.*

lid, there were so many Funerals. There came every day to our House Fathers to demand an Account of the Sons, we had robb'd them of; or Uncles to reproach us for the Death of their Nephews. As for the Nephews and Sons whose Fathers and Uncles far'd the worse for our Medicines, they came not to our House. The Husbands of the Wives we made away with were also very discreet, and did not scold us on that score. The Persons Afflicted, whose Reproaches we endur'd, had sometimes a Rashness in their Affliction, they call'd us Fools and Murderers; they thought no Names too bad for us. I was enrag'd at their Epithets; but my Master, who had been us'd to it, was not at all concern'd at it. Perhaps I should have accustomed my self to them as well as he, if Heaven, doubtless to take away one of the Flails of the Sick at *Valladolid*, had not giv'n me a Disgust to Physick, which I practic'd with so little Success.

There was a Tennis-Court in our Neighbourhood, where the Idle met every Day: Among whom was one who set up for Judge and Bully of the Place. He was a *Biscayan*, and his Name Don *Rodriguez de Mendragon*. He was about
thirty

thirty Years old, not very tall, but well
fet and ftrong. Befides two little Ferret
Eyes that roll'd in his Head, he had a
Hook'dNofe which hung over a red Muftachio that curl'd out to his Temple.
He fpoke fo hoarfe and fo haftily, that
he made every one afraid. He was the
Tyrant of the Tennis-Court. His Decifions among the Players were all arbi-
trary and imperious; and there was no
appealing from his Judgment without
running the risk of a Challenge. This
Signor Don *Rodrigo*, who, tho' he put
a *Don* before his Name, was no better
than a Butcher, had gain'd the Affections
of the Miftrefs of the Houfe. She was
a rich Widow of about forty Years old,
pretty well for her Perfon. Her Huf-
band had been dead about a Year and
a Quarter. I can't imagine how fhe could
take a liking to this Bully of the Racket ;
'twas not for his Beauty, fhe muft fee
fomething in him that no body elfe did.
Be it as it will, fhe had a Kindnefs for
him, and refolv'd to marry him. But
as all things were making ready for Con-
fummation, fhe fell fick ; and 'twas her
bad Luck to have me for her Phyfician.
If her Diftemper had not been a malignant Fevèr, my Remedy was fufficient
to

to make it one. In four Days time I put all the Tennis-Court into Mourning. The Miltrefs of it went the fame way I fent all my Patients, and her Relations took Poffeffion of her Eftate. Don *Rodrigo*, made defperate by the Lofs of his Miltrefs, or rather the Hope of a very advantageous Match, was not contented with flinging Fire and Flames at me, he fwore he would run me thro' the Guts, where-ever he met me. A charitable Neighbour gave me Information of his Oath, and advis'd me not to go out of our Houfe, for fear of meeting this Devil of a Man. This Advice, which I had no mind to negle&t, fill'd me with Trouble and Fear. The *Bifcayan* was always in my Mind, and before my Eyes. I could not be at Reft a Moment. This made me out of love with Phyfick; and I thought of nothing but how to deliver myfelf from the Apprehenfion in which I liv'd. I took my embroider'd Coat again ; and having bid my Mafter Adieu, notwithftanding the many Arguments he us'd, to perfuade me to ftay with him, I left the City at Break of Day, not without Fear of meeting Don *Rodrigo* in my Way.

CHAP.

CHAP. VI.

What Road he took when he left Valladolid *; and what Man he met by the*
Way.

I Made as much Hafte as I could when
I got out of the Town ; and every
now and then look'd behind me to fee
if I was not purfu'd by the terrible *Bif-*
cayan. My Head, was fo full of him,
that I took every Tree and Bufh to be
him. My Heart fail'd me at the leaft
Noife : And I did not think myfelf fafe
till I got two or three Leagues off
Valladolid. I then flackned Pace, and
jogg'd on pretty chearfully towards *Ma-*
drid, whither I propos'd to myfelf to
go. I was forry for nothing in departing from *Valladolid,* but leaving *Fabricio,*
my dear *Pylades,* to whom I had not
time to bid Adieu. I did not grieve for
lofing the Profeffion of a Phyfician ; on
the contrary, I begg'd God to forgive
me for having practis'd it at all. I was
well pleas'd however with the Money
I had in my Pocket, tho' it was the
Purchafe

Purchafe of my Murders. I was like
thofe Women that leave off Whoring,
but keep ftill the Money they made of
it. I had as many Reals as came to
five Ducats. That was all my Stock;
I depended upon it to carry me to *Madrid*, where I doubted not I fhould get
a good Place. Befides, I long'd mightily to fee that City, which I heard fo
much Talk of, as being an Epitome of
all the World's Wonders.

While I was meditating on what had
been told me of it, and pleafing my felf
with the thoughts of what I fhould fee
there, I heard a Man behind me coming
on, finging. He had a Snapfack at his Back,
a Guitar hanging about his Neck, and a
long Sword by his Side. He walk'd fo faft,
that he foon overtook me. 'Twas one
of the Journeymen Barbers that had been
imprifon'd with me about the Adventure of the Ring. We knew one another prefently, and were furpriz'd to
meet thus unexpectedly on the High-way.
I exprefs'd a great Joy at having him for
a Companion, and he did as much on
my account. I told him why I left *Valladolid* ; and he, on his part, inform'd
me that he had had a Quarrel with his
Mafter, and they had mutually bad one
ano-

another Adieu for ever. If I would have
ftaid at *Valladolid*, added he, there are
ten Shops I could have had my Choice
of; for, without Vanity, I may fay
there is not a Barber in *Spain* that knows
how to handle a Razor like me, or
curl a Muftachio: But I have a mind
to return to my own Country, from
whence I have been ten Years ab-
fent. I want to breath fome of my Native Air, and know how it goes with my
Relations. It will not be long before I
fhall be with them; for they dwell but
at *Olivedo* a great Village on this fide
Segovia.

I refolv'd to accompany the Barber to
that Village, and thence go to *Segovia*,
to get fome Convenience to convey my
felf to *Madrid.* We fell into Difcourfe
of indifferent things as we continued
our Journey. He was a good humour'd
merry Lad; and after we had travelled
together about an Hour, he ask'd me if
my Stomach was not come? I replied,
He fhould fee that at the firft Inn we
came to. Let us not ftay for that, fays
he, I have fomewhat to Breakfaft on in
my Budget. I always carry Provifions
with me when I travel the Road. I don't
burthen myfelf with Cloaths, Linen,
and

and fuch ufelefs Luggage. I put nothing
in it, but Provifion of the Mouth, my
Razors, and Wafhballs. I applauded his
Prudence, and confented to halt with'
him. I was hungry, and propos'd to
make a Meal on my Comrade's Cargo,
after what he had faid of it. We went
into a Bye-Place, and fat down on the
Grafs. The Barber pull'd out his Pro-
vender, which confifted of five or fix
Onions, a piece of Bread, and fomeCheefe.
But what he valued himfelf on, was a
Bottle, which he faid was full of rare
Wine. Tho' our Entertainment was not
very nice, yet we were fo hungry, that
neither of us found fault with it. We
empty'd the Bottle, which held about a
Quart, and did not contain any thing
worthy the Panegyrick the Barber be-
ftowed upon it. When we had thus
Breakfafted, we rofe, and proceeded very
gaily on our Journey. *Fabricio* had told'
me that this Barber had met with many Adventures; and he defiring me to
tell him mine, in hopes of hearing them,
I gave him Satisfaction. I then pray'd
him to oblige me, by giving me the Story of his Life. My Story, cry'd he,
'tis not worth telling. It has nothing in
it but plain Facts. However, fince we
have

have no better Subject to discourse of, I'll tell it you, such as it is. Accordingly he began it in the following manner.

CHAP. VII.

The Story of the Journey-man Barber.

*F*Ernand Perez de la Fuente my Grand-father, (I love to trace things from the Beginning) after having liv'd a Barber fifty Years in the Village of *Olmedo,* died, and left four Sons behind him: The eldest, call'd *Nicolas,* possess'd himself of his Shop, and succeeded him in his Profession. The second Son, *Bertrand,* took to a Trade, and became a Mercer. *Thomas,* the third, was a Schoolmaster. And *Pedro,* the fourth, finding he had a Genius for the *Belles Lettres,* sold a small Estate he had, and went to make the most of it at *Madrid.* The three other Brothers remain'd at *Olmedo,* where they married three young Women, Labourers Daughters, who brought them not much Money: But to make amends for it, they bless'd them with abundance

bundance of Children. They feem'd to outvie one another in getting them. My Mother, for her part, was fairly deliver-ed of fix in the five firft Years of her Marriage. I was one of them. My Fa-ther taught me to fhave betimes ; and when I was fifteen Years of Age, he put this Snapfack on my Back, ty'd a long Sword to my Side, and faid, Go, *Diego*, thou art now able to get thy Liv-ing ; go travel the Country, 'twill teach thee thy Trade better than ftaying at home : Go, and let me not fee thee at *Olmedo* again, till thou haft feen all *Spain*. Let me not fo much as hear thee nam'd, At thefe Words he embrac'd me cor-dially, and turn'd me out of Doors.

This was the Farewel I had from my Father. As for my Mother, fhe had not fuch a hard Heart. She feem'd trou-bled at my Going : The Tears trickled down her Cheeks ; and fhe flipt a Ducat into my Hand. I left *Olmedo* in this Condition, and took the Road to *Se-govia*. I had not gone Two hundred Yards before I examin'd my Budget. I long'd to fee what was in the Infide of it, and to have an exact knowledge of my Treafure. I found a Razor-cafe, with two Razors in it, very well worn,

a

a Leather to fet them upon, and a Bit
of Soap. Befides this, there was a new
Canvas Shirt, and a Pair of my Father's
old Shoes; and what rejoyc'd my Heart
more than all the reft, twenty Reals in
an old Rag. This was my Stock. You
may perceive by this that Mr. *Nicolas*
the Barber depended very much on my
Dexterity, fince he accouter'd me fo
indifferently. Neverthelefs, the Poffeffion of a Ducat and twenty Reals muft
needs be charming to a young Man. I
I thought my Purfe would be inex-
hauftibl:, and went on tranfported with
Joy, fometimes looking on my Rapier,
which hung at my Heels, and every now
and then got between my Legs, and was
like to overfet me.

I arriv'd in the Evening at *Aguinis* very hungry. I lodg'd at an Inn; and,
as if I was in Circumftances to fpend my
Money freely, demanded of my Landlord what he had for Supper? My Landlord loookd' upon me fwithfully; and perceiving what fort of Man he had to do
with, he faid, We'll fatisfy you, young
Gentlemen; you fhall be treated like a
Prince. He then led me into a little
Room, where, half an Hour after, they
brought me an old Rabbet, which, in all
pro-

probability had been the Mother of
many that that had made Ragouts laſt
Year. They accompanied this admirable
ble Diſh with ſome Wine, ſo good, ſays
he, the King does not drink better.
However, I perceiv'd it was prick'd ;
but I ſwallowed it as greedily as I did
the Rabbet, which being too tough to
be diſpatch'd by the Teeth, went down
in whole Peices. To finiſh my Treatment like a Prince, I was put into a
Bed much more proper to keep a Man
awake than aſleep. 'Twas ſo ſhort, I
could not ſtretch out my Legs, as ſhort
as I was myſelf. The Bottom was only
a little Straw, and that of the coarſeſt
ſort : A-top was a Sheet doubled, which
had perhaps ſerv'd a hundred Travellers
ſince the laſt Waſhing. Nevertheleſs,
my Stomach was ſo full of the old Co-
ny, and the delicious Wine my Landlord boaſted of, that, Thanks to my
Youth and my Conſtitution, I ſlept
ſoundly, and paſt the Night without In-
digeſtion. The next Day, when I had
Breakfaſted, and paid well for my Good
Cheer, I went on my Journey, and arriv'd ſafely at *Segovia*. I was no ſooner
there, than by good Luck I lit on a Shop
where I was receiv'd for my Board and
Lodging.

Lodging. I ſtaid tnere ſix Months only. A Journeyman Barber, whom I
came acquainted with, debauch'd me,
and I departed with him for *Madrid*.
I eaſily got a Place there on the ſame
Terms as at *Segovia*. 'Twas a well-ac-
cuſtom'd Shop. It ſtood near the Church
of St. *Creſs*; and its neighbourhood to
the Prince's Theatre brought a Croud of
Cuſtomers to it. My Maſter's two Journeymen and I were hardly enow to
Shave them. I ſaw People of all Conditions, and, among others, Players and
Authors. Two of the latter happen'd
to be one Day together in our Shop:
They talk'd of nothing but the Poets
and Poems of the Time. Among the
former I heard them name my Uncle,
which made me more attentive to what
they ſaid. Don *Juan de Zaraleta*, ſays
one of them, is an Author which the
Publick ought not to make account of.
He has no Fire nor Fancy. His laſt Play
is Intolerable. And what is *Louis Velez
de Guenera* worth, I pray? replied the
other; was there ever ſuch Stuff ſeen?
They then nam'd ſeveral other Poets,
whoſe Names I have forgotten. I only
remember they rail'd at them plentifully.
As for my Uncle, they made honourable

ble mention of him. They agreed both that he was a Man of Merit. Yes, cries one of them, Don *Pedro de la Fuente* is an excellent Author. There is a great deal of Pleasantry and Learning in his Works, which are picquant, and full of Salt. I don't wonder both Court and Town like him, and that he has several Pensions from the Grandees. He has sav'd a good Parcel of Money out of them. He has his Lodging and Diet at the Duke *de Medina Celi's*. He spends nothing; and must be very rich. I lost not a Word of what the Poets said of my Uncle. We had heard at home that he made a Noise at *Madrid* by his Writings; some People who pass'd thro' *Olmedo* told us so: But he never letting us hear from him, and seeming to shake us off, our Family did not trouble their Heads about him. However, I resolv'd not to lose such an Opportunity, but to make myself known to him as soon as I found how it was with him, and knew where he liv'd. One thing perplex'd me a little; the Authors call'd him Don *Pedro*. This *Don* gave me some Difficulty, and I was afraid it might be some other Poet, and not my Uncle. Nevertheless, I came to a Resolution to see whether it

was

was he, or no. I imagin'd he might be
become a Gentleman as well as a Wit.
In order to find him out, I dreſt myſelf
one Morning, and with my Maſter's
Leave went to viſit him, not a little
proud to be the Nephew of a Man
who had acquir'd ſuch a Reputation by
his Genius. Barbers are not the laſt
ſuſceptible of Vanity of any Men in the
World. I began to have a great Opinion of myſelf; and walking with a ſtate-
ly Air, inquir'd the Way to the Duke
de Medina Celi's. When I came to the
Gate, I ask'd the Porter for Signor Don
Pedro de la Fuente. The Porter hearing
him nam'd, pointed to a little Stair-caſe
at the farther End of a Court, and ſaid,
Go up thoſe Stairs, and knock at the
firſt Door on the Right-hand. I did as
he bad me : I knock'd at the Door. A
Young Man came out to me, of whom
I demanded if Signor Don *Pedro de la
Fuente* lodg'd there? Yes, replied he;
but you cannot ſpeak with him at preſent. I ſhould be glad to have one word
with him, ſaid I, becauſe I bring him
ſome News from his Relations. If you
brought News from the Pope, replied
he, I would not introduce you now into
his Chamber. He is Writing; and when

he Writes, one muſt have a care of diſturbing him. He will not be viſible till Noon: Go, and return at that time. I went thence into the City, which I walk'd about, contemplating the Reception I ſhould have from my Uncle; I believe, ſaid I to myſelf, he'll be overjoyed to ſee me. I judg'd of him by my ſelf, and expected that our Meeting would be a very joyful one. I did not fail of returning at the Time appointed. You are come very opportunely, ſays his Valet; my Maſter is going out; ſtay a little, I'll tell him you are here. He left me in the Anti-chamber, return'd a Moment after, and conducted me to his Maſter, who I preſently knew to be my Uncle, he was ſo like Uncle *Thomas.* I ſaluted him with a moſt profound Reverence, and told him I was the Son of Maſter *Nicolas ds la Fuente,* Barber, at *Olmedo:* That I had follow'd the ſame Trade as a Journeyman in *Madrid* three Weeks, and intended to travel all *Spain* to improve my ſelf. While I was ſpeaking. I obſerv'd my Uncle mus'd. 'Twas plain he was in ſuſpence whether to diſown me, or ſhake me off as dexterouſly as he could. He choſe the latter. He affected to ſmile; and ſaid, Well

Well, Friend, how do thy Father and thy Uncle do? How does it go with them? I then began to give him an Account of the copious Propagation of our Family. I nam'd him all the Children Male and Female, and added to the List their Godfathers and Godmothers. He did not seem to be much concern'd at what I said; and when I had done, *Diego*, said he, I approve mightily of thy Travelling the Country to perfect thy self in thy Trade: And I advise thee not to stay any longer in *Madrid*. 'Tis a Place destructive to Youth: Thou wilt be ruin'd here, Child: Thou'lt do better to go to the other Cities of the Kingdom; People are not so corrupted there. Go then, continued he; and when thou art about to depart, let me see thee again. I'll give thee a Pistole to carry thee thro' *Spain*. At these Words he push'd me softly out of the Room, and sent me Home.

I had not the Sense to perceive that he wanted to have me out of *Madrid*. I return'd to our Shop, and gave my Master an Account of my Visit. He had no more Thoughts than I of my Uncle Don *Pedro*'s Intention. I am not of his Opinion, said he; instead of running

K 2　　　　rambling

rambling about the Country, you had
better fix yourself in the City. Your
Uncle knows so many People of Quality,
he may easily get you a Place in a good
Family, and by degrees you may make
your Fortune there. I lik'd this Discourse
extremely, and two Days after went to
my Uncle again, to propose to him to
make use of his Credit to get me a
Place in some Nobleman's House : But
he did not approve of the Proposal.
A vain Man, who din'd every Day with
one Person of Quality or other, was
not willing to see his Nephew at the
Footman's Table, while he was at the
Lord's. Little *Diego* would have made
Signor Don *Pedro* blush. He fell upon
me therefore, and reprov'd me then
with a very angry Look. How ! you
young Rascal you ! Will you leave your
Trade ? What Rogues have been ad-
vising thee to thy Ruin ? Go to them ;
get out of my Apartment, and never
set foot here again, otherwise I shall
have thee chastis'd as thou deserv'st.
These Words stunn'd me, much more
the Tone with which my Uncle spoke
them. I retir'd with the Tears in my
Eyes, very much troubled that he should
be so cruel to me. But being naturally
lively

lively and proud, I soon gave over weeping. My Grief turn'd to Indignation, and resolv'd to leave so ill a Relation where I found him, having hitherto liv'd without him. I thought of nothing but cultivating my Talent. I minded my Business. I shav'd Day and Night : And to recreate my self now and then, learnt to play on the Guitarre. My Master on that Instrument was an old *Senor Essendero*, whom I shav'd. He had formerly been a Chanter in a Cathedral. His Name was *Marcos d'Obregon*. He was a discreet Person, and had as much Wit as Experience. He lov'd me as dearly as if I had been his own Son. He was Gentleman-Usher to a Doctor's Wife, who liv'd about thirty Yards off us. I us'd to go to him every Night when I had done Work ; and we two sitting on the Threshold of the Door, made a little Consort, with which the Neighbourhood was not at all displeas'd. Not that we had very good Voices, but we both perform'd our Parts pretty well, at least enough to please those that heard us. We particularly diverted Donna *Mergelina* the Doctor's Wife. She came into the Entry to hearken to us, and oblig'd us to give her some *Encores*,

K 3   when

when the Airs were to her Liking. Her
Husband was as well entertain'd with
us as she was. Tho' he was a *Spaniard*,
and an Old Man, he was not in the least
jealous of her. Besides, his Practice
took him up wholly; and as he us'd
to come home every Night from visiting
his Patients very much fatigued, so he
went to Bed betimes, and did not mind
our serenading his Wife. Perhaps he
thought our Musick was not so charming as to make any dangerous Impres-
sions upon her; and he had too much
Confidence in his Wife's Conduct to
suspect her. *Mergelina* was young and
handsome, but withal so coy, that she
would hardly suffer a Man to ogle her.
She did not think there was any harm
in listening to our Musick; and we
might sing or play as much as we pleas'd,
she took no Offence at it.

Coming one Evening to the Doctor's
Door, intending to divert myself there,
according to Custom, I found the old
Gentleman-Usher waiting for me. He
took me by the Hand, and said, he
would have me take a Walk before we
began our Consort. He then led me
into a Bye-street, where, thinking we
were private enough, he began his Discourse

courſe thus, in a melancholy Tone ;
Don *Diego*, I have ſomething to tell
you in particular. I am afraid, Child,
that we ſhall both of us repent amu-
ſing our ſelves every Night with Serenades at my Maſter's Door. I have certainly a Kindneſs for you. I am glad
I have taught you to play on the Guitarre, and ſing : But if I had ſo eſeen
the Miſchief that is likely to come of it,
I ſhould have made choice of another
Place for us to practiſe our Leſſons in.
I was frighted at what he ſaid, and de-
ſir'd him to explain himſelf ; for if we
were in any Danger, I ſhould be willing to get out of it as faſt as I could.
I'll tell you, replied he, what I have to
ſay, and then gueſs you the Danger.

When I enter'd into the Doctor's Service, which was about a Year ago, he
told me one Morning, preſenting me to
his Wife, That's your Miſtreſs, *Marcos* ;
you are to wait on her where - ever
ſhe goes. I was extremely taken with
Donna *Mergelina* ; I thought her wonderfully handſome, and was particularly charm'd with her fine Carriage.
Signor, replied I to the Doctor, I am
too happy in ſerving ſo lovely a Lady.
Mergelina was diſpleas'd at what I had
K 4   ſaid,

said, and cry'd, *You're a pretty Fellow
indeed, and take upon you more than becomes you. I shan't suffer such things to be
said to me.* Such rude Words from such
sweet Lips were a strange Surprize to
me. I could not reconcile them to
the Softness of her Air. Her Husband
was us'd to them, and valued himself
upon having a Wife of so rare a Character. *Marcos,* says he to me, my Wife
is a Prodigy of Virtue; and perceiving
she was putting on her Scarf, and preparing to go to Church, he bad me attend her. We were no sooner got into
the Street, than, what is not extraordinary in such Cases, several Men smitten
with the Beauty of Donna *Mergelina,*
said very kind things to her as she past
along. You can't imagine what silly and
ridiculous Answers she made them.
They were all amaz'd; and could not
conceive that there was a Woman in the
World who did not love to be flatter'd.
Do not you hear, Madam, said I, what
those Gentlemen say to you? One had
better be silent than give hard Words.
No, no, replied she, I'll have those inso-
lent Fellows to know that I am not a
Woman who will suffer them to fail in
their Respect to me. In short, she was
so

fo impertinent that I could not help
telling her what I thought of it, whether fhe lik'd it or no, I reprefented to
her, with as much Submiffion as I
could, that fhe did an Injury to Nature, and fpoil'd a thoufand good Qualities by her favage Humour ; that a
complaifant well-bred Woman might
render herfelf amiable without the Affiftance of Beauty ; whereas a beautiful
Woman, without good Breeding and
Complacency, would become contemptible. A great deal more I faid upon the
fame Subject, tending all to correct her
Manners. I was afraid fhe would have
refented my Leffons, and given me a fevere Reproof for them ; but fhe bore
them, contenting herfelf with taking notice of what I faid then, or at other
times to the fame Purpofe. I grew
weary of admonifhing her in vain, and
abandoned her to the Fiercenefs of her
Nature. In the mean time, what do ye
think ? This rude Temper, this proud
Woman is within thefe two Months
entirely alter'd. She's civil and good-
humour'd to every Body. She is not the
fame *Mergelina*, who always anfwer'd
Men rudely. She now fays the moft
obliging things in the World. She likes

K 5 now

now to be flatter'd, to be told she is
handsome, and that a Man cannot look
on her with Safety. One can hardly
imagine how she's chang'd ; and what
you ought to be most surpriz'd at, is,
You yourself are the Occasion of so great
a Miracle : Yes, my dear *Diego*, continues he, 'tis you that have thus meta-
morphos'd Donna *Mergelina*: You have
turn'd the Tigress into a Lamb ; in a
word, all her Thoughts run upon
you. I have observ'd it more than once ;
and either I don't know what sort of
Creatures Women are, or she is passionately in Love with you. This, my
Son, is the sad News I have to acquaint
you with, and the unhappy Conjuncture
we are fallen into.

I don't see, replied I to the old 'Squire,
that there is any thing in all this which
we need very much grieve for ; nor that
it is a Misfortune for me to be belov'd
by a pretty Lady. You talk like a Young
Man, *Diego*, said he ; you don't perceive
the Snake that's in the Grass. You have
regard to nothing but the Pleasure, but
I have respect to the Pains with which
it is attended. 'Twill all come out at
last. If you continue to sing at our
Door, you will inflame *Mergelina* still
more

more and more ; and fhe will perhaps in
the end become fo weak as to let Dr. *Olorofo* her Husband fee it. Tho' he is now
fo very complaifant, becaufe he thinks he
has no reafon to be jealous ; he will then
grow enrag'd againft thee, and be reveng'd
on her ; and you may imagine that neither you nor I fhall come off very well
on this Occafion. Well, Signor *Marcos*,
replied I, I fubmit to your Reafons, and
will follow your Advice. All that we
need do, fays he, is, to give over our
Serenades. Don't you appear before my
Miftrefs any more. When fhe does not
fee you fhe'll be quiet: Stay at home,
I'll come to you ; and we may play
there upon the Guitarre without running
any Rifk. Agreed, replied I ; and I pro-
mife you never to fet foot within your
Doors more. Indeed I refolv'd not to
fing again at the Doctor's Gate, but to
keep clofe to my Shop, fince I was a Perfon fo dangerous to be feen.

However, honeft *Marcos* found in a
little time that the Means he propos'd
to extinguifh Donna *Mergelina*'s Fires,
had a quite contrary Effect. The Lady
finding that we did not fing for two
Nights together, ask'd him why we gave
over our Confort, and what was the

Reafon fhe did not fee me? He anfwer'd, I was fo bufy that I had not a
Moment to fpare for Pleafure. She
feem'd fatisfy'd with that Excufe, and
bore my Abfence for three Days longer
pretty well; but then fhe loft all Patience, and faid to her Gentleman-Ufher,
You impofe upon me, *Marcos*; *Diego*
has fome other Reafon for not coming hither. Tell me what it is, I command you;
hide nothing from me. I invented a
new Excufe for him. Madam, faid I,
fince you will know all, I muft tell
you, that after we have been playing
our Confort, it has often hapned when
he came home, that the Buttery has
been lock'd up, and he has been forc'd
to go to Bed fupperlefs. How! Sup-
perlefs, cried fhe in a Paffion. Why did
not you tell me fo before? Poor Child,
go to him prefently; bring him hither
to Night: He fhall not go home with-
cut his Supper: I will always have
fomething got for him here.

What's this! faid the Gentleman-Ufher,
making as if he was furpriz'd at her
Difcourfe. Heaven! Is it you, Madam,
that talk after this Rate? What a
Change is here? How long have you
been fo compaffionate? How long I replied

plied. she, very briskly; Ever since you
came hither; or rather, ever since you
school'd me for my ill Nature, and reprov'd the Rudeness of my Manners.
But alas! added she, with a languishing
Look, I have gone from one Extreme to
another: From proud and insensible, I am
become too soft and too tender. I love
your young Friend *Diego*, and I can't
help it. His Absence, instead of weakning my Passion, strengthens it. Is it
possible, answer'd the old 'Squire, that
a Young Man, who is neither handsome
nor well-shap'd should be the Object of
so strong a Passion? I should pardon
your Sentiments, if they had been inspir'd by some Gentleman, a Man of
Worth. Ah! *Marcos*, interrupted *Mergelina*, I am not like the rest of my
Sex; or else with all your Experience,
you know not what to make of them.
If I can tell any thing, they love without
Consideration. Love is a Witchcraft of
the Mind that directs one to an Object,
and fixes one to it, maugre all our Resistance. 'Tis a Disease that seizes us
like the Madness of Dogs, and other
Animals. Therefore don't tell me that
Diego is unworthy of my Passion. 'Tis
enough that I love him, to find in him a
thousand

thousand Qualities that you do not see,
and perhaps he does not possess. 'Tis
in vain for you to represent to me
that his Face and his Shape are not
worth my Regard. To me he seems
as fair as the Day, and made on purpose
to charm. Further, his Voice has a
Sweetness that ravishes me; and he
plays on the Guitarre with a Grace pecu-
liar to himself. But, Madam, replied
Marcos, do you consider his Condition ?
that he is ———. I consider nothing
but him, interrupted she; and if I
were a Woman of Quality, I should not
mind that.

The Result of this Conference was,
that the Old Usher finding he was not
likely to gain any thing by his Arguments, gave over opposing his Mistress's
Inclination ; as a skilful Pilot gives way
to a Tempest which drives him from the
Port whither he was bound. He did
more to satisfie his Patroness. He came
to me, and taking me aside, told me
what had past between her and him.
You see, *Diego*, says he, we cannot a-
void continuing our Consorts at *Mergé-
lina's* Door. It must be so, Friend, the
Lady must see you again, or she'll do
some foolish thing or other which will
be

be more prejudicial to her Reputation. I was not fo cruel as to deny him. I replied, that I would come to her Houfe in the Evening with my Guitarre, and he might carry that welcome News to his Miftrefs. He did fo; and fhe was tranfported to hear it, waiting with Impatience for the time appointed to fee me, and liften to my Mufick.

In the mean while an unlucky Accident had like to have fpoil'd all. I could not go from my Mafter's before Night, which for my Sins prov'd very dark. I grop'd my way thro' the Street, and had gone about half my Journey, when a Window open'd, and I was faluted with a Showr, which, I can affure you, was not of Effence. I had all of it; and in thofe Circumftances could not tell what to refolve on. If I return'd home in that Condition, I fhould be laught at; and I could not think of going to *Mergelina* in fo filthy and unfavoury a Plight. However, I was fo eager to renew my Confort, that I got thither before I was aware of it, and found the old 'Squire waiting for me at the Door. He told me Dr. *Olorofo* was gone to Bed, and that we might divert ourfelves very freely. I replied, I muft, in the firft

place,

place clean myſelf. I then Inform'd him of the Diſgrace I had met with. He condol'd with me, and carried me to a Hall, where his Miſtreſs ſtaid for us. As ſoon as ſhe knew of my Adventure, and ſaw how it was with me, ſhe pitied me as much as if the greateſt Misfortune had befaln me. She afterwards fell a raving at the Perſon that had ſo ſerv'd me. Pray, Madam, ſays *Marcos*, don't be in ſuch a Paſſion: It does not deſerve it. How! replied ſhe, ſhould I not curſe the wicked Creature that has ſo treated this little Lamb, this Dove without Gall, who does not ſo much as complain of the Outrage that's done him? Ah! that I was a Man, I would this Minute revenge him.

Many other things ſaid ſhe, which ſhew'd the Exceſs of her Love; nor were her Actions leſs expreſſive of it than her Words; for while *Marcos* was wiping me with a Napkin, ſhe ran to her Chamber, and fetch'd a Box of Perfume; ſhe burnt odoriferous Drugs, and perfum'd my Cloaths. She afterwards ſprinkled Eſſences on them abundantly. The Fumigation and Aſperſion being over, this charitable Woman went her ſelf to the Kitchin for ſome Bread, Wine, and

and roasted Mutton, which she had order'd to be set aside for me. She made
me eat, and took pleasure in helping
me. Sometimes she would cut my
Meat, sometimes fill out my Wine,
whatever we could do to hinder her.
When I had supp'd, the Gentlemen of
the Consort prepar'd their Guitarre's,
and tun'd their Voices. We play'd a
Symphony, at which *Mergelina* was
charm'd. Indeed we assented to sing
some Airs, the Words of which humour'd her Passion; and it must be
remembred, that as I played, I now
and then cast a soft Look at her, which
was fresh Fuel to her Flame; and I began to think it no disagreeable Game.
Tho' the Consort lasted a good while,
I was not tir'd with it. As for the Lady, who thought the Hours were but
Moments, she would willingly have
hearkned to us all Night, if the old U-
sher, who thought the Moments were
Hours, had not often put her in mind
that it grew late. She gave him the
Trouble to repeat it ten times to her:
But she had to do with one that was
indefatigable therein; and would not
let her be quiet, till I left the House.
He was a Man of Prudence and Discretion;

tion; and feeing his Miftrefs gave herfelf over to the pleafing her Paffion,
he was afraid fomething ill might be-
tide us, if he did not prevent it. This
Fear was but too well grounded; the
Doctor either miftrufting fome fecret Intrigue, or being poffeft by that Devil
Jealoufie, who had fpar'd him till then,
cenfur'd our Conforts ; and not long
after forbad them, without telling his
Reafons for it, faying only, He would
not have Strangers entertain'd at his
Houfe. *Marcos* inform'd me of it ; and
as it had refpect to me in particular, I
was very much mortified at it. I had
conceived Hopes which I was loth to
lofe.

But to relate things as becomes a
faithful Hiftorian, I confefs it to you,
that I bore this Misfortune with Patience. It was not fo with *Mergelina* ;
fhe could not bear it. Dear *Marcos,*
cry'd fhe to her Ufher, 'Tis from you
alone I look for Affiftance. Manage it
fo, I pray you, that I may fee *Diego* in
private. What would you have of me ?
replied the old Man in a Fury ; I have
already humour'd you too much. I
fhall not contribute to the Difhonour
of my Mafter, by fatisfying your ar-
dent

dent. Defires ; nor, will I . facrifice your
Reputation, and cover my felf with Infamy. I, whofe Conduct, as a faithful
Domeftick, has always been unblameable, I had rather quit your Service than
do fo bafe an Action. Ah ! *Marcos*, interrupted the Lady, whom thefe laft
Words frighted, you kill me when you
talk of leaving me. Cruel as you are ;
will you abandon me, after having
brought me into this miferable Condition ? Reftore to me my Pride, and that
favage Temper which you took from
me. Ah, that I had ftill thofe happy
Defects ! I fhould now be at eafe, whereas your indifcreet Remonftrances have
ravifh'd from me the Repofe I once enjoy'd. You have corrupted my Manners by endeavouring to correct them.
But ah ! continued fhe, weeping, why
do I blame you, why reproach you unjuftly ? No, no, Father, you are not the
Author of my Misfortune. 'Tis my
ill Fate that prepares fo much Affliction
for me. Don't take notice, I conjure
you, of my extravagant Difcourfe. My
Paffion, alas ! diforders my Mind. Pity
my Weaknefs : All my Confolation is
in you ; and if my Life is dear to you,
do not refufe me your Affiftance. Saying

ing this, she wept afresh, and her Tears
choak'd her Words. She pull'd out her
Pocket Handkerchief, and throwing it
over her Face, fell into a Chair like a
Person overwhelm'd with Grief. Old
Marcos, who perhaps knew the Business
of his Post as well as any Gentleman-
Usher in *Spain*, could not stand out a-
gainst so moving a Spectacle. It touch'd
him to the quick. He wept as well as
his Mistress, and said to her very ten-
derly, Ah! Madam, you are enough to
seduce any body. I cannot resist your
Afflictions. It overcomes my Virtue:
I promise you my Succour; and don't
wonder Love has the Power to make
you forget your Duty, since Compassion
only is capable of withdrawing me
from mine. Thus this old Usher, not-
withstarding his unblameable Conduct, devoted himself very obligingly
to *Mergelina*'s Passion. He came one
Morning to acquaint me with all this;
and told me when he left me, that he
had already contriv'd a way to procure
me a secret Interview with the Lady.
This gave me new Hopes. But two
Hours after I had other sort of News.
An Apothecary's Man, one of our Cus-
tomers entred our Shop to be shav'd.
                              While

While I was fetting my Razor, he faid,
Do you know, Signor *Diego*, what's the
Matter with your Friend the Old Gentleman-Ufher *Marcos d'Obregon*, and
why Dr. *Olorefo* has turn'd him away?
I replied, No. 'Tis certainly true, anfwer'd he; he was turn'd off juft as I
came hither. I learnt it from Signor *O-
lorofo* himfelf, who came to our Houfe,
and difcourfing with my Mafter, told
him, he had difmifs'd his old Ufher,
being refolv'd to put his Wife under the
Care of a faithful, fevere, and vigilant
Duegna, defiring him to recommend him
to one. I underftand you, faid my Mafter, interrupting him : You would have
fuch a one as Dame *Melancia*, who was
Governantee to my Wife, and who is ftill
in my Houfe, tho' I have been a Widow-
er thefe fix Weeks. I can ill fpare her;
but will part with her to you, in whofe
Honour I have a particular Intereft. You
may truft her with the Guardianfhip of
your Forehead. She's the Pink of *Duegna's*, and a Dragon where the Chaftity
of the Sex is concern'd. During the
twelve Years that fhe liv'd with my
Wife, who, as you know, wanted neither Youth nor Beauty, I never faw
the Shadow of a Gallant in my Houfe.
And

And truly fhe at firft had no very eafy Task of it. I muft own the Defunct had once a very great Inclination to Coquetry ; but Dame *Melancia* reclaim'd her, and inftill'd into her a Love of Virtue. In fine, this Governantee is a Treafure ; and you'll thank me a thoufand times for making a Prefent of her to you. The Doctor exprefs'd himfelf to be mightily obliged to my Mafter for this Favour ; and they two agreed that the *Duegna* fhould this very Day fupply the Place of the old Ufher.

This News gave a terrible Difturbance to the Idea's of Pleafure which I began to entertain my felf with ; and foon after *Marcos* came himfelf to confirm all that the Apothecary's Man had told me. Dear *Diego*, fays he, I am overjoy'd that Dr. *Olorofo* has turn'd me out of his Houfe. How much Trouble will it fave me ? Befides difcharging me from a bafe Employment, what Perplexity fhould I have been in to bring you and *Mergelina* together ? Thank Heaven, I am deliver'd from that Trouble, and the Danger which attended it. On your part, you, my Son, ought to comfort yourfelf for the Lofs of a few fweet Moments, by confidering theCares,

Anxie-

Anxieties and Pains that would have follow'd after. I hearkned to *Marcos*'s Leſſons the more attentively, becauſe I gave over all Hopes of ſeeing *Mergelina* again. I was not one of thoſe obſtinate Lovers who are ſharpen'd by Obſtacles; and tho' I had been one of them, the Character of Dame *Melanchia* was enough to diſcourage me. However, as terrible a Dragon as ſhe had been repreſented to me, I found two or three Days after, that the Doctor's Wife had thrown this *Argus* into a Sleep, or corrupted her Virtue; for as I was going to ſhave one of my Neighbours, a good old Woman ſtopp'd me in the Street, asking me if my Name was not *Diego de la Fuente?* I replied, Yes. Then you are the Man, I look'd for, anſwer'd ſhe. Come to night to Donna *Mergelina's* Door, and when you are there, make it known by ſome Sign, and you ſhall be let into the Houſe. What Sign? ſaid I; That ſhould be agreed upon before-hand. I can counterfeit a Cat to the Life: I'll mew before the Door ſeveral times. 'Tis enough, replied this Agent of Love. I'll tell her your Anſwer. Your Servant, Signor *Diego.* Heaven bleſs you: Ah what a kind Creatue you are: I wiſh I

was

was but Fifteen Years old for your fake, I would not feek you for another. At thefe Words the Meffenger of Gallantry left me ; and you may well imagine that her Meffage rais'd a furious Storm in my Mind. Farewel *Marcos*'s Morality. I waited for Night impatiently : And when I thought Dr. *Olorofo* was a-bed, I went to his Gate. I mew'd feveral times, as a Signal that I was come, and did it fo cleverly, that it was without doubt an Honour to the Mafter who fhew'd me fo fine an Art. A Moment afterwards *Mergelina* came foftly to the Door, open'd it herfelf, and fhut it as foon as I was in the Houfe. We went to the Hall where our laft Confort was perform'd, and there was only a Light in the Chimney. We fat down clofe to each other for the Convenience of Difcourfe, and were both in Confufion ; a Confufion, 'tis true, caus'd by the Pleafure of our Meeting ; but mine had alfo a Mixture of Fear. My Princefs in vain affur'd me that we had nothing to apprehend on account of her Husband. I fhook every Joint of me ; and 'twas plain that it was not all the Trembling of a Lover. Madam, faid I, how could you deceive the Vigilance of your Governantee?

nantee ? After what I have heard of
Dame *Melancia*, I did not think it poffible for me ever to hear from you,
much lefs to fee you again in private.
Donna *Mergelina* fmil'd at this Difcourfe,
and anfwer'd me, You will not be furpriz'd at this private Meeting of ours,
when I have told you what has pafs'd
between my *Duegna* and me. When fhe
entred this Houfe, my Husband carefs'd
her in an extraordinary manner, telling
me he gave me up to the Conduct of
that difcreet Lady, who was a Sam-
ple of all the Virtues, a Looking-Glafs
that I was to have inceffantly before my
Eyes, to learn Difcretion by her. He
added, This admirable Perfon govern'd
an Apothecary's Wife, a Friend of mine,
twelve Years, and that in fuch a manner, that fhe made a perfect Saint of
her. This Panegyrick, which Dame
Melancia's four Looks confirm'd, coft me
many a Tear, and flung me into Defpair. I imagin'd how I was to be do-
cumented by her from Morning to Night,
and reprimanded all Day long. In a
word, I expected to become the moft
miferable Woman in the World, which
made me not to matter how I treated a
Duegna, from whom I look'd for no

Vol. I.   L   Mercy :

Mercy : So I refolv'd to begin with her ;
and affoon as we were alone, I faid to
her, I doubt not you are preparing to
make me fuffer as much as you can
from you : But I muft tell you before-
hand, I am not very patient. I fhall,
on my part, give you all the Mortifica-
tions that lie in my Power. I muft be
plain with you, I have in my Breaft a
Paffion which all your Remonftrance will
never cure me of. So take your Meafures accordingly. Be as vigilant as you
can, I muft own I'll do my utmoft
to be too hard for you. At thefe Words
the *Duegna* alter'd her Look ; and inftead
of a fevere Lecture, which I was in expectation of, fhe faid with a Smile, I am
charm'd with your Humour, and will
be as frank as you ; I find we were made
for one another. Ah ! fair Lady, you
know me ill, if you judge of me by what
the Doctor your Spoufe faid of me, or
by my auftere Afpect. I am far from
being an Enemy to Pleafure. I never
undertake to keep the Glory of Huf-
bands, but in order to do Services to
their pretty Wives. I have a long time
learnt to diffemble, and can fay that I
am doubly happy, fince I at once enjoy
the Convenience of Vice, and the Reputation

putation of Virtue. Between you and me, the World are all Virtuous at this rate only ; It costs too much to be entirely fo. Tis enough now-a-days if one has the Appearances of Virtue. Let me be your Guide, continued the Governantee. We will make old Dr. *Olorofo* have as good an Opinion of his Wife and me, as the Apothecary Signor *Apuntador* had of his and me. Poor *Apuntador!* how many Tricks have we play'd him : His Spoufe was a lovely Creature, fo good natur'd, reft the Soul of her, I'll vouch for her, fhe fpent her Youth finely. She had I don't know how many Lovers whom I introduc'd into her Houfe, without her Husband's perceiving any thing of the Matter. Therefore, pray, Madam, make a more favourable Judgment of me, and be perfuaded that, whatever Talent the old Ufher had, you will lofe nothing by the Change. Perhaps I may be more ferviceable to you than he was.

I leave you to imagine, *Diego*, whether I was pleas'd or no with the *Duegnia's* difcovering herfelf to me fo frankly. I thought her the moft fevere of Women : But one knows not what to judge of our Sex. Her Sincerity made me put

Confidence in her. I embrac'd her with
such Transport, that she found I was
overjoyed to have so complaisant a Governantee. I open'd my self freely to
her, and entreated her to contrive
some way or other that we might have
a private Meeting ; and she has
done it. She it was that employ'd the
Old Woman who spoke to you this
Morning, and who was often an Agent
of her's and the Apothecary's Wife :
But what's the best of all in this Adventure, continued *Mergelina*, smiling,
is, that *Melancia*, upon my telling her
what a sound Sleeper my Husband is, is
this very Moment a-bed with him, and
supplying my Place. So much the
worse, Madam, said I ; I don't like the
Contrivance. Your Husband may wake,
and find out the Deceit. He will not
perceive it, replied she hastily : Don't
be in pain about that, nor let a ground-
less Fear disturb the Pleasure you ought
to take in being with a Young Lady
who wishes you so well. The Doctor's
Wife observing that I could not help
being afraid still, left nothing undone
she could think of to put Courage into
me ; and she try'd so many Ways, that
at last Love got the better of my Fear,
and

and I was ready to take hold of that,
Opportunity; when all of a sudden,
in the height of my Joy and my Paſſion, we heard a terrible Knocking at
the Door; which put the Blind God to
Flight, with all his Train of Smiles and
Sports. *Mergelina* immediately hid me
under a Table in the Hall. She put out
the Light; and, as had been managed
between her and her Governantee, in
caſe ſuch an Accident hapned, went
ſtreight to the Door of her Husband's
Chamber. In the mean time the Knocking continued; the whole Houſe rung
with it. The Doctor got up, and put
on his Morning-Gown, calling *Melancia.*
The *Duegna* jumpt out of Bed, tho' the
Doctor, who thought it had been his
Wife, bid her lie ſtill. *Melancia* ran
to her Miſtreſs, who ſtaid for her at the
Door; and the Governan'ee making as
if ſhe had met her coming out of the
Chamber, cry'd, Pray. Madam, go to
Bed again, I'll ſee who it is. *Mergelina*
undreſt herſelf as faſt as ſhe could, and
laid herſelf down by the Doctor, who
had not the leaſt Suſpicion that he was
impos'd on. 'Tis true, this Scene was
play'd in the Dark by two Actreſſes, one

of them was an incomparable one, and
the other had a great Difposition to become fo.

The *Duegna* going to the Gate with
a Light in her Hand, open'd it, and
return'd foon after to the Doctor, faying, Be pleas'd to rife, Sir, our Neighbour *Fernandez de Buendia* the Bookfeller is fallen into an Apopleſtick Fit.
You are fent for, and defir'd to make
what hafte you can. The Doctor put
on his Cloaths as faft as he could, and
ran away to the Bookfeller's. His Wife,
attended by the *Duegna*, came in her
Morning Gown to the Hall, and drew
me out from under the Table more dead
than alive. Fear nothing, *Diego*, fays
Mergelina: Be of good Courage. She
then told me in few Words all that had
pafs'd; and would fain have renewed the
Converfation which the Incident had
broken off: But the Governance would
not let her. Madam, faid fhe, your
Husband may come back in a Moment;
The Bookfeller may be dead. Befides,
added fhe, feeing the Fright I was in,
What can you make of this poor Creature? He is not in a Condition to come
off as he fhould do. You had better
fend him home now, and let him come
again

again to Morrow. Donna *Mergelina* confented to do fo, but with Reluctance.
She was always for the Time Prefent;
and I believe fhe griev'd heartily that fhe
could not give her Husband the new
Bonnet with which fhe defign'd to cap
him. For my part, I was not fo afflicted
for the Lofs of Love's dear Favours, as
I rejoyc'd for having efcaped the Danger I was in. I return'd to my Mafter's,
and fpent the reft of the Night in think-
ing on my Adventure. I was in fuf-
penfe whether I fhould go again the next
Night. I was afraid ftill of fome new
Difgrace; but the Devil, who always
puts one forward on the like Occafions,
reprefent d to me, that I fhould be a
Blockhead now not to pufh my Fortune. He filled my Head with Idea's of
Mergelina's Charms, and the Joys that
were promis'd me in the Poffeffion of
them. This determin'd me to make a-
nother Attempt; and I refolv'd to do
it with a better Heart than I had done
before. In this good Difpofition I went
to *Mergelina's* Door the Night following, about Eleven a Clock; it was very
dark, not a Star to be feen. I mew'd
twice or thrice, to give notice of my being there; and no body coming to me,

I not

I not only mew'd again, but counterfeited all the different Cries of a Cat, which I learn'd of a Shepherd at *Olmedo.* I perform'd my Part so well, that a Neighbour coming home, and taking me for one of those Animals, took up a Stone, and threw it at me with all his Force, crying, Curse on your Squalling. The Stone hit me on the Head, and stunn'd me with the Blow. I found I was wounded ; and that was enough to cure me of my Gallantry. I lost my Love with my Blood, went Home, and wak'd all the House. My Master dress'd my Wound, which he took to be dangerous. However, it heal'd in three Weeks time. I have not since heard of *Mergelina* ; and suppose Dame *Melancia* disengag'd her from me, to provide her with a Lover more for the *Duegns's* Interest. I don't much trouble myself about it ; and soon after departed from *Madrid*, to continue the Tour of *Spain,* which I intended to make.

C H A P.

CHAP. VIII.

How Gil Blas *and his Companion met a Man soaking Crusts of Bread in a Fountain; and the Discourse they had together.*

SIgnor *Diego de la Fuente* told me other Adventures of his; but they are not worth repeating. I was however oblig'd to hear them, tho' they were all very long. He led us to *Ponte de Duero*; and we staid in that Village the rest of the Day, and supp'd on Pease Soup and a Hare, the latter not very young nor very fresh. Assoon as it was light, we set out the next Day, having stor'd ourselves with pretty good Wine and Bread, taking with us also half of the Hare which we left over Night.

When we had travell'd six Miles, our Stomachs began to come; and observing there was a Juft of Trees about a hundred Yards off the High Road, we went thither to sit down under the Shade. We met there a Man of Eight and twenty Years of Age, who was

L 5 soaking

foaking fome Cruſts of Bread in a Fountain. He had by him a long Rapier and
a Snapſack, which he carried at his
Back. We ſaluted him civilly, and he
did the ſame by us. He then offered us
forne of his Cruſts, demanding with a
Smile, Whether we would do as he did?
We ſaid, With all our Hearts, on condition he would permit us to joyn our
Fare with his, and accept of part of it.
He agreed to it; and we produc'd what
we had, and the Stranger was very well
pleas'd with it. So, Gentlemen, cries
he, I perceive you are well provided:
You are Men of good Forecaſt. I have
not the Precaution that you have. I truſt
to Chance: Nevertheleſs, as it is with
me, I muſt tell you without Vanity, that
I ſometimes make a ſhining Figure. I
am often treated like a Prince, and have
Guards attending me. I underſtand
you, ſays *Diego*; you would let us know
that you are a Player. You gueſs right,
replied the other; I have been a Player
ever ſince I was Fifteen Years old. I
could act ſeveral Parts when I was a
Child. I muſt be plain with you, cry'd
the Barber, ſhaking his Head, I can
hardly believe you; I know the Players too well for't. Thoſe Gentlemen,
don't

don't use to travel like you on Foot,
nor feed on Bread and Water. I am
afraid you rather snuff the Candles.
Think of me what you please replied
the Actor, I have acted several Top
Parts, especially Love ones. If that's
true, says my Comrade, I felicitate you
upon it ; and Signior *Gil Blas* and my
felf rejoyce that we have the Honour to
Breakfast with a Person of so great Importance. Saying this, we fell to, all
three of us, and soon pick'd the Bones
of the Remains of the Hare. We empty'd our Flasks with so much dispatch
that we had not time to speak ; but after we had done Eating and Drinking,
we renew'd the Conversation. I am
surpriz'd, said the Barber, to the Player,
that Matters are no better with you.
Your Appearance is much too mean for
a Hero of the Stage. Pardon me, if I
speak so freely to you. So freely I cry'd
the Actor, you don't know *Melchior Zapata*. I thank my Stars, I am not telty.
I love that every Body should be free
with me, as I am with every body. I
confess I am not rich : You see my Coat
here shews my Profession ; and so will
all the rest of my Wardrobe. He then
open'd his Snapsack, and pull'd out some
Tinsel

Tinfel Ornaments, a dirty Plume of
Feathers, and fome red Buskins. This
is my Equipage, Gentlemen, continued
he; and in truth it is not as good as a
Man could wifh for. I wonder at it,
replied *Diego*, fure you have no Wife nor
Daughter. Yes, I have a young Wife, and
a handfome one, replied *Zapata:* But my
damn'd Luck would have it, that fhe
muft prove Virtuous, forfooth. I married
her in hopes fhe would not let me ftarve;
but fuch is my ill Fate, that fhe ftands
upon her Reputation. 'Tis very hard,
that among all the Strollers, there fhould
but be one honeft Woman, and fhe fhould
fall to my fhare. 'Tis indeed very hard,
fays the Barber. Why did you not marry one of the Company at *Madrid?*
You could not have fail'd there. That's
right, replied the Actor; but we Strollers muft not pretend to fuch Heroines
as Town-Actreffes. An Actor of the
King's own Company can afpire to no
more than that. If one would take a
Wife in the City, one might be furnifh'd as well out of the Play-houfe as
in it. Did you never try, fays my Companion, to get into the King's Company? Muft a Man have infinite Merit to
be admitted amongft them? Infinite
                    Merit *!*

Merit ! replied *Melchior* ; there are Twenty of them, enquire into their Characters, you'll find above half of 'em are
fit for nothing but to hug a brown Muf-
ket ; Yet, for all that, 'tis no eafy Matter to get to be one of them. It muft
be done either by Money or Friends, and
then whatever a Man's Merit is, he fhall
be admitted. I ought to know it ; for
I have been hooted and hifs'd like a
Devil, tho' I deferv'd to be clapt for
my Performances. I tore my Lungs,
and imitated the moft popular Actors
of the Stage : But nothing would do.
The Town would not bear in me, what
they clapt in others ; fuch is the Power
of Prejudice. Thus finding I did not
take ; and having nothing to make my
way for me, in fpite of thofe that hifs'd
me, I am returning to *Zamora* to my
Wife and my Companions, who have
not met with very good Luck there neither. I wifh we may not be obliged to
beg our Way to the next Town. If we
do, 'twill not be the firft Time. Saying
this, the Stage Emperor rofe up, threw
his Snapfack over his Shoulder, put on
his Sword, and with a grave Air cry'd,
May the Heavens, Gentlemen, fhowr
their Favours upon your Heads. *Diego*
replied

replied in the same Tone, May you find your Wife at *Zamora* another Woman, and in a better Temper to keep you from starving. Assoon as Signor *Zapata* had turn'd his Back upon us, he fell to his Declamations and Gesticulations. The Barber and I hifs'd him, to teach him more Discretion. He thought he heard still the Hisses at *Madrid*, look'd back ; and finding 'twas we only, who made our selves merry at his Expence, instead of being offended at it, he took it in good part, and went away laughing aloud, as little Reason as he had for it. We also return'd to the High-Road, and proceeded on our Journey.

CHAP

CHAP. IX.

In what Condition Diego *found his Family ; and how merry* Gil Blas *and he made themselves before they separated.*

WE lay the next Night in a little Village, whose Name I have forgot, between *Moyades* and *Valpuesta*, and came the next Day about Eleven a Clock to the Plain of *Ulmedo*. Signor *Gil Blas*, says my Companion, This is the Place where I was Born, and I am transported at the Sight of it ; so natural 'tis for Men to love their Country. Signor *Diego*, answer'd I, A Man who loves his Country so well as you seem to do, should methinks not have talk'd so freely of it as you have done. *Ulmedo* appears to me to be a City, and you represented it only as a Village. It must be a great Town, if it is not a City. I beg *Ulmedo*'s Pardon, replied the Barber ; but I must tell you, t at af er having seen *Madrid*, *Toledo*, *Saragossa*, and other great Cities, which I have done

in

In my Travels in *Spain*, I look upon little ones as Villages. As we drew nearer to *Olmedo*, we perceiv'd a great number of People were gather'd together; and when we came up to them, found three Tents set up at a distance from each other, in which were Cooks and Butlers making ready for a Feast. Some were preparing Boil'd Meat and Roast Meat: Others Pies and Fricassees: Others filling Bottles: Others washing Glasses. What I took most particular Notice of, was a great Stage built in the middle of the Place, adorn'd with painted Paper, on which were several Motto's in *Greek* and *Latin*. The Barber no sooner spy'd the Inscriptions, than he cry'd, The *Greek* there smells very much of my Uncle *Thomas*. I'll lay a Wager 'tis his Doing: For between you and me, he's a Person of great Ability. He can say an infinite Number of College Books by heart. The worst of it is, he's ever repeating 'em in all Companies, which every one is not pleas'd with. My Uncle has, more than this, Translated the *Latin* Poets, and *Greek* Authors. He's Master of Antiquity, as may be seen by the fine Remarks he has made. If it had not been

for

for him, we fhould not have known that in the City of *Athens*. Children cry'd when they were whipp'd. We owe that Difcovery to his profound Erudition.

When my Comrade and I had made our Obfervations on what we had feen, we were curious to know for what were fuch Preparations. We were about enquiring, when *Diego* fpy'd his Uncle Signor *Thomas de la Fuente*, who it feems had the ordering of the Feaft. We ran up to him; but the Schoolmafter did not at firft know his Nephew *Diego*, fo much was he alter'd in Ten Years time. But finding at laft it was the fame, he embrac'd him very affectionately, and cry'd, Ah, my dear Nephew! Art thou come once more to the Place of thy Nativity? Wilt thou again revifit thy Houfhold Gods? And art thou reftor'd fafe and found to thy Family? Oh, thrice and four times happy Day! a Day worthy a Place among the Red-letter'd in the Calendar. I have abundance of News, Friend, to tell thee. Thy Uncle *Pedro*, the Wit, is become the Victim of *Pluto*. He dy'd three Months ago. The Mifer in his Life-time was ever afraid that

that he fhould want Neceffaries. He
had great Penfions from feveral Grandees, and yet he fpent but ten Piftoles
a Year for his Maintenance. He had a
Valet, but he ftarv'd him as well as
himfelf. He was more mad than the
Greek Ariftippus, who order'd his Slaves
to throw away his Riches in the D fart
of *Lybia*, as things that were Incum-
brances. Thy Uncle was continually
heaping up Gold and Silver. For whom?
For Heirs he would never look upon.
He dy'd worth Thirty thoufand Ducats,
which thy Father, thy Uncle *Bertrand*,
and I have divided among us. We can
now provide for our Children. My
Brother *Nicholas* has already difpos'd of
thy Sifter *Therefa*. She is newly married
to one of our Alcaides, *Connubio junxit
ftabili, propriamque dicabit*. 'Tis for her
Wedding that this Feftival is going to
be kept. It is we that have fet up thefe
Tents here for the Three Heirs of *Pedro*; each of us has one, and each pays
the Expence of a Day. I wifh thou
had'it come fooner, to have feen the
Beginning of our Rejoycings. The Day
before Yefterday, which was that of the
Wedding, thy Father was at the Expence :

pence: He gave a noble Entertainment,
and the Company ran at the Ring afterwards. Yefterday the Mercer bore
the Charge, and diverted us with a Pa-
ftoral Comedy. He drefs'd up ten handfome Boys and Girls like Shepherds
and Shepherdeffes. He us'd all the Points
and Ribbands in his Shop to equip 'em.
They danc'd and fung moft part of the
Day: But tho' they perform'd their Parts
very dexteroufly, yet the People were
not very much taken with it. I find Pa-
ftoral is out of doors.

This Day's Expence is to be mine ; and
I have provided a Show of my own Invention, to entertain the Townfmen of
Olmedo. Finis coronat Opus. I have
caus'd a Stage to be rais'd, upon which,
God willing, my Difcipls fhall reprefent
fent a Piece compos'd by myfelf, inti-
tul'd, *The Amufements of* Mulei Bugentuf *King of* Morocco. 'Twill be extremely well play'd ; for my Scholars
pronounce as well as the Actrs of *Madrid.* They are Youths of *Penafiel* and
Segovia, who board at my Houfe. Excellent Actors! Indeed I have taken
fome Pains with them: What they fay,
will be done matterly, *ut ita dicam.* As
to

to the Piece itself, I shall say nothing.
I will have the Pleasure of the Surprize. All I shall observe to thee on that
Head, is, that 'twill transport the Spectators. 'Tis one of those Tragical Subjects that move the Soul by Images of
Death; for I am of the same Opinion
with *Ariſtotle!*, that Poets should ex-
cite Terror. Well, If I had wrought
for the Stage, I would have brought
nothing on it but bloody Princes and
murdering Heroes. I would have bath'd
my self in Blood. I would not only have
kill'd the principal Persons in my Plays,
but even the Guards themselves. I would
have cut the Throat of the Candle-
Snuffer. In fine, I love the *Terrible.*
'Tis my *Gout.* Those kinds of Poems
always take. They bring many to the
House, and get the Authors Fame.

While he was speaking, we spy'd a
great Croud of People coming out of
the Town. They were the New-mar-
ried Couple, attended by their Relations and Friends. Twelve Fiddlers went
before, and made a horrid Noise with
their Discord. We met them: and *Diego* discover'd himself to the Company,
who shouted for Joy. Every body was
eager

eager to accoft him. He had fomething
to do to receive all their Civilities in a civil manner. All his R·lations and all that
were prefent embraced him. After which
his Father faid, Thou art welcome, *Diego*; thou findeft thy Parents fomewhat
better in the World than when thou
left'ft them. I fhall explain my felf farther another time. Then the Company
proceeded into the Plam, entred the
Tents, and fat down at the Tables which
were prepared for them. I did not leave
my Companion. We both din'd with
the Bridegroom and B.ide, who feem'd
to be well match'd. Dinner held a long
while, becaufe the Schoolmafter had
the Vanity to order three Courfes to be
ferv'd u:, that he might out-do his Brethren, who had not come off fo mag-
nificen ly. After Dinner all the Guefts
expref'd a great Impatience to fee Signor *Thomas*'s Piece reprefented, not
doubting, faid they, but the Production
of fo fine a Genius muft be well worth
hearing. We drew near the Theatre,
where all the Fidlers fat in a readinefs to
play between the Acts. Every one was
filent, in expectation of the Opening the
Play. At laft the Actors appeared on
the

the Stage ; as did alſo the Author, with the Poem in his Hand. He had reaſon to ſay the Piece was Tragical ; for in the firſt Act the King of *Morocco* , by way of Recreation, kills a hundred *Moor-iſh* Slaves, ſhooting at them with his Bow and Arrows. In the Second he cuts off the Heads of Thirty *Portu-gueſe* Officers, whom one of his Captains had made Priſoners of War. And in the Third, this Monarch, weary of his Wives, ſets Fire to the Palace wherein they were lodg'd, and reduc'd both it and them to Aſhes. The *Moor-iſh* Slaves and the *Portugueſe* Officers were Figures made of Reed very artfully ; and the Palace was compos'd of Paper, which, when 'twas ſet a fire, there were a Thouſand doleful Cries that ſeem'd to iſſue from amidſt the Flames. This finiſh'd the Piece ; and all the Field rang with the Applauſes which ſo fine a Tragedy met with. This juſtified the good Taſte of the Poet ; and ſhew'd that he knew how to make a good Choice of his Subjects.

I thought there was nothing more to be ſeen, if the *Amuſements of Mulei Bur-*

Bugentuf were over; but I was miftaken. There were Prizes to be diftributed. For *Thomas*, to render the Entertainment the more folemn, had caus'd fome of his Scholars to make Exercifes, which they were to read to the Auditory that had heard the Play; and thofe that did beft were to have Books given them, which he had purchas'd with his own Money at *Segovia*.

Two Benches were therefore brought on the Stage, and a Cafe of Books very neatly Bound. All that were to perform came up to Signor *Thomas*, who ftood as ftiffly as the Prefident of a College. He had a Paper in his Hand, wherein was written the Names of thofe that were to carry off the Prizes. He gave the hrft to the King of *Morocco*, who read his Part with a loud Voice. Each Scholar, as he was nam'd, went refpectfully to receive a Book of the Pedant. He then was Crown'd with Laurel, and made to fit down on one of the two Benches, expos'd to the View of the admiring Spectators. As defirous as the Schoolmafter

was

was to fend away the all Company contented, he could not accomplish it.
For having diftributed all the *Prizes*
among certain Youths whofe Parents
paid him beft, the Mothers of fome
of the negl-ected Scholars took fire,
and accufed the Pedant of Partiality.
Thus this Feaft, which had till then
done him fo much Honour, was like
to end like that of the *Lapithæ*

The End of the Second Book.

THE

THE
HISTORY
OF
GIL BLAS
OF
SANTILLANE.

BOOK III.

CHAP. I.

Of Gil Blas's *Arrival at* Madrid, *and the* First Master *he serv'd in that City.*

I Staid some time with the young Barber; and hearing there was a Merchant in *Olmedo,* who was going to *Segovia* from *Valladolid* with four light

Vol. I. M Mul s.

Mules, I got into his Acquaintance, and
rode one of them to *Segovia*, where he
invited me to his Houſe, and kept me
there two Days, ſo far was I got into
his good Graces. When he found I
was about to depart for *Madrid* by the
Muletier, he gave me a Letter in charge,
deſiring me to deliver it with my own
Hand, as 'twas directed. I took it, not
knowing it was a Letter of Recommendation. However, I carried it to
Signor *Matheo Meléndez* a Linen Draper at *Madrid*; who had no ſooner read
the Contents of it, but he ſaid very o-
bligingly to me, Signor *Gil Blas, Pedro
Palaeio* my Correſpondent writes to me
in your Favour ſo preſſingly, that I muſt
beg of you to take a Lodging at my Houſe.
He has alſo deſired me to help you to
a good Place, which I ſhall with pleaſure endeavour to do, not doubting of
ſucceeding in it to your Content.

I accepted of *Melendez*'s Offer with
the more Joy, for that my Finances grew
daily leſs and leſs. I was not however
a Burthen to him long. When I had
been with him Eight Days, he told
me he had juſt been recommending me
to a Gentleman of his Acquaintance,
who wanted a Valet de Chambre, and
he

he believ'd he would take me. The Gentleman came himself soon after. Signor, says *Melendez*, pointing to me, you see there the Young Man I spoke to you about. He's a sober Lad, and I'll anfwer for his Honefty. The Gentleman look'd fixedly upon me, and faid my Phyfiognomy pleas'd him, and that he would hire me for his Servant. Come along with me, continued he, I'll fhew you what you muft do. So bidding the Merchant Good-morrow, he led me to the broad Street near St. *Philip*'s Church. We went into a pretty good Houfe, of which he took up one Wing. We mounted a Stair-cafe of fix Steps, and came to a Room which had two Doors, one within another ; the firft had a little Lattice Window. Thro' that Room we paft into another, where was a Bed and other Furniture, rather neat than rich.

As my new Mafter had made his Obfervations of me at *Melendez*'s, fo did I alfo in my turn examine him with a great deal of Attention. He was above Fifty Years old ; had a grave, referv'd Look, but withal there was good Nature in it ; and his Temper anfwerd his Afpect. He ask'd me feveral Que-

ftions

ttions about my Family. And my Account
of my felf giving him Satisfaction ; *Gil
Blas.* fays he, I take thee to be a fenfible Youth, and am glad I have met
with thee: Thou fhalt thy felf have
no reafon to be forry. I will allow thee
Six Reals a Day for thy Wages and
Board, befides the Vails thou wilt have
in my Service. 'Tis no hard Matter to
pleafe me. I don't eat at Home. All
thou wilt have to do, is, to brufh my
Cloaths in the Morning, to drefs me,
and the reft of the Day is thy own ;
only take care to be at home early in
the Evening, and ftay for me at my
Door. I require no more of thee.
Having thus told me my Bufinefs, he
took Six Reals out of his Pocket, and
gave me for the Ufe before-mentioned;
after which, we went out of the Houfe
again. He lock'd the Doors. and took
the Keys with him. Friend, faid he,
do not follow me. Go whither thou
wilt ; but let me find thee on the Stairs
when I come home at Night. Saying
this, he left me to fpend the reft of the
Day as I thought fit.

Thou haft got a rare Mafter, *Gil Blas,*
faid I to my felf. Six Reals a Day for
Brufhing his Cloaths, and Dreffing him
a Morn-

a Mornings, the reft of thy Time all thy own! This is the ealieft Place fure that over Man had. No wonder I was fo defirous to fee, *Madrid*. My good Genius put me upon it. I cannot be happier in my Circumftances. I walk'd up and down the City all Day, looking upon every thing that was new to me, and that was not a little. In the Evening I fupp'd at an Eating-houfe in our Neighbourhood ; and then went to the Place where my Mafter order'd me to wait for him. He came three quarters of an Hour after me, and feem'd well pleas'd to find me fo punctual. 'Tis very well, fays he ; I love that Servants fhould be exact to a Minute. At thefe Words he open'd the Doors of his Apartment, and afterwards lock'd them upon us. It being dark, he took a Tinderbox, ftruck a light, and lighted a Candle. I then help'd to undrefs him. When he was a-bed, I put a Candle in his Chimney, as he bad me, and took the other with me into the Anti-chamber, where I lay in a Bed without Curtains. He rofe the next Day between Nine and Ten. I brufh'd his Cloaths. He gave me fix Reals, and difmifs'd me till Night. When he went out, I obferv'd

M 3 that

that he took great Care to faften his
Doors. We faw one another no more
till Night. Such was our Way of Living, which I thought was very pleafant. But the pleafanteft of it all was,
that I did not know my Mafter's Name.
Melendez knew it not himfelf, he having no more knowledge of him, than
that he us'd to come to his Shop, and
buy Linen of him. Our Neighbours
could not fatisfy my Curiofity any
better. They all told me my Mafter
was a Stranger to them, tho' he had liv'd
in thofe Lodgings Two Years; that he
kept Company with no body there-
abouts : And fome of them, who were
apt to judge too rafhly, concluded thence,
that he was not fo good as he fhould
be. They went farther afterwards, and
fufpected him to be a Spy for the King
of *Portugal* ; bidding me take care of
my felf. I was mightily troubled at
what they faid, for fear, if it fhould
happen to be true, I might perhaps vifit
fome of the Dungeons in *Madrid*. As
innocent as I was, I could not help being afra'd. My paft Misfortunes render'd the Magiftracy terrible to me. I
had twice had Experience, that if it did
not murder the Innocent, it had at leaft
no

no regard to the Laws of Hofpitality;
and that it was always a fad thing to fall
into its Hands. I confulted *Melendez* on
fo nice an Occafion. He could not tell
what to advife me. Tho' he did not
think my Mafter was a Spy, yet he knew
not what elfe to make of him. I refolv'd to obferve him, and to leave him,
if I found him an Enemy to the State.
But I thought to myfelf, I liv d fo eafily, that I ought to be very fure of it.
To this end I examin'd ftrictly all his
Actions; and to fift him, faid one Night,
as I was undrefling him, I know not,
Sir, how a Man can live fo as to avoid
evil Tongues. 'Tis a vile World; and
fome of our Neighbours are as bad as
any in it; they deal altogether in Scandal. You can't imagine how they talk
of you. Well, *Gil Blas*, replied he, and
what can they fay of me? Malice, anfwer'd I, never wants Matter: Virtue
it felf is often turn'd to its Purpofe.
Our Neighbours fay we are dangerous
People; that the Court ought to have
an Eye upon us. In a Word, you pafs,
Sir, for the King of *Portugal*'s Spy.
Saying this, I look'd on my Mafter as
Alexander did on his Phyfician, and
made ufe of all my Penetration to fee

M 4   whether

whether I could difcover any thing. I fancy'd I perceiv'd fome Alteration in my Patron, which agreed well enough with the Conjectures of our Neighbours. He appear'd very penfive; but prefently recovering himfelf, he faid, with a great deal of Compofure, *Gil Blas*, don't mind what our Neighbours fay; it is not worth our troubling ourfelves about it. Let 'em think as ill as they pleafe of us, as long as we give them no Occafion for it.

He faid no more, but went to Bed, and I did the fame, not knowing what Judgment to make of him. The next Day, as we were preparing to go out, we heard a great Knocking at the Door. My Mafter open'd the Innermoft, and looking thro' the Lattice, he faw a Man well dreft, who accofted him thus, Signor, I am the Alquazil, and am come to tell you that Monfieur the Corregidor defires to fpeak with you. What would he have with me? replied my Patron. The Alquazil anfwer'd, I don't know that; you'll foon be inform'd of it. I am his humble Servant, replied my Mafter; I have no Bufinefs with him. Saying this, he clapp'd the Door upon him very haftily, as if he did not much

much like what the Alquazil faid. He
gave me my Six Reals, bidding me go,
he would ftay within that Morning,
and had no farther Occafion of me.
This made me judge that he was afraid
of being apprehended, and to avoid it,
kept at home. I left him ; and to fatisfie myfelf in the Matter, hid in a
Place where I could fee him when he
went out. I was refolv'd not to ftir
till I faw what would come of it ; and
about an Hour after I obferv'd him
to come out with an Air of Affurance,
which confounded my Sufpicions, but
did not cure me of them; for I had
no very good Opinion of him. I imagined that his Looks were artificial ;
that he ftaid behind to carry off his Gold
and Jewels, and perhaps was going to
fave himfelf by fudden Flight. I defpair'd of feeing him again, and was
in doubt whether I fhould wait for him
at Night ; but I alter'd my Mind, and
went to my Poft at the ufual Hour. I
was very much furpriz'd to fee him
return. He went to Bed without
fhewing the leaft Concern, and rofe
the next Day with the fame Compofure of Mind.

M 5   While

While he was Dreffing himfelf, we heard a knocking at our Door, as it was the Day before. My Mafter look'd thro' the Lattice. He perceiv'd the Alquazil was there again, and demanded what he would have? Open the Door, replied the Alquazil; it is Monfieur the Corregidor. At fo redoubled a Name my Blood chill'd in my Veins. I was curfedly afraid of thofe Gentlemen ever fince I had fallen into their Hands, and would gladly have been a hundred Leagues off *Madrid.* As for my Patron, he was not fo frighted. He open'd the Door, and receiv'd the Judge with Refpect. You fee, fays the Corregidor, I am not come with a Train after me. I would do what is to be done without making a Noife. As ill a Character as you have in this City, I think there is fo much due to you, as you appear like a Gentleman. Pray, what's your Name, Sir? and what Bufinefs brought you to *Madrid?* My Lord, replied my Mafter, I am a Native of *New Caftile,* and my Name is Don *Bernard de Caftil Blazo.* As to my Bufinefs here, I walk about to fee Plays, and divert my felf daily with fome pleafant Companions. You have doubtlefs, fays
the

the Judge, a great Income. No, my Lord, anfwer'd my Patron, I have no Income at all, nor Lands, nor Houfes. How do you live then ? replied the Corregidor. I will fhew you, fays my Mafter : At thefe Words he lifted up the Hangings, open'd a Door that I had not obferv'd before, and after that another within it, which led to a Clofet, where was a great Cheft full of Pieces of Gold. He defired the Judge to fatisfy himfelf, and went on in this manner :

You know, my Lord, that the *Spaniards* don't love Labour : And of all the *Spaniards* in the World, I believe I love it leaft. I am fo lazy that I can't bear any Employment. If I would turn my Vices into Virtues, I might call that Lazinefs a Philofophical Indolence : That 'twas the Effect of a Mind taken off from the Things which are moft defired by Men. But I muft own that I am lazy by my Complexion, and fo lazy, that if I were to work for my Living, I fhould ftarve. That I might live according to my Humour, and fave the Trouble of a Steward, I turn'd all my Eftate, which confifted of feveral confiderable Inheritances, into Money. That
Money

Money is in this Cheft, above Fifty thoufand Ducats, which are more than I
fhall want, if I live to an hundred Years
old, being now near threefcore. And
I fpend but a Thoufand a, Year. I am
not folicitcus for the future; becaufe,
thank my Stars, I am no ways addicted
to the three Things that commonly ruin Men. I don't love Feafting nor Gaming, and have done with Women. I
am not one of thofe old Coxcombs
that doat on the Sex when the Seafon
is paft, and fhall never be at any Charge
to purchafe their Favouis.

You are a happy Man, fays the Corregidor. They injur'd you who took
you to be a Spy. A Man of your Temper is by no means fit for it. Live on
in your Way, Don *Bernard*, added he ;
inftead of giving you any Difturbance,
I will hereafter be your Defender, and
defire your Friendfhip, and I offer you
mine. My Lord, cry'd my Mafter, I
accept with Joy and Refpect fo obliging
an Offer. By giving me your Friendfhip, you add to my Wealth, and make
my Happinefs compleat. The Alquazil
and I heard, this Converfation in the
next Room. Don *Bernard* could hardly
tell how to return the extraordinary
Civilities

Civilities of the Corregidor: And my
Master's Example put me upon exert-
ing my self to do Honour to the Al-
quazil. I made him a hundred low
Bows; tho' at the bottom, I had that
Contempt and Aversion for him, which
every honest Man has naturally for an
Alquazil.

CHAP. II.

The Surprize *Gil Blas* was in to meet
Captain Rolando *at* Madrid: *And
several curious Things related to him
by that Robber.*

DON *Bernard de Castil Blazo* having
waited upon the Corregidor to the
Street, return'd immediately to see that his
Chest was fast, and his Doors well lock'd.
We then went out both of us much better
satisfied than we were before, Don *Bernard* having the Corregidor to his Freind,
and I being secure of my Six Reals a
Day. I resolv'd to go and tell this
Adventure to *Melendez* ; and as I drew
near his House, I spy'd Captain *Rolando*. I was in a dreadful Surprize, and
could

could not help trembling at Sight of
him. He knew me again, came up
to me very gravely, and keeping
still his Air of Superiority, order'd me
to follow him. I shook all the while,
and obeyed him in my Fright. He'll pay
my old Reckoning, said I to myself:
Whither will he carry me ? Perhaps there
is some subterranean Habitation in this
City also. 'Egad, if I thought so, I would
let him see that I have not the Gout in
my Toes. I walk'd behind him, observing narrowly at what Place he stopp'd,
resolving to run for it, if I did not
like it.

Rolando rid me of my Fears, by entring a famous Tavern. I followed
him. He called for the best Wine, and
bid the Landlord get Dinner. While
Dinner was preparing, Captain *Rolando* began his Discourse to me, thus :
Thou may'st well wonder, *Gil Blas*, to
see thy old Commander here ; and thy
Wonder will be encreas'd, when thou
hearest what I am going to tell thee. The
Day I left thee in our subterranean
Dwelling, while I and my Companions
went to *Mansilla*, to sell the Mules and
the Horses we took the Day before,
we met the Corregidor of *Leon's* Son in
his

his Coach, attended by four Men on Horseback, well arm'd. We kill'd two of them, and the other two fled. The Coachman, afraid of his Master's Life, cry'd, Ah, Signors, For God's fake don't murder the only Son of the Corregidor of *Leon*. These Words, instead of gaining the Pity of my Cavaliers, enraged them against the Son of the Coregidor. Don't let the Son of a mortal Enemy of our Fellows escape us, said one of my Companions. How many of our Profession has he slaughter'd? Let us be reveng'd, and offer this Victim to their *Manes*. The rest of my Cavaliers approv'd of his Speech; and my Lieutenant was preparing to act the Part of the High-Priest in this Sacrifice; when I held him by the Arm, and cry'd, Hold, why will you spill Blood, without Necessity? Let us be content with this Young Man's Purse, since he does not resist. It would be barbarous to cut his Throat. Besides, he is not accountable for his Father's Actions; and his Father does but his Duty when he condemns us to Death, as we do ours, when we ease Travellers of their Burthens.

I in-

I interceded Thus for the Corregidor's
Son ; and my Intercession was not ineffectual : We only took all the Money
he had, and carried off with us the
Horses of the two dead Men, which
we sold, with the rest, at *Mansilla.* We
return'd afterwards to our subterranean
Habitation, where we arriv'd next Day
a little before Light. We were very
much surpriz'd to find the Trap-Door
lifted up ; and that Surprize of ours was
still greater, when we found *Leonarda*
ty'd to a Table. She told us what had
pass'd, in two Words. We admir'd how
thou could'st deceive us. We did not
think thee capable of playing us such a
Trick ; and we forgave thee, for the
Contrivance. As for us, as soon as we
had unty'd our Cook, I order'd her to
get us something good for to eat ; and
took my Comrades with me to see our
Horses well look'd after. The old Negro, who had had nothing given him in
four and twenty Hours, was almost in
the Agony. We would fain have sav'd
him, but he was too far gone, and appear'd so near his End, that we left
the poor Dog as we found him. We
ourselves went to Breakfast ; and having satisfied our craving Appetites, slept
away

away the rest of that Day. When we
awoke, we heard from *Leonarda* that
Domingo had breath'd his Last. So we
carried him into the Vault, where thou
may'st remember thou usedst to lie, and
buried him as formally as if he had had
the Honour to have been one of our
Companions.

Four or five Days after, as we were
scouring the Road, we met three Troops
of St. *Hermandad*'s Officers at the Entrance of a Wood. We spy'd no more
than one Troop at first, and despis'd
them, tho' superior in Number to us.
We attack'd them ; and while we were
engag'd, the two other Troops that had
not yet come in Play, bore down upon
us so warmly, that our Valour was of
no Use to us. Our Lieutenant and two
of our Cavaliers were kill'd on this Oc-
cation. Myself and two more, which
were all our Company, were surrounded and taken. Two of the Troops of
St. *Hermandad* conducted us to *Leon* :
The third went to destroy our Retreat,
which was found out in this manner :
A Peasant of *Luceno* crossing the Forest
in his Way home, by chance perceiv'd
our Trap-Door lifted up, the same Day
ou carriedst away the Lady. He suspected

pected that it was our Dwelling; and not having the Courage to enter, he contented himself to observe the Place, and make those Remarks by which he might find it again. He cut the Bark off some of the neighbouring Trees in several Places, and notch'd others all the Way from one Space to another, till he was out of the Wood. He then went to *Leon* to give Information of it to the Corregidor, who was the more pleas'd with i , because his South'd been lately robb'd by our Company. He presently got together those three Troops of St. *Hermandad*'s Officers to apprehend us, and the Peasant was their Guide.

I was a Show for the Citizens of *Leon*, on my Arrival in that City. Had I been a *Portuguese* General, brought thither Prisoner of War, the People could not have flock'd about me more. Behold the famous Captain! cry'd they, the Terror of the Country : He deserves to be torn in pieces by Horses, and so do his Companions! We were brought before the Corregidor who began to insult me. Heav'n, tir'd out with the Disorders of thy Life, says he, has given such a Rogue at last into my Hands. My

My Lord, replied I, if I have been
guilty of Crimes, you cannot at leaſt
reproach me with the Death of your
Son. I ſav'd his Life: You ſhould conſider me a little for that. Sirrah, cry'd
he, 'Tis not by ſuch Raſcals as thou
art, that Men of Honour are obliged to
act generouſly. But if I had a mind to
ſave thee, the Duty of my Office will
not let me. Having ſaid this, he order'd us to be ſhut up in a Dungeon,
where my Companions did not long
languiſh; for at three Days end they
were taken out to act a Tragical Part
in the Market-place. As for me, I remain'd in the Dungeon three Weeks,
imagining that my Execution was de-
ferr'd to render it the more terrible;
and I expected a new ſort of Death:
But the Corregidor then ſending for me,
ſaid, Hear thy Sentence, Thou art dif-
chaig'd. Had it not been for thee, my only
Son had been murder'd on the High-way.
As I am his Father, I cannot in Gratitude forget that piece of Service: And
as I am a Judge, not having it in my
Power to pardon thee, I wrote to Court
in thy Favour. I have procured a Pardon for thee, and thou may'ſt go where
thou pleaſeſt: But have a Care how thou
offendeſt

offendeſt again. Let this happy Event
inſtruct thee to leave off thy wicked
Courſe of Life. What he ſaid made an
Impreſſion upon me, and I departed for
Madrid, with a Reſolution to follow
his Advice, and live peaceably in that
City. I found my Father and Mother
dead. Their Eſtate was in the Poſſeſſion
of an old Relation, who gave me ſuch
a kind of Account of it as Truſtees generally do. I had no more than Three
thouſand Ducats, which perhaps was
not a fourth part of what belong'd to
me. But what ſhould I do in that Caſe?
I had got nothing by a Law-Suit. So I
took it, and, to avoid Idleneſs, bought
an Alquazil's Place. My Brethren would,
out of Decency, have oppos'd my
Admiſſion, had they known my Hiſto-
ry. But by good Luck they either knew
it not, or made as if they did not,
which is all one. Indeed, in this Honourable Society it behoves every Body
to hide his Actions as well as he can.
Heaven be prais'd, we have nothing to
ſay againſt one another on that ſcore:
The Devil take the beſt. Nevertheleſs,
Friend, continues *Rolando*, to ſpeak my
whole Mind to thee, I do not at all like my
Profeſſion. It requires too much Tricking
and

and Cunning for me. Here one can
only commit private and fubtle Ro-
gueries. My firft Trade was more to
my *Gout.* My new one is fafer, tis true;
but the former is more pleafant, and I
love Liberty. I am difpos'd to fell my
Place, and take to the Mountains at the
Source of the *Tagus.* I know there is a
Retreat there, inhabited by a Band of
Catalans, the bravest Fellows in the
Kingdom.' If thou wilt go with me,
we'll add to the Company. I fhall be
Captain's *Second* ; and that they may
make no Objection to thee, I'll affure
them that I faw thee fight twice by
my Side. I will wonderfully extol thy
Valour. I will praife thee more than a
General does an Officer whom he would
have advanc'd. I ll take no notice of
the Trick thou didft put upon us, left
they fhould fufpect thee. They fhall
know nothing of that. Well, what fay'ft
thou? Wilt thou follow me? I wait
for thy Anfwer. Every one has his particular Inclinations, replied I : You are
made for hardy Enterprizes, and I for a
quiet, eafy Life. I underftand you, faid
he : The Lady you took from us has
ftill the Poffeffion of your Heart, and
no doubt you live an eafy Life with her

at

at *Madrid.* Confefs, Monfieur *Gil Blas,*
that you have her with you here; and
live together on the Piftoles ycu carried
off from our Under-ground Dwelling. I
told him he was in an Error; and while
we were at Dinner, related to him the
Story of that Lady, and all that had hapned to me fince I left the Band. When we
had din'd, he reviv'd his Difcourfe of the
Catalans. He own'd that he refolv'd to
join them, and again tempted me to go
with him: But perceiving that I declin'd
it, he gave me a ftern Look, and faid
very gravely, Since thy Soul is fo bafe as
to prefer thy flavifh Condition to the
Honour of being admitted into a Company of brave Men, I abandon thee to
the Poverty of thy Spirit. But heark-
en to what I fay to thee, and keep it
always in Memory, Forget what thou
haft heard from me to day. Mention me
to no body. If I hear thou doft fo much
as name me in Converfation —— Thou
know ft me, and that's enough. At thefe
Words he call'd for the Reckoning, paid
it, and we went our Way.

CHAP

CHAP. III.

*He is dismiss'd the Service of Don
Bernard de Castil Blazo, and enters
into that of a Beau.*

A'S we were going out of the Tavern,
and taking leave of one another, my
Master pass'd by. He saw me, and I
observ'd that h more than once cast his
Eye upon the Captain. I imagin'd he
he was surpriz'd to see me with such a
sort of a Man; for the very Looks of
him were enough to let one into his
Character. He was tall, hard-visag'd;
and tho' he was not ugly, yet he had
something in his Face that was shocking,
and had the Air of a Rogue.

I was not out in my Conjectures. I
found at Night that Don *Bernard*'s Head
was full of the Captain, and that he
was well dispos'd to believe every thing
I knew of him, if I durst tell him. *Gil
Blas*, says he, what tall Fellow was it
that I met you with? An Alquazil, Sir,
replied I; thinking that would have
been

been fufficient to fatisfie him. But he ask'd me feveral other Queftions about him ; and obferving that I was in fome Confufion, occafiou'd by *Rolando's* Threats, which were frefh in my Memory, he faid no more, but went to Bed. Next Morning, when I had dreft him as u-fual, he gave me Six Ducats, inftead of Six Reals, faying, There, Friend, I give thee that for this Day's Service. Go, find out another Mafter. I will not enter-tain a Valet that has got fuch an Ac-quaintance. I anfwer'd, in my Juftifica-tion, that I knew this Alquazil, by ha-ving prefcrib'd him Phyfick, when I practis'd it at *Valladolid.* Very well, re-plied my Mafter, your Excufe is very fine ; but you fhould have made it laft Night. I was cautious of doing it then, faid I, for fear you fhould have been of-fended at it ; and that was the caufe of my Confufion. Yes, yes, replied my Patron, you were very cautious. I did not think you had been fo cunning, continu'd he, clapping me gently on the Shoulder, Go, Child, I difmifs you.

I went immediately to inform *Me-lendez* of this bad News. He heard me out, and faid, Don't trouble thy felf ; I'll help thee to a better Place. And ac-cordingly,

cordingly a few Days after he inform'd me that he had got the best Master in *Madrid* for me. *Gil Blas*, cried he, thou little think'st thou art going to be so happy as I shall make thee. I have recommended thee to Don *Matthias de Silva*, a Man of the first Quality, one of those young Lords who go under the Denomination of *Beaux*. I have the Honour to be his Draper and Mercer. He buys Silks and Linen of me upon Tick, it is true; but we seldom lose by these Gentlemen in the End. They marry rich Heiresses or Widows, who pay their Debts for them; and if they don't, we charge their Goods at such Rates, that if we have one part in four, we come off pretty well. Don *Matthias's* Steward is my particular Friend. We'll go to him: He will present you to his Master; and you may depend upon it, he'll use you well, upon my Account.

As we were going to Don *Matthia's* Palace, the Draper said to me, Methinks it is very necessary that you should know the Character of the Steward. His Name is *Gregorio Rodriguez*. He was not worth a Groat, between you and I, when he first came into Businefs ; but finding he had a Genius for it, he purfu'd it, and has got a good Eſtate out of two round Families, in which he ferv'd as Steward. I muſt tell you he's very vain, and will have the other Domeſticks cringe to him. They muſt all apply themſelves to him, if they want any Favour of their Maſter. For if they ſhould obtain it without his Participation, he'll always contrive ſome Way or other to hinder its taking Effect. Do you govern yourſelf, *Gil Blas,* by this Rule therefore, and never fail to make your court to him, even more than to his Maſter. Try all Ways of getting into his good Graces. His Friendſhip will be of great uſe to you. He'll pay you your Wages punctually, and do ſomething more for you. If you pleaſe him, he may now and then give you a little Bone to pick, while himſelf ſecures the great ones. He does what he will. Don *Matthias* minds nothing but his Pleaſures, He never looks into his Affairs. Is not that a rare Houſe for a Steward ?

When we came to the Palace, we ask'd for Signor *Rodriguez,* and were told we ſhould find him in his Apartment. He was there, and with him a kind of Pea-

fant

fant, with a blue Bag full of Piftoles.
The Steward, who appear'd to be of a
more fallow Complexion than a Girl
worn out with Celibacy, met *Melendez*
with open Arms. The Draper open'd
his in like manner, and they embrac'd
both with Demonftrations of Friendfhip, in which there was at leaft as much
Art as Nature. Their Salutations over,
they talk'd of me. *Rodriguez* having
examin'd me from Head to Foot, faid
very civilly, I was exactly fuch a one as
Don *Matthias* wanted, and that he
would gladly undertake to prefent me
to him. Upon this, *Melendez* let him
know what a Kindnefs he had for me ;
praying the Steward to take me into his
Protection. After which he left us together : And affoon as he was gone, fays
Rodreguez, I'll introduce you to my Mafter when I have difpatch'd this Countryman, of whom he took the blue
Bag, faying, Let's fee, *Talego*, whether
the Money be right. He told out 500
Piftoles, and cry'd, 'Tis very well, the
Sum is exact. Upon which he gave the
Countryman an Acquittance, and fent
him away. The Piftoles he put into the
Bag again. Then addreffing himfelf to
me, faid, Now we'll go to my Mafter's

Levee.

Levee. He generally rises about Noon
'Tis an Hour past, and I suppose he's
got up. As the Steward said, we found
him in his Morning-Gown, lolling in
an Elbow Chair, his Leg over one Arm
of it, and his Head over-t'other, and his
Nose full of Snuff. He was discoursing
with a Footman who supplied the Place
of a Valet. My Lord, says the Inten-
dant, I take the liberty to present a
young Man to you in the room of him
you turn'd off the Day before Yester-
day. *Melendez* your Draper will answer for him. He assures me the Lad
has Merit; and I believe you'll be satisfied with him. 'Tis enough, replied
the young Lord, that you bring him to
me. I take him into my Service. He
shall be my Valet de Chambre. That
Business is done, *Rodriguez*, added he.
I have something else to say to you. You
are come very *apropos*. I was going to send
for you. I have bad News to tell you,
dear *Rodriguez*, I had ill Luck last Night.
Besides the hundred Pistoles I had of
you, I lost 200 upon Honour. You
know of what Consequence it is for
Persons of Quality to discharge such a
Debt. 'Tis indeed the only one that
the Punctilio of Honour obliges us to
pay

pay with Punctuality. As for the reft, they are not to be minded. You muft therefore get me 200 Piftoles prefently, and fend them to the Countefs of *Pedrofa.* Sir, fays the Steward, 'tis much eafier to fay it than do it. Where, an't pleafe you, fhall I find fuch a Sum? Your Tenants do not bring me a Maravedi, tho' I threaten them hard. I muft take care of your Family, whatever is done for't ; and they fuck my very Blood to anfwer the Expence. Hitherto I have gone thro' with it ; but I can't hold out longer without a Miracle. All that you fay fignifies nothing, cries Don *Mathias,* interrupting him : Your Particularities ferve only to vex me. Don't think, *Rodriguez,* that I'll change my Courfe of Life, or take care of my Eftate. A fine Employment that for a Man of Pleafure as I am. Truly, Sir, replied *Rodriguez,* as Matters go, I forefee you will foon have that Care taken off your Hands. You teaze me to Death, fays the young Lord, a little haftily. Let me ruin myfelf without knowing it. I tell you I muft have 200 Piftoles. I muft have them. I will go again to the little Old Man, who has already lent you fo much at Intereft, re-

N 3 plies

plies *Rodriguez,* I don't care whom you go to, says Don *Matthias,* so I have the Money. Go to the Devil for't, if you will.

As he was speaking these Words, hastily and angrily, the Steward went out, and a Young Man of Quality, call'd Don *Antonio Centelles,* enter'd. What's the Matter, Friend, says the latter to my Master? You are cloudy, and seem in a Passion. Who has put you into such an ill Humour? I'll lay a Wager 'tis the Man I met. Yes, replied Don *Matthias*; it is my Steward. Every time I speak to him, it is always thus. He will be talking of my Affairs to me. He tells me I shall eat myself out of House and Home. A Wretch! —— He'll lose nothing by it, however it goes. I am just in the same Case, cries Don *Antonio.* I have such another impertinent Steward. When the Coxcomb, after my repeated Orders, brings me any Money, he does it as if he gave it to me. He is full of his Advice. Sir, cries he, you'll undo yourself. Your Rents are seiz'd. I am forc'd to interrupt him, and cut him short in his Discourse. The worst of it is, says Don *Matthias,* we cannot do without these Men. They are a necessary Evil. They are so, replies

replies *Gentelles.* But hold, I have one
of the pleafanteft Thoughts come into
my Head that ever Man had. With that
he burft out into of Fit of loud Laughter; and then continued, Nothing can
be better contriv'd. We'll turn thefe
ferious Scenes into comick, and divert
ourfelves with what has fo much vex'd
us. 'Tis this: I will demand of your
Steward as much Money as you have
occafion for. Do you do the fame by
mine. Let them then lecture us as
much as they pleafe, we fhall hear them
with Indifference. Your Steward fhall
bring me his Accounts. My Steward
fhall do the fame by you. You will hear
of nothing but my Extravagances, I
fhall her of nothing but of yours. 'Twill
be a pretty Frolick, will it not?

They both tickled themfelves with
the Thoughts of it; and were laughing
at it. when their Mirth was interrupted
by *Gregorio Rodriguez,* who return'd,
follow'd by a little old Man that had
fcarce a Hair upon his Head, fo bald
was he. Don *Antonio* would have gone.
Adieu, Don *Matthias,* fays he; we fhall fee
one another again by and by. I leave you
with thefe Gentlemen. You have doubtlefs fome Bufinefs of Confequence to-

N 4   gether.

gether. No, no, reply'd my Mafter, ftay,
this fage old Perfon is an honeft Man
who lends me Money at 20 *per Cent.*
How! 20 *per Cent.* cries *Centelles,* in a
Surprize: You light of honefter Men
than I do. I am forc'd to pay dear
for every Peny I borrow: 40 *per Cent.*
is my Common Rate. Extortion! fays
the old Ufurer. What Rogues they
are? Don't they think there's another
World? I do not wonder People rail fo
much at Ufury. 'Tis the Exorbitancy
of it that makes it fo difhonourable.
If all my Brethren were like me, we
fhould not be decry'd fo much. For
my part, I generally lend my Money only to do my Neighbour a Kindnefs. Ah!
if the Times were as they have been, I
would offer you my Purfe without Intereft; and as bad as they are now, I
can hardly in my Confcience take even
fo little as 20 *per Cent.* But they fay
there is no Silver in the Mines; that the
Bowels of the Earth are drain'd of it;
and it's Scarcity makes me encroach upon
Morality. How much do you want?
continued he, addreffing himfelf to my
Mafter. Two hundred Piftoles, replied
Don *Matthias.* I have Four hundred in
a Bag, fays the Ufurer. You may have
                                    half

half of them. Saying this, he pull'd a
blue Bag from under his Cloak, which
feem'd to me to be the very Bag in which
the Peafant *Talego* brought the Five hundred Piftoles to *Rodriguez*. I guefs'd
immediately what was the Meaning of
it ; and foon after perceiv'd that *Melendez* had not mifinform'd me, when he
boafted of the Steward's Dexterity.
The Old Man empty'd the Piftoles on
the Table ; the Sight of which made
my Mafter greedy of all. . He was fmit-
ten with the Totality of the Sum. Signor *Difcomulgado*, fays he to the Ufurer,
I have thought better of it, and find my
felf to be a Blockhead. I ask'd to borrow only what I had pafs'd my Word
for, not thinking that I had not a Peny
in my Purfe. I will take the whole
Four hundred .Piftoles, to fave the
Trouble of fending for you again. I
intended, replied the Ufurer, to lend part
of this Money to a Clergyman, who
has enter'd fome Maidens in a Nunne-
ry, and is about furnifhing their Lodgings for 'em ; but fince you have occafion for all of it, 'tis at your Service. All
you have to do, is, to provide Security.
As for Security, cries *Rodriguez*, interrupting him, and taking a Paper out of

his

his Pocket, you fhall have very good.
Signor Don *Matthias* need only fign this
Bill ; 'twill entitle you to Five hundred
Piftoles upon *Talego*, a rich Peafant of
Mondejar. 'Tis very well, replies the U-
furer : I am not very difficult. Then the
Steward prefented a Pen to my Mafter ;
who, without reading it, fet his Name
to the Bill, whiftling all the while he
was writing.

This Affair over, the old Man bad my
Mafter Adieu. Don *Matthias* ran and
embrac'd him, crying, Till next Time,
Signor *Defcomulgado*, I am yours. I
can't imagine why they fhould treat
Ufurers as Rafcals. I think you are Men
neceffary to the State. You are the Confolation of a Thoufand Heirs, and the
Refource of all the Lords, whofe Expence exceeds their Income. Very true,
fays *Centelles* ; the Ufurers are Men of
Honour, who cannot be too much honour'd. Let me alfo embrace this worthy
Perfon, for the fake of his 20 *per Cent.*
Saying this, he approach'd the Old Man
to hug him : And thefe two Beaux
pufh'd him from one to t'other, by
way of Diverfion, as a Ball is ftricken
at Tennis. After they had done with
him, the Steward, who deferv'd it as
much

much as he, and a great deal more, took him away. They were no sooner gone, than Don *Matthias* sent the 200 Piftoles to the Countefs of *Pedrofa*, by the Lackey that was in the Room with me. The other 200 Piftoles he put up in a long Silk Purfe, which he ufually carried about with him. Being highly pleas'd to find himfelf fo well in Cafh, he demanded with a great deal of Gayety of Don *Antonio*, What fhall we do to Day ? Let us confult. You talk like a Man of Senfe, replies *Centelles* ; let us deliberate upon the Matter. While they were confidering it, two other Lords enter'd the Chamber, Don *Alexio Segiar*, and Don *Fernand de Gamboa*, both of them near about the fame Age with my Mafter, who was Twenty eight or Twenty nine Years old. Thefe Four Gentlemen embrac'd as if they had not feen one another in ten Years before. After which Don *Fernand*, who was a Boon Companion, faid, addreffing himfelf to my Mafter, Where do you dine to Day ? If you are not engag'd, I'll carry you to a Tavern where you fhall drink the Liquor of the Gods. I fupp'd there, and did not come away till between five and fix this Morning.

Would

Would to Heav'n, cry'd my Mafter, I had done the fame, I fhould not have loft my Money then. For my Part, faid *Centelles*, I found out a New Diverfion laſt Night. I love change in my Pleaſures. Nothing but Variety can render Life agreeable. One of my Friends carried me to the Houfe of a Cuſtomhoufe Officer; a Set of Men who do their own and the State's Bufinefs together. Every thing was magnificent, and the Entertainment very elegant: But the Mafter of the Houfe had fomething in him extremely ridiculous. Tho' he was but an ordinary Fellow at the Beginning, he pretended mightily to Quality, and his Wife to Beauty, tho' fhe was horribly ugly. They had both a *Bifcayan* Brogue in their Talk, which made the filly things they faid ſtill more pleafant. Their Children, in number five or fix, with their Preceptor, were all fet to Table. Judge you what their Breeding was.

I fupp'd, cries Don *Alexio Segiar*, with the Actrefs *Arfenia*. We were fix of us, *Arfenia*, *Florimonda*, with a Coquet, a Friend of hers, the Marquis *de Zeneta*, Don *Juan de Alencado*, and
your

your Servant. We spent the Night in Drinking, and Talking merrily. What Pleasure was it ! 'Tis true, *Arsenia* and *Florimonda* are not over-stock'd with Wit; but then they are wanton Jades, and that's as good as witty. They are brisk, frolickfome Wretches : And I love 'em a thousand times better than your prim, precise Dames that pique themselves of Sense and Virtue.

***

C H A P. IV.

How Gil Blas *became acquainted with Valets belonging to Beaux. An admirable Secret they taught him to acquire the Reputation of a Man of Wit : And the singular Oath they made him take.*

THESE Lords continued to divert themselves in this manner, till Don *Matthias*, whom I was all the while dressing, was ready to go out with them. He then bad me follow him ; and all these Four Rakes went together to the Tavern Don *Fernand de Gamboa*

Gamboa had propos'd to them. I march'd behind them, with three other Valets; for each of thofe Gentlemen had one. I obferv'd with Aftonifhment that each of thofe Valets copied after his Mafter, and gave himfelf the fame Airs. I faluted them as their new Comrade. They returned my Salute : And one of them, after having look'd .fome time ftedfaftly upon me, faid, I perceive, Brother, by your Air, that you have never yet ferv'd a young Lord. No, replied I ; I have not been long in *Madrid.* So I thought, faid he, you have a Country Look ftill: You feem timerous and confus'd. You don't know how to behave yourfelf. But no Matter; we fhall make fomething of you. You flatter me, replied I. No, no, fays he; there's no Man fuch a Blockhead, but we can improve him. Depend upon it we'll do your Bufinefs for you.

He need fay no more to give me to underftand that I had a Company of rare Sparks for my Brother Valets; and that I could not have fallen into better Hands to learn my Trade. At our coming to the Tavern, we found an Entertainment prepar'd for them. Signor
Don

Don *Fernand* had befpoke it in the
Morning. Our Mafters fat down to
Table, and we ftood ready to ferve
them. They were extremely pleafant
all the while they were at Dinner ; and I took great Delight to
hear them talk. Their Character, their
Thoughts, and Expreffions diverted
me. What Fire ! What Fancy ! They
feem'd to me to be a new Species of
Men. After the Defert was brought
in, we fpread the Table with Bottles of
the moft excellent Wine ; and left them,
to go to Dinner ourfelves, in a Room
where the Cloth was laid on purpofe
for us.

I foon found that the Cavaliers of
my Fraternity had more Merit than I
at firft imagin'd. They were not contented with affuming the Manners of
their Mafters ; they affected the Language alfo : And thefe Rogues imitated
them fo well, that there was no Difference, except the Quality Air. Their
Air was free and eafy. I was charm'd
with their Wit, and defpair'd of ever
becoming fo agreeable as they were.
Don *Fernand's* Valet, becaufe his Mafter treated the others, had the Ma-
nagement of the Feaft : And that we
might

might want nothing, call'd the Land-
lord, and said, Master *Andrew Manthano*,
give us tenBottles of your most excellent
Wine ; and, as you are us'd to do, put
them down in our Masters Reckoning.
With all my Heart, replied the Host :
But Master *Gasper*, added he, you know
Signor Don *Fernand* owes me a great
many Reckonings already. If by your
Means I could touch a little Money. Oh,
Sir, answer'd the Valet, don't be in any
Pain on that Score. I'll answer for him.
My Master's Debts are as good as old
Gold. 'Tis true, some ill bred Creditors
have seiz'd our Rents ; but we shall out
them in a little while, sell our Estates,
and clear off all, without enquiring
into the Particulars of your Bill. *Man-
tuano* brought the Wine, notwithstanding the Rents were seiz'd ; and we
drank it before the Creditors were
outed. We wassed one another's Healths
by the Sirnames of our Masters. Don
Antonio's Valet call'd Don *Fernand*'s *Gamboa*, and Don *Fernand*'s Valet call'd Don
Antonio's *Centelles*. My Name was *Silva*
with them ; and we got as fuddled by
degrees, under those borrow'd Names,
as the Lords who bore them.

Tho'

Tho' I was not fo brilliant as my Brethren, they express'd themselves to be
very well satisfied with me. *Silva*, said
one of the loosest of 'em, we shall make
something of thee. I find that thou
hast a Genius at bottom, but thou
dost not yet know how to use it. The
fear of speaking ill, hinders thy speaking any thing at a venture; and I must
tell thee, that 'tis by venturing any thing
in Conversation, that Men now-a-days
acquire the Name of Wits. Would'st
thou shine? Follow the Vivacity of
thy Nature, and say every thing that
comes uppermost. Thy Impudence will
pass for a noble Boldness. If thou can'st
but crack one Jest among a hundred Im-
pertinences, the foolish things thou say'st
shall be taken no notice of; and thou
shalt be deem'd a Man of Merit. This
is what our Masters practise so success-
fully; and thus every Man should do
that aims at the Reputation of a di-
stinguish'd Wit,

Besides, that I had too great a Desire already to pass for a fine Genius,
the Secret to succeed in it appear'd so
easy to me, that I thought I ought not to
neglect it. I made a Trial of it on the
Spot; and the Wine I had drank, gave
Success

Succefs to the Experiment; that is, I talk'd right or wrong, whatever came into my Head ; and had the good Fortune, among many Extravagances, to mingle fome Points of Wit, which were mightily applauded. This Effay fill'd me with Confidence. I redoubled my ufual Vivacity, to produce fome agreeable Sally; and Chance was fo much my Friend, that my Efforts were not ineffectual.

So now, fays one of my Brethren, the fame that had fpoke to me in the Street, Doft thou not begin to mend upon it ? Thou haft not been with us above two Hours, and thou art already another Creature. Thou wilt alter for the better more and more every Day. This it is to ferve Perfons of Quality. It raifes the Mind. City Places do not do fo. Without doubt, replied I ; and hereafter I will dedicate my Services to the Nobility. Well faid, cry'd Don *Fernand's* Valet, almoft drunk. 'Tis not for Citizens to have fuch fuperior Genius's as we have. Let's take an Oath, Gentlemen, among our felves, never to ferve fuch Fellows. Let us fwear by *Styx*. We all laught at *Gafper's* Thought; we applauded it ; and every Man with his Glafs in his Hand, took the Burlefque Oath. We

We sat at Table till it pleased our Masters to retire. 'Twas Midnight first. And my Brethren took it for an Excess of Sobriety that they went home so soon. Indeed these Lords went from the Tavern, only to visit a famous Coquet who liv'd in the Court Quarter, whose House was open Night and Day to Men of Pleasure. She was about Thirty five Years of Age. She wore extremely well, and was so agreeable in Company, that 'tis said she sold the Remains of her Beauty, as dear as she did the First-Fruits. She had always with her two or three Coquets of the first Order, which drew a great Concourse of Lords to her House. They gam'd in the Afternoon; they supp'd at Night, which they spent in drinking, and making themselves merry. Our Masters stay'd there till Morning. So did we, without being tir'd; for while they were with the Mistresses, we diverted our selves with the Maids. At last, when Day broke, we separated, and went each to his Rest. My Master, according to Custom, rose about Noon, dress'd himself, and went out. I waited upon him to the House of Don *Antonio Centelles*, where we found one Don *Alvaro de Acuna*,

Acuna, an old Debauchee. All the young
Men who would render themselves a-
greeable, put themselves into his Hands.
He form'd them for Pleasure. He taught
them how to shine in the World, and
waste their Estates. He was not afraid
of spending his. That Business was
done long before. After the natural Embraces of these Gentlemen were over,
Centelles said to my Master, S'Death,
Don *Matthias*, thou could'st not come
hither more *apropos*. *Alvar* is come to
carry me to dine with a Citizen who
treats the Marquis *de Zenatt*, and Don
Juan de Moncado to day. Thou shalt
go with us. What's the Citizen's Name?
says Don *Matthias*. *Gregorio de Noriega*,
replies Don *Alvar*; and I'll tell you in two
Words what this young Man is. His
Father, who is a rich Jeweller, is gone
to trade in Jewels in foreign Countries,
and left with him, when he went, a
very good Income. *Gregorio* is a Coxcomb, who has a towardly Disposition
to ruin himself, and set up for a Beau
and a Wit, in spite of Nature. He has
desir'd me to instruct him. I govern
him; and can assure you, Gentlemen, I
have put him in a right Way. His Income is already pretty well diminished.

I

I don't doubt it, cry'd *Centelles.* I see him, methinks in an Alms-house. Come, Don *Matthias,* continued he, let us scrape Acquaintance with this Man, and contribute to his Ruin. With all my Heart, replied my Master; I love dearly to see those Mechanick Fops reduced, who pretend to our Airs and Manners. Nothing, for Example, pleas'd me better, than when the Collector's Son was so beggar'd by Gaming and Vanity, in making a Figure like a Lord, that he was forc'd to sell his House over his Head. As for him, replies *Antonio,* he does not deserve to be pitied. He's as great a Fop in his Misery, as he was in his Prosperity.

Centelles and my Master accompanied Don *Alvar* to *Gregorio Noriega's. Mogicon* and I went with them, overjoyed that we were like to come in for Snips, and contribute also to the Citizen's Ruin. When we came there, we found several Men very busy in getting Dinner ready. The Fumes of the Ragouts were most grateful Odors to us. The Marquis *de Zenete,* and Don *Juan de Moncado* were just arriv'd. The Master of the House appear'd to be what *Alvar* said, a great Coxcomb. He, in vain, affected

affected to affume the Airs, of a Beau.
He was a wretched Copy of fo excellent
an Original ; or rather a Blockhead that
would fain have put himfelf off for a
Man of Sence. Reprefent to yourfelf a
Man of this Character, among five
Sparks a rallying him, each of them
making a Jeft of him, and endeavouring
to draw him into Extravagances. Gentlemen, fays Don *Alvar*, after the firft
Compliments were over, I recommend
Signor *Gregorio de Noriega* to you, for
an accomplifh'd Cavalier. He has a
thoufand fine Qualities. Do you know
how he has improv'd himfelf? Put it
to the Experiment. He is equally Mafter of all the Sciences, from Logick to
Orthography. You do me too much
Honour, fays the Citizen, interrupting
him with an awkard Smile ; I could turn
that Argument upon you, Signor *Alvar*;
you, who are ftyl'd one of the Foun-
tains of Learning. I did not think,
cry'd Don *Alvar*, that I fhould have
drawn upon my felf fo witty a Panegyrick. But to fay the Truth, Gentlemen, Signor *Gregorio* cannot fail of
acquiring a Reputation in the World.
As for me, cries Don *Antonio*, what I
take to be moft charming in him, and
value

value infinitely above his Orthography, is, the judicious Choice he makes of the Perfons he frequents. Inftead of confining himfelf to a City Converfation, he keeps Company with none but young Lords, not minding what a Charge it puts him to. This fhews a Greatnefs of Soul, and that he knows how to fpend Eftate with Delicacy and Difcernment. Thefe Ironical Difcourfes made way for a thoufand of the fame nature. They all fell upon poor *Gregorio*; and he was fuch a Fool as not to perceive it. On the contrary, he took every thing to be meant as it was faid, and was mightily pleas'd with his Guefts. He even imagin'd that they did him a Favour, to turn him into Ridicule. In fine they play'd upon him all the while they were at Dinner. They ftaid with him all Day and all Night too. We drank what we would as well as our Mafters, and were both in a handfome Pickle when we left him.

CHAP. V.

Gil Blas *sets up for a Gallant Man,
and gets Acquaintance with a pretty Girl.*

I Slept some Hours, and rose in a gay
Humour. Remembring the Advice
Melendez gave me, I went, while my
Master was yet asleep, to make my Court
to our Steward, who seem'd to take my
Respects very graciously. He ask'd me
how I lik'd this way of Living? I replied, 'Twas new to me; but I did not
despair of accustoming myself to it;
which indeed I did effectually, and in
a little time too. I chang'd Humour,
and from grave became frolicksome.
Don *Antonio's* Valet complimented me
on my Metamorphosis; and told me that
I wanted nothing now to finish me for
a Cavalier but an Affair of Gallantry,
which was absolutely necessary to render a young Man compleatly polite.
That all our Comrades were belov'd
by

by fome fair Lady; and that he, for
his part, was in the good Graces of
two Ladies of Quality, I believ'd the
Rafcal ly'd. Monfieur *Mogicon*, fays I,
you are a jolly, handfome Fellow ; but
I can't underftand how Women of Quality can fall in Love with a Man of
your Condition. Oh! as for that, replied he, they don't know who I am.
I make Conquefts in my Mafter'sCloaths,
and even with his Name, as thus : I am
dreft like a young Lord ; I imitate the
Manners of one ; I go to the publick
Places ; I ogle all the Women I meet,
till I fix on one that gives me Encouragement ; I follow her, and get
into Talk with her. I call myfelf Don
Antonio Centelles. I demand an Affignation. The Lady feems coy. I prefs her.
She complies, *& cætera.* By this means,
Child, continues he, I have Affairs of
Gallantry upon my Hands, and I advife thee to follow my Example. I had
too great a Defire to become a Gallant
Man, not to take his Advice. Befides,
I did not find any Repugnance in myfelf to an Amorous Intrigue. I defign'd
therefore to transform my felf into
a young Lord, and feek out fome Gallant Adventures. I durft not difguife

myfelf in our Palace, for fear Notice
fhould be taken of it. I took one of
the fineft Suits in my Mafter's Wardrobe. I bundled it up, and carried it
to a Barber's, a Friend of mine, where
I might drefs and undrefs myfelf commodioufly. I made myfelf as fine as I
could. The Barber affifted me in doing
it; And when I thought we had
done enough, I march'd toward the Walks
of St. *Jerom*, where I doubted not
but I fhould meet with more Opportunities than one to enter upon Gallantry.
But before I got there, I light upon
an Adventure, which I was wonderfully
charm'd with. As I was croffing a
Bye-ftreet, I faw a Lady richly drefs'd,
and very well fhap'd, go out of a little Houfe into a Hackney-Coach which
waited at the Door. I ftept to look after her, and faluted her in a way which
fhew'd I was not a little taken with her.
She, on her part, to fhew that fhe deferv'd my Attention, perhaps, more
than I thought fhe did, lifted up her
Veil for a Moment, and difcover'd one
of the prettieft Faces I ever faw. The
Coach drove away; and I ftaid behind
in the Emotion this Apparition had
caus'd in my Breaft. A lovely Creature,
faid

said I to myself; she'll furnish me, I'll warrant her. If the two Ladies that are in Love with *Mogican* are as handsome as this, he's a happy Dog. I should think myself so, if I had such a Mistress. As I was making these Reflexions, I chanc'd to cast my Eye at a Window of the House whence this amiable Person came, and perceived an Old Woman, who beckon'd to me to enter. I flew into it, and found the venerable, discreet Matron in a Parlour, neatly furnish'd. She took me for a Marquis at least; and saluting me very respectfully, said, I doubt not, my Lord, you have an ill Opinion of a Woman, who, without knowing you, made a Sign to you to enter the House; but you will alter it, perhaps, when you know that I deal with all the World in this free Way. You look to be a Court Lord. You judge well, my Dear, cry'd I, stretching out my Right Leg, and falling away a little to the left, I may without Vanity say, I am of one of the best Families in *Spain*. You have the Air, replied she; and I must own I love to do good Offices to Persons of your Quality. 'Tis my *Foible.* I took notice of you at my Window, and ob-

ferv'd you ogled a Lady who had juft
then parted with me. Do you like her?
Tell me truly. Yes, cried I; I am fmit-
ten with her, upon my Honour. I
never faw fo charming a Creature.
Bring us together, and depend upon
my Gratitude. You have done Services of this kind for other Perfons of
my Quality, and know by that how
'well we are us'd to pay for them. I
have told you, fays fhe, that I am
devoted to ferve the Quality. I delight
to be ufeful to them. I entertain here,
for Example, certain Ladies, whom an
Appearance of Virtue hinders from feeing their Gallants at Home. Very
well, cry'd I ; and 'tis probable you
have been doing as much for the Lady we talk of. No, replied fhe, 'tis a
young Widow of Quality, who is willing to have a Lover; but fhe is fo
nice, I cannot tell whether you would
fucceed, whatever may be your Merit.
I have already recommended three very
likely Gentlemen, but fhe has refus'd
them all. 'Sdeath! my dear, faid I,
with an Air of Confidence, do but
bring me into her Company once, and
I'll anfwer for the reft ; I want to have
fome Diologue with fo nice a Lady,

I

I never yet met with one too nice for me. Well then, answer'd the Old Woman, Come hither to morrow at this Time, and you shall satisfy your Curiosity. I will not fail, replied I. We shall see whether a young Lord may not pretend to a Conquest.

I return'd thence to the Barber's, without looking out for other Adventures, and very impatient to see the End of this. The next Day, when I had adjusted myself to the best Advantage, I went at the time appointed to the Old Woman's. My Lord, says she, you are punctual; and I am glad of it. The Business is worth the Trouble. I have seen our young Widow; and we have had a great deal of Discourse about you. I was bid not to speak of it; but I am so much your Friend, that I can't help it. She is as much taken with you, as you are with her; and you are in a fair Way to be happy. Between you and me, this Lady is a choice Bit. Her Husband did not live long with her. He was but a sort of a Shadow. She is as good as a Virgin. The Old Woman meant without doubt, one of her Virgins, who know how to pass their Celibacy without wanting

Hus-

Husbands. The Heroine of the Aſ-
ſignation arriv'd ſoon after in a Hack-
ney Coach. Aſſoon as ſhe came into
the Hall, I accoſted her with five or ſix
foppiſh Bows; and then approaching
her very familiaily, ſaid, My Princeſs,
behold a Lord that's taken in your Snare.
Your Image has not been out of my
Mind ever ſince I ſaw you Yeſterday;
and you have driven out a Dulneſs that
had began to take footing there. TheTri-
umph is too glorious for me, replied ſhe,
lifting up her Veil; but I muſt not rejoyce too much. Young Lords love
change; and nothing is ſo hard to keep
as a Courtier's Heart. Ah! my Queen,
cry'd I; if you pleaſe, let's leave that
to the future, and think now of the
preſent. You are Fair; I am in Love.
If my Love is agreeable to you, let
us engage without Reflexion: Let us
embark like Mariners, and not dread
the Dangers of the Sea. Let us think
only of Pleaſure. At theſe Words I
threw myſelf at her Feet in a Tranſport of Joy; and to imitate the *Beaux*,
I preſs'd her very petulantly to conſent
to my Happineſs. She ſeem'd to be
complying; but would not yield at the
firſt Meeting: So ſhe puſh'd me back:
Hold

Hold, cry'd she, you are too forward:
you act like a Rake : I am afraid you are
a young Debauchee. Puh, Madam, said
I, do you hate what all Women that
are not Vulgar love. None but Citizens
are afraid of a Rake. Your Reasons,
reply'd she, are too powerful to be re-
sisted. I perceive 'tis to no Purpose to
dissemble with you young Lords. A
Woman must come half way. Know
therefore, the Victory you have gain'd,
continued she, with seeming Confusion,
as if her Modesty had been injur'd by
that Confession, you have inspir'd me
with Sentiments I never felt before ;
and I want nothing now but to know
who you are, to make me chuse you for
my Lover. I take you to be a young
Lord, and a Man of Honour : However,
I am not sure of it ; and as prejudiced
as I am in your Favour, I will not give
my self to one I don't know.

I call'd to mind in what manner Don
Antonio's Valet told me he us'd to extri-
cate himself out of such Difficulties ;
and resolving, like him, to pass for
the Matter ; Madam, says I to my Widow, I shall make no Scruple to tell you
my Name. It is too noble for a Man
to be ashamed of it. Did you never

hear

hear talk of Don *Matthias de Silva*?
Yes, replied she, I have seen him at a
Friend's of mine. As impudent as I
was become, this Answer of her's puz+
led me a little; but I recollected my
self in a Moment, and put my Genius
to the stretch to come off cleverly. Ah!
my Angel, replied I, You know a Lord
that I know also. I am of the same
Family. His Uncle married a Sister-in-
law of an Uncle of my Father's. We
are, as you see, very nearly related. My
Name is Don *Cesar*. I am the only Son
of the illustrious Don *Fernand de Ribera*, who was kill'd fifteen Years ago in
a Battle on the Frontiers of *Portugal*. I
might give you a particular Account of
the Action, which was very hot; but
It would be to lose the Moments which
are precious in Love, and may be em-
ployed much more agreeably.

I became more pressing and passionate
after this Discourse. My Princess was
not at all mov'd by it. The Favours she
gave me, only made me long for others
which she refus'd. The cruel Creature
left me in this Condition, went to her
Coach, and drove away. Tho' I was
not entirely happy, yet I was pleas'd
with my good Fortune. If I have not
obtain'd

obtain'd the Favour I preſt for, ſaid I to
myſelf, 'tis becauſe my Goddeſs is a Lady of Quality, who would not appear
forward, nor comply with my Deſires
at the firſt Interview. Her high Birth
makes her delay my Joys for a few Days.
With all theſe favourable Thoughts of
her, I could not ſometimes help thinking
ſhe might be a cunning Gypſy, and did
it to draw me in. However, I lov'd
to think the beſt; and the moſt
advantageous Opinion I had of her
had the Predominancy in my Mind.
We agreed, when we parted, to meet
again the next Day; and the Hopes of
enjoying then the Height of my Wiſhes,
gave me a Taſte of them before Hand.
With theſe pleaſing Fancies in my Head,
I return'd to my Barber's. I chang'd
my Cloaths, and went to my Miſter,
whom I knew to be at a Tennis-Court.
I found him at Play, and obſerv'd that
he gain'd, by his Looks: For he was
not one of thoſe inſenſible Gameſters
that make or ruin themſelves without
changing Countenance. He was merry
and inſolent when he got, and ſuſly
when he loſt. From the Tennis-Court
he went in a very gay Humour to the
Prince's Theatre. I waited upon him to

the

the Play-house Door, where putting a
Ducat into my Hand, he cry'd to me,
There, *Gil Blas*, since I have had good
Fortune to Day, be thou so much the
better for it. Go, divert thyself with thy
Comrades, and come to me at Midnight at *Arsenia*'s, where I shall sup with
Don *Alexio Segiar*. At these Words he
went into the House, and I stay'd without, studying with whom to spend my
Ducat, according to the Intention of the
Founder. I was not long at a loss about
it. *Clarin*, Don *Alexio*'s Valet, falling
in my Way, I took him with me to the
first Tavern, and we staid there till
Midnight. From thence we went to *Arsenia*'s, whither *Clarin* had Orders to
come as well as I. A little Lackey, o-
pen'd the Door, and conducted us into
a Hall, where *Arsenia* and *Florimonda*'s
Women were making merry, while
their Mistresses were doing the same with
our Masters. The coming of two good
Guests, who were already half fuddled,
could not be disagreeable to two such
Baggages as they were, especially, considering they were Players. But how
was I astonish'd, when, in one of them, I
discover'd my Widow, my adorable Widow, who I took to be a Countess or a
? O   Mar-

Marchionefs. She was no lefs furpriz'd
to find her dear Don *Cæfar de Ribera*
reduc'd to a Valet de Chambre. We,
however, look'd upon one another fome
time, without being out of Countenance.
We had both of us a great mind to
burft out a laughing; and we did not
long forbear it. After which, *Laura,* fo
my Princefs was call'd, taking me afide,
while *Clarin* talk'd with her Companion, and giving me her Hand, whifper'd
me, Since it is fo, Signor Don *Cæfar,*
let us not reproach one another, but do
each other Juftice, You play'd your
Part admirably, and I did not act mine
ill ; What fay you ? Did not you take me
for one of thofe pretty Women of Quality who delight in Intrigue ? 'Tis true,
replied I ; but be you who you will,
my Queen, I have not chang'd Sentiments in changing Forms. Accept of
my Services, and fuffer Don *Matthias*'s
Valet to finifh what Don *Cæfar,* fo happily began. Well, faid fhe, I love thee
better as thou art now, naturally, than I
did before. Thou art as a Man, the
fame as I am as a Woman : That's
the greateft Encomium I can beftow upon thee. I admit thee among the number of my Adorers. We have no need
of

of the Agency of the Old Woman. Thou
may'ſt come hither freely. The Ladies
of the Theatre live without Conſtraint,
higdelly-pigdelly among the Men. The
Publick ſees it, laughs at it ; and what
then ? Are we not made for their Diverſion ?

We left off here, becauſe there were
others in the Room. The Converſation
became general, brisk, wanton, and full
of very intelligible *Double Entendres*. Every one ſaid ſomething, and eſpecially my
amiable *Laura, Arſenia*'s Woman, ſhew'd
that ſhe had a great deal more Wit than
Virtue. We could often hear our Maſters and the Players laugh aloud ; and
gueſs'd by that, their Converſation was
of the ſame nature with ours. If all the fine
things which were ſaid that Night at *Arſenia*'s were written down, it would make
a Book of great Inſtruction for Youth.
The time of departing, that is, Day-
break, coming upon us, we each retir'd
with our Maſters, *Clarin* with Don *A-
lexio*, and I with Don *Matthias*

C H A P.

CHAP. VI.

Of the Discourse of some Lords about the Players of the Prince's Company.

IN the Forenoon my Master receiv'd a Billet from Don *Alexio Segiar* to desire him to come to him. We went to his House, and found there the Marquis *de Zenete*, and another young Lord whom I had not seen before. Don *Matthias*, says *Segiar* to my Master, presenting that Cavalier to him, This is my Kinsman Don *Pompeyo de Castro*. He has been bred up from his Youth in the Court of *Portugal*. He arriv'd at *Madrid* last Night, and returns to morrow to *Lisbon*. He can give me but this one Day. We must make the most of so precious a one; and I thought I should want you and the Marquis *de Zenete*, to help me out in it. Upon this my Master and Don *Alexio's* Kinsman embrac'd; and many a Compliment pass'd between them. I was mightily pleas'd with what Don *Pompeyo* said,

said, he seeming to be a Man of as much Judgment as Wit.

They din'd at *Segiar's:* And those Lords, after Dinner, Gam'd till Play-time. They then went together to the Prince's Theatre, to see a New Trage-dy, call'd *The Queen of* Carthage. When the Play was done, they return'd to sup at the same Place where they had din'd. Their Conversation roll'd at first on the Play they had heard, and afterwards on the Players. As for the Play, cries Don *Matthias,* I have no O-pinion of it. *Æneas* is flatter there than in the *Æneid;* but it was play'd di-vinely. What does Don *Pompeyo* think of it? He does not seem to be of the same Sentiment. Gentlemen, says the Cavalier, smiling, I observ'd you were so charm'd with the Actors, and espe-cially with the Actresses, that I dare not give you my Opinion. Very well, cries Don *Alexio,* interrupting him; have a care what you say of our Actresses be-fore us, who are the Trumpets of their Fame, drink with them every Day, and are their Guarantees. We'll give Cer-tificates for them if you require it. I doubt it not, replied his Kinsman; you will warrant their Lives and Manners as
well

well as their Merit, I fee you are fo much
their Friends.

Your *Lisbon* Players, fays the Marquis *de Zenete*, fmiling, are without doubt
much better than ours. Moft certainly, replied Don *Pompeyo*; there are fome
at leaft that have no Defect. Thefe
are fure of your Certificate, fays the
Marquis. I have no Correfpondence
with them, replies Don *Pompeyo*. I never drink with them : I am therefore
qualified to judge of them without Prejudice. Tell me truly, Do
you really take your Players to be an
excellent Company ? Not I, fays the
Marquis ; I'll fpeak but for very few of
them. I'll give up all the reft. Will
not you allow that the Actrefs who
play'd the Part of *Dido*, did it incom-
parably ? Did fhe not reprefent that
Queen with all the Grandeur and all the
Grace that fuit the Idea we have of
her ? Did you not admire to fee with
what Art fhe engages a Spectator, and
makes him feel the Emotions of all
the Paffions fhe expreffes ? She is perfect Miftrefs of all the Beauties of De-
clamation. I grant, reply'd Don *Pompeyo*, fhe knows how to Move and
Touch : Never Player had more Bowels ;
and

and the Reprefentation was fine : But
fhe is not an Actrefs without Fault.
Two or three things in her Playing
fhock'd me. When fhe would denote
Surprize, fhe rolls her Eyes in a furious
manner, which does not become a Princefs. Add to this, that by heightning
her Voice, which is naturally low, fhe
fpoils the Sweetnefs of it, and makes it
harfh. Befides, in more than one Place
of the Play, fhe did not feem to underftand what fhe faid : But I will rather think her Thoughts were diftract-
ed, than accufe her of want of Underftanding.

By what I can fee, fays Don *Matthias*
to the Critick, our Players are not like
to have any Panegyricks from you. Pardon me, replies Don *Pompeyo*, I difcover
a Talent thro' their Defects ; nay, I
muft own to you, I was charm'd with
the Actrefs who play'd the Woman's
Part in the Interlude. She has a fine
Genius ; and gave a Grace to every thing
fhe faid. If there was a Jeft in it, fhe
feafon'd it with a malicious Smile, and
added new Charms to it. One may
blame her fometimes for giving too much
way to her natural Fire, and paffing the
bounds of an honeft Boldnefs. But we
                                    muft

muſt not be too ſevere, I would only
have her correct an ill Cuſtom. Often,
in the middle of a Scene, in a ſerious
Place, ſhe on a ſudden interrupts the
Action, to pleaſe a fond Deſire of
Laughing, with which ſhe is tak n. You'll
ſay the Pit clap her then. Therein indeed ſhe is happy.

And what do you think of the Men
cries the Marquis, interrupting him,
you'll ſurely have no Mercy on them,
ſince you ſpare the Women ſo little. No,
ſays Don *Pompeyo*, there are ſome of the
young Actors very promiſing; and I
was eſpecially very well pleas'd with the
fat Actor that play'd the Part of *Dido*'s firſt Miniſter. He ſpeaks naturally,
and like our *Portugueſe* Players. If you
were pleas'd with him, ſays *Segiar*, you
muſt ſurely be charm'd with the Player
that acted the Part of *Æneas*. Is he
not a fine Actor? an Original? An Original indeed, replied the Critick. He
has Tones which are particular to him,
and very ſharp ones. He's almoſt always
out of Nature. He precipitates the
Words in which the Senſe lies, and
dwells on the others; nay, he raiſes his
Voice on Conjunctions. He diverted me
extremely, and particularly where he
                              expreſs'd

exprefs'd to his Confident the Violence he did to himfelf to leave *Dido*. Grief cannot be declar'd more comickly. Very fine, Coufin, fays Don *Alexio*; you will at laft make us believe the Court of *Portugal* have no refined Gout. Do you not know that the Actor you talk of Is mightily admir'd? Did you not hear how he was clapt? That's no Proof of his Merit, replies Don *Pompeyo*; the worft Actors are commonly the greateft Favourites of the Pit, and have the moft Claps. The Audience likes what's glaring, and neglects what's juft, as *Phædra* informs us, by an ingenious Fable; which fuffer me to relate to you as follows.

The Citizens of a certain City met at a great Square to fee fome Pantomimes act their Buffoonries. Among thefe Actors there was one whom the People applauded every Moment. This Buffoon, when the Show was almoft over, wou'd needs clofe it with fomething New. He came alone upon the Stage, bent down, cover'd his Head with his Cloak, and fet himfelf to counterfeit the Cry of a Sucking Pig. He did it fo well, that they all believ'd he had a Pig under his Cloak. They cried out

to

to him to throw open his Cloak and
Robe. He did so ; and the People
finding there was nothing under them,
repeated their Applauses with more Fury
than ever. A Peasant, who was among
the Spectators, was shock'd with so many
Tokens of their Admiration : Gentlemen,
cries he, you are in the wrong to be so
charm'd with this Buffoon. He is not
such a rare Actor as you take him to be,
I can act a Sucking Pig better than he ;
and if you question it, come here to
morrow, and you shall be Witnesses of
it, yourselves. The Citizens, prejudiced
in favour of the Pantomime, met again
the next Day, rather to hiss the Peasant
than see what he could do. The Two
Rivals appear'd on the Theatre. The
Buffoon began, and receiv'd the same
Applauses as the Day before. Then the
Peasant bending down in his Turn, and
covering his Head with his Cloak, took
a true Sucking Pig, which he had under
his Arm by the Ear, and the Pig
squeek'd heartily. However, the Audience gave the Preference to the Pantomime, and hiss'd the Peasant ; who
pulling out the Sucking Pig, and shewing it to them, said, Gentlemen, 'tis
not

not I that you hifs; 'tis the Pig itfelf.'
See what Judges you are.

Coufin, cries Don *Alexio*, thy Fable is
a little too clofe a one. Neverthelefs, fpite
of thy Sucking Pig, we fhall not give
up our Actors and Actreffes. Let's
change the Difcourfe : We have had e-
nough of this. You will go to morrow then, as defirous as I am to keep
you longer. I fhould be glad to ftay,
replies his Kinfman, if I could. I have
already told you that I came to the
Court of *Spain* about a State Affair. I
fpoke to the Prime Minifter yefterday.
I am to fee him again to morrow Morning, and fhall depart a Moment after to
return to *Lisbon*. Thou art become a
Portugueze, fays Don *Alexio*; and in all
likelihood will return no more to *Madrid*. I believe not, replies Don *Pompeyo*. I have the Happinefs to be belov'd
by the King of *Portugal*. I live pleafantly at his Court : Yet, as gracious as
he is to me, can you think it ? I was
very near leaving his Dominions for
ever. On what Occafion, cries the Marquis? Pray tell us. Moft willingly, replies Don *Pompeyo* ; and my Story is contain'd in what I am about to relate to
you.

C H A P.

CHAP. VII.

The Story of Don Pompeyo de Caftro.

DON *Alexio*, continues he, knows, that from my Youth I took an Inclination to Arms; and feeing our Country was in Peace, I went to *Portugal*; from whence I crofs'd over to *Africa* with the Duke of *Braganza*, who gave me a Poft in his Army. I was a Cadet, and not one of the richeft in *Spain*, which fpurr'd me on to fignalize myfelf in feveral Actions; and that made me taken notice of by the General. I did my Duty fo well, that the Duke advanc'd me, and put me in a Condition to continue in his Service with Honour. After a long War, the End of which you are not ignorant of, I fettled at Court; and the King, on the Recommendation of the General Officers, allow'd me a confiderable Penfion. To fhew how fenfible I was of that Monarch's Generofity, I let no Opportunity

tunity flip to exprefs my Gratitude by
my Affiduity. I was near him at all
Hours when the Courtiers were admitted into his Prefence. By this Conduct I infenfibly became belov'd by
him, and received new Benefits from
him.

Having one Day diftinguifh'd myfelf in
a Ring-courfe and Bull-fight, the whole
Court extoll'd my Strength and Dexterity; and when, loaded with their Applau-
fes, I got home, I found a Billet which
inform'd me, that a Lady, the Conqueft
of whom ought to rejoyce me more
than all the Honour I had acquir'd that
Day, defired to fpeak with me; and
that I need only come to a certain
Place appointed, in the Dusk of the
Evening. I was indeed more pleas'd
with this Letter than all the Applau-
fes before mentioned; and imagin'd that
the Perfon who fent it was a Woman of
the firft Quality. You don't doubt but
I was punctual at the Time and Place.
An Old Woman waited there to be my
Guide; and introduc'd me by a little
Door into the Garden of a great Houfe,
whence fhe carried me into a rich Clofet, full of rich Decorations, faying,
Stay there. I'll go tell my Miftrefs of
your

your coming. I examin'd the Riches of the Cloſet, which was enlighten'd by Wax-Candles in Golden Sconces: And this convinc'd me the Lady muſt be as noble as I conceiv'd her to be. If every thing I ſaw aſſur'd me of the Nobility of her Birth before ſhe came, her Appearance, her Grand and Majeſtick Air confirm'd me in that Opinion; which however was a wrong one.

Signor Cavalier, ſays ſhe, after the Step I have taken in your Favour, it would be in vain to endeavour to conceal the tender Sentiments I have for you. The Merit which the Court were Witneſſes of this Day, in regard to you, was not the firſt Motive of them: It only haſtned the Diſcovery of 'em. I have ſeen you more than once. I inform'd myſelf of you; and your Character is ſo good, that I reſolv'd to follow my Inclination. Do not think, continues ſhe, that you have made a Conqueſt of a Dutcheſs. I am only the Widow of a Captain of the King's Guards; but what will render your Victory glorious, is, the Preference I give you of one of the greateſt Lords in the Kingdom. The Duke of *Almeida* loves me, and ſpares for nothing to pleaſe me.

He

He could never succeed ; and I suffer his Caresses, only out of Vanity.

Tho' I found by this Difcourfe that I had to do with a Coquet, yet I was not difpleas'd at the Adventure. Donna *Hortenfia*, for that was her Name, was ftill in the Flower of her Youth, and her Beauty charm'd me. Befides, I was offer'd the Poffeffion of a Heart which a Duke fought after in vain. What a Triumph was that for a young *Spanifh* Cavalier! I threw my felf at *Hortenfia's* Feet, to thank her for her Goodnefs to me. I faid all a Gallant Man could think of; and fhe had reafon to be fatisfy'd with my Tranfports. Thus we parted the beft Friends in the World, after we had agreed to meet every Evening that the Duke *d' Almeida* did not come thither ; which I was promifed to have exact Intelligence of. They did not fail me ; and at laft I became the *Adonis* of this new *Venus*!

But the Pleafures of Life are not of eternal Duration. Whatever Meafures the Lady took to keep our Commerce from my Rival, he came to the knowledge of what it imported us very much he fhould be ignorant of : One of the Lady's Maids, in difguft, told him all.

all. This Lord, naturally Generous, but Proud, Jealous, and Paſſionate, was en-rag'd at my Audaciouſneſs. Choler and Jealouſy diſorder'd his Mind ; and hear-kening only to his Fury, he reſolv'd to be reveng'd of me after an infamous Manner. One Night when I was at *Hortenſia's*, he waited for me at the Garden-door with all his Valets, arm'd with Sticks. Aſſoon as I came out, he caus'd thoſe Raſcals to ſeize me, and or-der'd them to beat me to Death. Strike, ſays he, let him periſh under your Hands. I will thus chaſtiſe his Inſolence. At theſe Words his People aſſaulted me all together, and gave me ſo many Blows that they laid me for Dead on the Place. After which they retir'd with their Maſter, for whom this cruel Spectacle had been a very pleaſant one. About Day-break ſome Perſons came by, who obſerving I breath'd ſtill, had the Cha-rity to carry me to a Surgeon ; and I falling into the Hands of a skilful one, was perfectly cur'd in two Mon hs time. I then went to Court, and liv'd there as I us'd to do. I left off viſiting *Hor-tenſia*, who took no Step to let me ſee her again, becauſe the Duke had at this Price forgiven her Infidelity.

As no body was ignorant of my Adventure, nor took me for a Coward, every one admir'd that I should sit down so quietly under such an Affront; for I did not say what I thought, and I seem'd not to resent it. Some believ'd that, as stout as I was, the Rank of the Offender kept me in Awe, and oblig'd me to put up the Offence. Others, with more reason, mistrusted my Silence, and look'd on the peaceable Situation of my Soul as a deceitful Calm. The King was of the latter Opinion; and imagin'd that I would not suffer such an Outrage without Revenge, as soon as I had an Opportunity. To find out my Design, he took me into his Closet one Day, and said to me, Don *Pompeyo,* I know the Accident that has happen'd to you; and must confess I am surpriz'd to find you so easy under it. You certainly dissemble. Sir, replied I, I know not who the Offender is. I was attack'd in the Night by Men who are unknown to me. 'Tis a Misfortune I must bear as well as I can. No, no, says the King; don't think that I can be so put upon. I have heard all. The Duke of *Almeida* has mortally affronted you. You are Noble, and a *Castilian.* I know what

these

thefe Qualities will engage you to do.
You have form'd a Refolution to be reveng'd. Tell me what you intend to
do: I require you. Fear nothing; you
fhall not repent of trufting me with your
Secret.

Since your Majefty will have me, replied I, I muft inform you what I have refolved to do in this Matter. Yes, my Lord, I
do meditate Revenge for the Affront I
have fuffer'd. Every Man that bears
fuch a Name as mine is accountable to
his Race. You know how bafely I
have been treated: And to be reveng'd
in a manner anfwerable to the Offence,
I propofe to affaffinate the Duke of *Al-*
meida, by ftabbing him with a Dagger,
or fhooting him thro' the Head: After
which I'll make my Efcape, if I can,
into *Spain*. This is my Defign. 'Tis
rafh, fays the King, yet I cannot condemn it, after the cruel Outrage the
Duke of *Almeida* has done you. He deferves the Chaftifement you have referv'd
for him: But do not execute your Enterprize fo foon. Let me find out fome
Way to make the Matter up between
you. Ah! my Lord, cry'd I, a little
angrily, Why did you oblige me to reveal my Secret to you? What Way can

there

there be found out? If it is not one
that gives you Satisfaction, said he, interrupting me, you may do what you
intend. I shall not abuse the Confidence you put in me: I will not betray
your Honour. Be under no manner of
Concern on that score.

I was extremely desirous to know how
the King would have this Business accommodated. It was thus: He talk'd
to the Duke of *Almeida* about it. Duke,
says he, you have affronted Don *Pom-*
peyo de Castro. You are not ignorant that
he is a Man of an illustrious Family,
a Gentleman whom I love, and who
has done me Service. You ought to
give him Satisfaction. I shall not refuse it, replies the Duke. If he com-
plains of my Fury, I am ready to do
him Reason by way of Arms. There
must be another Reparation, cries the
King. A *Spanish* Gentleman understands
the Point of Honour too well to fight
fairly with a base Assassin. I cannot call you any thing else; and you
cannot expiate the Indignities of your
Action, but by presenting a Stick your
self to your Enemy, and offering to receive his Blows. Heaven! cries the
Duke, Would you have a Man of my
Rank,

Rank, my Lord, so debase himself? so stoop to a Gentleman, and receive Blows from him? No, replies the Monarch; I'll oblige Don *Pompeyo* to promise me that he will not strike you: But do you ask his Pardon when you present the Stick to him; that's all I require of you. 'Tis too much, my Lord, says the Duke, hastily; I had rather be still expos'd to the Danger I run from his conceal'd Resentment. Your Life is dear to me, replies the King; and I would prevent this Affair's having any ill Consequence: That it may end with as little Dislike as may be to you, I myself will be the only Witness of the Satisfaction I order you to give the *Spaniard*. The King stood in need of all his Power over the Duke, to bring him to consent to do so mortifying a thing. He brought him to it at last. He then sent for me, and told me what Discourse he had had with the Duke of *Almeida*, demanding if I would be content with the Reparation they two had agreed upon. I replied, Yes; and would be so far from striking the Offender, that I would not take the Stick he presented to me. The Matter being thus regulated, the

P 3   Duke

Duke and I met one Day, at a certain
Hour, in the King's Apartment. His
Majesty took us into his Closet : Come,
says he to the Duke, acknowledge your
Fault, and deserve a Pardon. My Enemy then made Excuses to me, and presented me a Stick he had in his Hand.
Don *Pompeyo*, cries the King at the instant, Take the Stick, and let not my
Presence hinder you from doing Justice
to your injur'd Honour. I discharge
you from the Promise you made me,
not to strike the Duke. No, my Lord,
replied I; 'tis sufficient that he puts
himself in a Posture to receive the Blows.
An affronted *Spaniard* demands no more.
Well, says the King, since you are
both content with this Satisfaction, you
may now determine the Matter in a re-
gular Way, at the Points of your
Swords. That's what I earnestly desire, cries the Duke ; and nothing but
that can make me reconcile myself to
the shameful Step I have been taking.
At these Words he went out, full of
Rage and Confusion ; and two Hours
after he sent to tell me he waited for
me in a Bye-Place ; I went thither, and
found him there in a Disposition to
fight it out to the last. He was not a-
bove

bove Five and Forty Years of Age. He
wanted neither Courage nor Skill. The
Parly was equal between us. Come,
Don *Pompeyo*, says he, let us end our
Difference. We both of us have reason
to be angry; you for the Treatment you
met with from me; and I for having
ask'd your Pardon: Saying this, he drew
so quickly that I had scarce time to be
upon my Guard. He push'd at first
very vigorously; but I had the good
Fortune to parry all his Passes. I push'd
at him in my Turn; and found I had
to do with a Man who knew as well
how to defend himself as to attack. I
know not what might have happen'd,
had not his Foot slipt in retiring, and
that Slip threw him on his Back. I
then held my Hand, and said, Rise.
Why do you spare me? replied he:
your Mercy is an Affront to me. I
shall take no Advantage of your Misfortune, says I: 'Twould be an Injury to my Glory. I say once more, Rise,
and let us continue the Combat. Don
Pompeyo, replied he, getting up, After
so generous an Action, Honour will
not permit me to fight against you.
What would the World say of me, if
I should kill you? I should pass for a

P. 4   Scoun-

Scoundrel, that took away the Life of a Man who might have taken mine. I shall not put it in any danger, and I find my Gratitude gives birth to soft Transports which succeed the furious Emotions that before ruffled my Soul. Don *Pompeyo*, continues he, let us cease hating one another; let's do more. let us be Friends, Ah! my Lord, cry'd I, I accept of your agreeable Proposal with Joy. I swear to you from this Moment a sincere Friendship; and to give you present Proofs of it, I add to it, that I will never set foot within *Hortensia's* Doors again, tho' she should desire it. No, says he, I ought rather to yield the Lady to you, since she prefers you in her Heart. But you Love her, reply'd I, interrupting him; and her Kindness to me may be troublesome to you, I'll sacrifice it to your Ease. Ah! too generous *Castilian*, cries the Duke, holding me fast in his Arms, how am I charm'd with your Sentiments? What Remorse do they create in my Mind! With what Grief, with what Shame do I remember the Outrage you have received. The Satisfaction I gave you in the King's Cabinet, appears to me now to be too small; I will make better Reparation for the Affront; and to blot
out

out the Infamy of it for ever, I offer you
one of my Neeces, who is at my Dif-
pofal. She is a Rich Heirefs of Fifteen
Years of Age, and fairer ftill than fhe is
young. I return'd the Duke's Compliments as refpectfully as the Honour he
did me to receive me into his Alliance
deferv'd. I Married his Neece a few
Days after; the whole Court commended this Lord for making the Fortune of
a Young Gentleman, whom he had
cover'd with Infamy: And my Friends
rejoyced with me, that an Adventure,
which might have ended fo fatally, had
fuch an happy Iffue. Ever fince that
Time, Gentlemen, I have liv'd very
pleafantly at *Lisbon*. I am belov'd by
my Spoufe, and ftill love her; the Duke
of *Almeyda* is always giving me New
Tokens of his Friendfhip, and I may fay
without boafting, that I am ftill well
with the King of *Portugal*. The Importance of my prefent Journey to *Madrid*, affures me that I am ftill in his
Efteem.

P 5   C H A P.

CHAP. VIII.

By what Accident Gil Blas *was obliged to look out for a New Place.*

THUS did Don *Pompeyo* finish his Story, which Don Alexio's Valet and I hearkened to in an Outer Room, for they had taken care to dismiss us from theirs before he began it. We stay'd behind the Door, and listen'd so attentively that we did not lose a Word. After this, these Lords drank on, but they left off before Morning, because *Pompeyo* was to be early with the Prime Minister, and desir'd to have a little Rest. The Marquis de *Zenete* and my Master embraced that Gentleman, bid him farewell, and left him with his Kinsman.

We went to Bed for this Time before Day-light, and when Don *Matthias* a-woke he gave me a New Employment. *Gil Blas*, says he, Take Pen, Ink and Paper, and write Two or Three Words for me, which I will dictate to thee. I make thee my Secretary. So, says I to
my-

myself, this is a new Bufinefs for me;
As a Lackey, I follow my Mafter every-
where; as Valet de Chambre, I Drefs
him; and Write for him as Secretary,
Heaven be prais'd, I am going like the
Threefold *Hecate*, to act three different
Parts. Thou doft not know, continues
my Mafter what my Defign is, but be
difcreet and I'll tell thee; 'tis as much as
thy Life is worth to fay any Thing. As
I meet every Day with Perfons who
boaft of Ladies Favours: To give them
as good as they bring, I'll have Counterfeit Letters in my Pocket, which I
will pretend came from Women, and
read 'em to them. This will divert me, and make me happier than
my Fellows, who are at the pains to obtain Conquefts, meerly for the Pleafure
of publifhing them; whereas I will
publifh them, and be at no Pains in ob-
taining them; But, added he, fo difguife thy Hand, that the Billets may not
appear to come all from one Perfon.

I took Pen, Ink and Paper, made my
felf ready to obey Don *Matthias*'s Commands, and he dictated a Billet to me in
the following Terms. *You was not laft
Night at the Place of Affignation. Ah! Don
Matthias, what can you fay in your Jufti-
fication.*

fication ? How was I mistaken : You have justly punished me for believing that all the Amusements, all the Business in the World, should give way to the Pleasure of your seeing Donna Clara de Mendoza. This Billet being done, he dictated another to me, as from a Woman which had left a Prince for him ; and after this a Third, from a Lady who told him if she could be sure he would be discreet, she would take a Voyage with him to the Island of *Venus.* He not only caus'd me to write the Letters, but to set the Names of Persons of Quality to them. I cou'd not help telling him I thought that was too nice and perilous a Matter, but he desir'd me to give him Advice only when he ask'd it. I was forc'd to hold my Tongue and to follow his Orders. This Affair dispatch'd, he rose, and I help'd dress him. He put the Letters in his Pocket, went out, and I waited on him to Don *Juan de Moncado,* who that Day treated five or six Gentlemen his Friends. There was Plenty of all Things, and of Joy, which gives the best Relish to them at all Festivals. Every one of the Guests contributed to keep up the Conversation, some by Witticisms, others by Stories of which they made themselves always
the

the Heroes. My Mafter did not lofe fo
fair an Opportunity to value himfelf on
the Letters he had made me write; he
read them out to the Company, and
with fo confident an Air, that every one
but his Secretary might have been deceived by it. Among the Gentlemen to
whom he read them, there was one
nam'd Don *Lovez de Velafco*. This Man
who was very grave, inftead of doing
like the reft, and congratulating the
Reader on the Favours he had received
from thofe Ladies, demanded of him,
fullenly, if the Conqueft of *Donna Clara*
came Cheaply? Very eafily, reply'd Don
Matthias; fhe made all the Advances; fhe
met me in the Walks; fhe lik'd me, fent
after me, underftood who I was, wrote
me a Billet, appointed me to come to
her at fuch an Hour in the Night, when
all the Family was a-bed but her felf and
her Woman. I went to her Houfe, was
introduced to her Appartment——— I
muft beg Pardon if I fay no more: It is
not confiftent with Difcretion.

At this Laconick Recital, *Signor de
Velafco* chang'd Countenance; and it was
plain he had an Intereft in the Lady that
was the Subject of it. All thofe Billets,
fays he to my Mafter, cafting a furious

Look

Look at him, are Counterfeited, and especially that you boast to have received from *Donna Clara de Mendoza*: There is not a more reserv'd Lady in *Spain*: A Gentleman every way equal to you in Birth and Merit, has Courted her these Two Years, and has scarce been able to obtain the most Innocent Favours; and may flatter himself, that if ever she granted any others, it would be to himself only. How, Sir! do you say the contrary? replies Don *Matthias* in a merry way: I agree with you she is a Lady of nice Honour. And I too am a Man of nice Honour; consequently you ought to be satisfy'd that nothing but what was very Honourable past between us. Don *Lopez*, interrupting him, said, This won't do, Sir; let us have none of your Rallery: you are an Impostor: *Donna Clara* never had an Assignation with you by Night: I can't bear your injuring her Reputation. I need not tell you any more. At these Words, he broke up abruptly, and went away in a manner that shew'd this Affair wou'd have ill Consequences. My Master, who was brave enough for a Man of his Character, despis'd Don *Lopez's* Threats. What a Coxcomb he is? cry'd he, bursting out a Laughing; Knight Errants

Errants vindicate the Beauty, of their Miſtreſſes; He will vindicate the Vertue of his; which I think is much more extravagant.

Velaſco's withdrawing, which *Moncado* in vain endeavoured to hinder, did not break up the Company. The Gentlemen took little Notice of it, and went on Carouſing till Morning: By Five a Clock my Maſter and I were got to Bed. I was very ſleepy, and made account to have a good long Nap of it; but I reckon'd without my Hoſt, or rather without our Porter, who awak'd me an Hour after, to tell me there was a Youth demanded to ſpeak with me. The Duce take the Porter, cry'd I, gaping; Doſt thou not know that I have not been in Bed an Hour? Tell the young Man I am aſleep, and that he muſt call again. He ſays he muſt needs ſpeak with you this Minute, reply'd the Porter. Upon which I got up, ſlipt on my Coat and Breeches and went down, curſing the Perſon whom I was going to. Friend, ſays I, be pleas'd to tell me what preſſing Affair procures me the Honour of ſeeing you ſo early. I have a Letter, anſwer'd he, to give into Don *Matthias*'s own Hand, and he muſt read it this Inſtant, 'tis of that

vaſt

vaſt Conſequence : I deſire you would introduce me to him. Believing 'twas a Matter of Importance, I took the liberty to wake my Maſter. Your Pardon, Sir, for diſturbing your Reſt, ſaid I ; but the Importance—What woud'ſt thou have with me? cry'd he, interrupting me. My Lord, ſays the Young Man who accompanied me, I have a Letter to deliver you from Don *Lopez de Velaſco*. Don *Matthias* took the Billet, open'd it ; and having read it, ſaid to Don *Lopez*'s Valet, Child, I don't riſe before Noon, whatever Diverſion is propos'd to me to tempt me , think then, if I will riſe at Six a Clock in the Morning to fight. Tell thy Maſter, if he is at the ſame Place at Two a Clock, I'll be with him. Go, carry him that Anſwer. At theſe Words he ſunk down in his Bed and fell aſleep again.

He roſe, and dreſt himſelf very compoſedly between One and Two a Clock, ſaying, when he went out, that I need not follow him. But I was too impatient to ſee what became of him, to obey his Commands. I walk'd after him till I came to St. *Jerom*'s Walks, where I perceiv'd Don *Velaſco* ſtay'd expecting him. They drew and fell to it immediately :

diately: The Battle was long. They push'd both with great Vigour and Dexterity. At last Victory declared for Don Lopez : He ran my Master through. Don *Matthias* fell, and Don *Lopez* fled, very well fatisfy'd with the Vengeance he had taken. I made what haste I could to assist my Master : I found him just departing. The fight drew Tears from me, and especially when I consider'd that he had made me the Instrument of his Death. But notwithstanding my Grief, I thought of what I had to do for my own Interest on this Occasion. I return'd Home immediately, without saying any Thing, I bundled up my Cloaths and other Goods I and by mistake put some of my Master's among them. I carry'd the Bundle to the Barber's, and then reported about Town the fad Accident of which I had been a Witness. I told every body that would hear me, and did not fail to make a Report of it to *Rodriguez.* He feemed to be less afflicted than studious about the Measures he was to take: He affembled Don *Matthias's* Domesticks, order'd them to follow him, and went with 'em to St. *Jerom's* Walks. We lifted our dying Master up, and carry'd him Home, for he Breath'd still, but Dy'd Two

Hours

Hours after. Thus perish'd Signor Don
Matthias de Silva, for reading *Mala pro-*
pos, some Counterfeit Billetdeux.

CHAP. IX.

What Person he enter'd into the Ser-
vice of, after the Death of Don
Matthias de Silva.

SOME Days after the Funeral of Don
Matthias, his Domesticks were all
paid off and dismiss. I took up my
Quarters at my Barber's, with whom
I liv'd very Friendly, and lik'd living
there much better than at *Malendez's*.
Having Money in my Pocket, I was not
in haste for a Service; besides, 'twas not
now every Place that would please me.
I would wait on no ordinary Person, and
resolv'd to be very Scrupulous in my
Choice of a Master. I did not think the
best too good for me; so favourable an
Opinion had I conceived of a Young
Lord's Valet preferable to all others.

While

While I was waiting for a Place equal to my Merit, I thought I could not spend my Time better than by passing some of my idle Hours with my fair *Laura*, whom I had not seen ever since we made the Discovery of our selves. I durst not Dress my self like Don *Cæsar de Ribera*, nor, unless it was for a Disguise, put on that Habit, without passing for a Madman ; my own Cloaths were still pretty fresh, and, by the Barber's Assistance, I adjusted my self the middle way, between Don *Cæsar* and *Gil Blas*. Thus equipp'd, I went to *Arsenia*'s House, where I found *Laura* in the same Room we formerly met in, and by her self. Is it you ? cry'd she, as soon as she saw me; I thought you had been lost ; 'tis a Week ago that you promised to see me : I perceive you are a Man of your Word, especially with the Ladies.

I excus'd my self, on Account of the Death of my Master, the Affairs I had had to do ; and added very gallantly, that in the midst of all of 'em the amiable *Laura* ran still in my Mind. If it be so, reply'd she, I have no more Reproaches to make you, and must own that I thought of you too. As soon as I heard of Don *Matthias*'s Misfortune, I
form'd

form'd a Defign that perhaps will not difpleafe you. I have heard my Miftrefs
fay often, that fhe wanted a Man to be
a fort of a Steward, and keep an exact
Account of all the Money given him for
the Expences of the Houfe : I have caft
my Eye on your Lordfhip : I fancy you
may go thro' fuch an Employment well
enough. And I fancy, reply'd I, I fhou'd
do it to a Miracle ; I have read the OEco-
nomiques of *Ariftotle* : and for keeping
Accounts, 'tis my Mafter-piece. But
Child, continued I, I have one Scruple
upon me concerning my ferving *Arfenia.*
What Scruple? fays *Laura.* I have taken
an Oath, reply'd I, not to ferve a Citizen:
Nay, I have Sworn it by *Styx.* If *Jupiter*
durft not break that Oath, judge you
whether a Valet may ? What do you
mean by a Citizen ? cries the Woman of
Arfenia ! What do you take us Players to
be ? Do you level us with the Wives of
Mechanicks or Attorneys? Know, Friend,
that Actreffes are Noble and Arch-Noble,
by the Alliances they contract with great
Lords. On this Foot, fays I, I may accept the Place you have cut out for me :
I fhall not demean my felf. No no, replies fhe, to pafs from the Service of a
Beau, to that of a Stage Heroin Tis ftill
the

the fame World. We go Cheek by Jowle
with People of Quality : We have the
fame Equipages ; we live as well, and in
the main, act the fame Parts of Life.
Indeed, Where's the Difference between a
Marquis and a Player, take them all the
Day long ? If the Marquis is three quarters of the Day above the Player by Birth,
the Player for the other Quarter is ftill
more above him by the Part of Emperor
or King which he Acts. This methinks,
is a Compenfation for our want of Nobility and Grandeur, and equals us with
the Lords and Ladies of the Court. Yes,
truly, reply'd I, you are Tallies one to a-
nother. I find Players are not fuch Scoun-
drels as I took 'em for, and you have
given me a great defire to ferve Perfons of
fo much Honour. Come then, fays fhe,
Two Days hence, I need no more Time
to difpofe my Miftrefs to take thee : I'll
fpeak in thy Favour ; and having an Af-
cendant over her, I'm fatisfy'd I fhall
fucceed in it.

I thank'd *Laura* for her Good-will. I
let her fee that my Gratitude wou'd have
no Bounds, and affur'd her of it with
Tranfports which left her no room to
doubt it. We had a long Converfation ;
and it had been longer, if a Foot-Boy had

not

not come and told my Princefs that *Arfenia* wanted her. We then parted : I went
Home in fweet hopes of an Employ to
my liking, and was punctual to *Laura's*
Appointment Two Days after. I expected thee, faid *Arfenia's* waiting Woman, to inform thee that thou art In-
tendant of this Houfhold. Follow me,
I'll prefent thee to my Miftrefs. At thefe
Words fhe led me thro' an Appartment
confifting of five or fix Rooms within one
another all richly furnifh'd.

What Luxury ! What Magnificence !
I thought my felf in the Houfe of a Vice-
Queen, or rather, that I faw all the
Riches of the World heap'd together in
one Place. True, there were the Riches
of feveral Nations, and that Apartment
might be defin'd to be the Temple of a
Goddefs, where each Traveller brings
an Offering of the Rarities of his Country. I faw the Goddefs fitting on a Sat-
tin Couch, fhe look'd Charming and
Plump with the Fumes of the Sacrifices :
fhe was in a gallant Difhabillé, and her
fairHands were preparing a newHead-drefs
for her to Act her Part in the next Day.
Madam, fays her Woman, This is the
Steward I fpoke of ; I will affure you,
you cannot have a better. *Arfenia* look'd
atten-

attentively upon me, and I had the good
luck not to difpleafe her. So, *Laura*, cries
fhe, 'Tis a prettyLad, and I doubt not but
I fhall like him. Child, added fhe to me,
I receive you into my Service, and have
only one Word to fay to you. You will
have no Reafon to be diffatisfy'd with
me, if I have none to be fo with you.
I anfwer'd, I would do my utmoft to
give her Content. And perceiving we
were agreed, I went for my Cloaths,
and took immediate Poffeffion of my
Poft in her Houfe.

CHAP. X.

Which is not longer than the pre-
ceding One.

'TWAS near Play Time. My Miftrefs
bid me wait on her, with *Laura*, to
the Theatre. We enter'd her Shift, where
fhe took off her ordinary Drefs, and put
on a more Pompous one to Play in.
When the Curtain was drawn, *Laura*
took me with her to a Place where we
could

could fee and hear the Actors perfectly
well. I did not like the greateft Part of
them, occafion'd without doubt by what
I heard Don *Pompeyo* fay to their Prejudice. However, feveral of them were
clap'd, and fome of thofe put me in mind
of the Fable of the Sucking Pig.

Laura told me the Names of the
Actors and Actreffes, as they came upon the Stage. She not only nam'd them,
but with Characters that were as divert-
ing as they were malicious. This Actor
fays fhe, is a Blockhead, that a Bully ;
that Minx whom you fee there, and who
looks fo fmirkingly, is call'd *Rofanda* ;
the Company has but a bad Bargain in
her, fhe ought to be lifted in the Band
that's raifing for the Vice-Roy of *Mexico*,
and to be fuddenly Ship'd off: Behold
that Bright Star advancing there, that
Setting Sun ; 'tis *Cafilda* ; if fhe had re-
quir'd a piece of Marble out of every
Lover, to build a Pyramid, as did here-
tofore a Princefs of *Egypt*, fhe might have
rais'd one as high as the Heavens. In
fine, *Laura* rail'd at them all alike, the
Baggage fpar'd not even her own Miftrefs. However, I muft own my Weaknefs ; I was charm'd with *Laura*, tho'
her Character was not morally good. She
rail'd

rail'd with a Grace that made me in
love even with her Malice. She rose between the Acts to see if *Arsenia* wanted
her; but instead of coming to her Place
again, she stay'd chatting with the Fellows behind the Scenes. I follow'd her
once to watch her, and observ'd she had
abundance of Acquaintance. I told three
Players that stopt her, one after another,
to talk to her, and I saw they did it with
great Familiarity, I was not pleas'd with
it, and it was then the first time of my
Life that I knew what Jealousy was:
I went back to my Place so Thoughtful
and Sad, that *Laura* perceiv'd it as soon as
she return'd. What's the matter with
thee, *Gil Blas?* said she in a Surprize.
What Humour has taken thee since I left
thee? thou art melancholy and pensive.
? Tis not without Reason, my Princess,
reply'd I, your Aires are a little too free,
I saw you speak to the Players. A fine
Reason for you to be melancholy, said she,
smiling: Does that trouble you? You
must bear a great deal more, if you live
among Actors: you must learn our familiar Ways: No Jealousy, Child: Jealous
Folks: in the Comick World, pass for
Fools. Indeed there are no such Creatures here: Fathers, Husbands, Brothers,
Q Uncles

Uncles, Coufins, are, with us, the eafieft Perfons upon Earth, and very often make their Fortunes by it.

After having exhorted me to take Umbrage at no Body, and mind nothing I fee, fhe declar'd I was the happy Mortal who had found the way to her Heart, affuring me fhe wou'd always love me, and me only. Upon this, Affurance, which I might have fufpected, without paffing for a Diftruftful Perfon, I promis'd not to be allarm'd ; and I kept my Word. I faw her that very Moment Talk and Laugh with Men. When the Play was done, we return'd Home with our Miftrefs. *Florimonda* came thither foon after with three Old Lords, and a Player, who were to fup there. Befides *Laura* and me, there were a Cook, a Coach-man, and a Foot-boy in the Houfe : We join'd all five to get the Supper ready. The Cook, who underftood her Bufinefs as well as Dame *Jacinta*, prepar'd the Difhes, the Coach-man affifting her ; the Waiting-woman and the Foot-boy laid the Cloth, and I fet out the Buffett, where were placed feveral Veffels of Silver and Gold, and other Offerings which the Goddefs had receiv'd. I furnifh'd it alfo with Bottles of different Wine, and ferv'd serv'd as Butler; to shew my Mistress I was fit for any thing. I observ'd the Looks of the Players during the Entertainment. They carry'd themselves like Ladies of Importance: They imagin'd themselves to be Women of the first Quality. Instead of giving the Lords the Title of *Excellency*, they gave 'em only that of *Lordship*, calling them plainly by their Names. 'Tis true, the Lords themselves spoil'd them, by rendring them so familiar with them. The Player, on his side, accustom'd to act the Hero, behav'd himself with those Lords *sans Ceremonie*: He toasted their Healths, and one wou'd have thought expected to have been toasted in his Turn.

Floridor, a vain empty Fellow, who got his first Name on the Stage, by representing a Thing of as little Wit and as much Vanity as himself, a Composition of Levity and Grimace; this same *Floridor*, from wearing a Livery, is admitted to sit down with Gentlemen and Persons of Condition, and even to call *Ovid* and *Terence*, two celebrated *Wits*, his Friends.

By the Behaviour of my Mistress and *Florimonda* with the Old Lords, I thought to my self, what *Laura* told me, the

Q 2 Marquis

Marquis and the Player were equal all
Day; she might have added, they are
much more so at Night, which they
spent together over their Cups. *Arsenia*
and *Florimonda* were naturally Wanton;
a thousand bold Touches escaped them
in their Discourse, intermix'd with small
Favours and Toyings, which were sa-
voury Things to those Old Sinners.
While my Mistress was amusing one of
them with some innocent Banter, her
Friend, who sat between the two others,
did not act the *Susannah*. As I was considering this Picture, which had but too
many Charms for a Lad of my Age,
Fruit was brought in. I then fill'd the
Table with Bottles and Glasses, and va-
nish'd to sup with *Laura*, who waited
for me. What dost thou think of those
Lords, says she, *Gil Blas?* They are,
doubtless, replied I, Adorers of *Arsenia*
and *Florimonda*. No, cry'd she, they are
Old Lechers who visit all Coquets alike,
and engage with none in particular:
They ask but a little Complacency of
them, and are Generous enough to pay
well for the Trifles that are granted
them. *Florimonda* and my Mistress have
no Lovers at this time, I mean, no such
Lovers as assume the Authority of Husbands:

bands; and wou'd have all the Pleasures of a House, because they are at all the Expence. As for me, I am glad of it, and maintain, that a Coquet of Sense ought to avoid such Engagements. Why shou'd they suffer any one Man to be their Master? They had better live meanly by getting a Peny a Time, than flourish on such hard Terms.

When *Laura*'s Tongue was once set a-going 'twas not an easy Matter to stop it. Words cost her nothing. What a Flux of Language! She told me a hundred Adventures, what had happen'd to the Actresses of the Prince's Company; and I concluded, from her Discourse, that I cou'd not be better plac'd, to acquaint my self perfectly with Vice. I was unhappily of an Age when it does not strike People with Horror; and the Truth is, the Baggage knew how to give such Colour to it, that nothing appear'd but what was Delicious. She had not Time to tell me the tenth part of the Exploits of the Actresses, for we were but three Hours together. The Lord and the Player retir'd with *Florimonda*, whom they saw Home.

When they were gone, *Arsenia* putting some Money into my Hand, said, There,

Gil Blas, are 10 Pistoles for thee to go to Market with. Five or six of our Gentlemen and Ladies Dine here to Morrow, be sure take Care that we want for nothing. With this Money, Madam, reply'd I, I'll engage to buy enough to Entertain the whole *Troop*. Pray, Friend, says she, interrupting me, correct your Expressions. You must never say *Troop*, but *Company*. You call a parcel of Banditti a *Troop :* The same is the Phrase when you speak of Beggars and Authors; but when you talk of *Players*, you must always say a *Company*, especially if you are speaking of the Actors of *Madrid*, who very well deserve to be call'd a *Company*. I ask'd my Mistress's Pardon, for making use of so disrespectful a Term. I humbly entreated her to excuse my Ignorance, protesting that for the future, whenever I speak of Messieurs the Players of *Madrid*, in a collective manner, I would always say the *Company*.

CHAP.

CHAP. XI.

How the Players live together, and af-
ter what Manner they Treat the Au-
thors.

NExt Morning I went to Market to
exercife my Employment of Steward: 'Twas a Faſt-Day, but by my
Miſtreſs's Order I bought ſome good
fat Pullets, ſome Rabbets, Partridges,
and other Poultry. As Meſſieurs the
Players were not entirely ſatisfied with
the Manners of the Church, they did not
then exactly follow her Commandments.
I brought home as much Proviſion as
would have ſerv'd a dozen honeſt Gentlemen for three Days in Carnival-time.
The Cook had Work enough all the
Forenoon. While Dinner was getting
ready, *Arſenia* roſe, and was at her Toi-
let 'till Noon, when Signors *Roſmairo* and
Ricardo came. After them, arrived two
Actreſſes, *Conſtantia* and *Celinaxra*, and
a moment after *Florimonda*, accompanied
with a Man who had the Air of a moſt

Q 4

foppiſh

foppifh Cavalier: His Hair was ty'd
behind with Colour'd Ribbands, his
Hat was cock'd, and in it he wore
a Red Feather: His fine Shirt was
fhewn at his Bofom : His Gloves and his
Pocket-handkerchief hung at his Sword's
hilt; and he wore his Cloak with a
grace particular to himfelf. Tho he had
a good Mien, and was well Shap'd, I
immediately faw fomething very fingular in him. This Gentleman, faid I to my
felf, muft needs be an Original. I was
not deceiv'd, his Character was a moft
diftinguifhing one. As foon as he enter'd
Arfenia's Appartment, he ran with open
Arms to the Actors and Actreffes and
embraced them with more Familiarity
than the young Beaux who affociated
with my Mafter made ufe of. I did not
change my Opinion when I heard him
open his Mouth ; he dwelt upon every
Syllable, and pronounced his Words in
an Emphatick Tone, with Looks and
Geftures accommodated to the Subject.
I had the Curiofity to ask *Laura* who
that Cavalier was ? Thou may'ft well
defire to know, fays fhe, 'tis impoffible
to fee and hear him, and not be curious
to know more of him ; his Name is *Signor Carlos Alonfo de la Ventoleria* ; he
was

was formerly a Player, he left the Stage
out of Humour, and has had sufficient
Reason to repent it. Didst thou take
notice of his black Hair? 'Tis a borrow'd *Teint* and so is that of his Eye-
brows and Mustachio ; he is Older than
Saturn. But his Parents having forgot
to have him Register'd when he was
born, he takes advantage of their negli-
gence, and says he's Twenty good Years
younger than he really is ; he is the full-
est of himself of any Man in *Spain*. He
almost reach'd his Fifteenth Year before
he could either write or read, and then
he took a *Preceptor*, who taught him to
Spell in *Greek* and *Latin*. He has abundance of Stories by Heart, which he has
told so often that at last he believes them,
he outs with them in all Companies ;
and one may say, that he frequently
shews his Wit at the Expence of his Memory. 'Tis said he is a great Actor ; I
must take other Peoples Word for it : I
confess I don't like him, I have heard
him sometimes rehearse here, and among
other Defects, found he has an affected
Pronunciation, and a quivering Voice
that gives it an Antick and ridiculous
Air.

Such

Such was the Picture that my Doxy
made of this Honorary Player, and indeed, I never saw a Man of a Prouder
Aspect ; he affected to speak finely, and
did not fail to take out of his Budget
Two or Three Stories, which he related
with a studied and imposing Air. On
the other Hand, the Actors and Actresses,
who did not come there to hold their
Tongues, were not mute ; they entertain'd themselves with their absent Companions, after a most uncharitable manner ; but that goes for nothing with
Players and Authors. They made no
Conscience of Back-biting their Neighbours. You don't know, Ladies, says *Ro-*
Sanairo, what our Dear Brother *Cesarino*
has done lately, he bought some Silk-
Stockings, some Ribbands and Gloves,
and had them brought this Morning, to
the House by a little Page, as if a Countess had sent them. What deceit there is
cries *Signor de la Ventoleberia*, with the
Air of a Coxcomb ; in my Time People
had more Integrity, we did not think
of putting such Tricks upon one another.
'Tis true, the Ladies took Care to spare
our Invention, they often made us Pre-
sents. S'death, cries *Ricardo*, with as much
Vanity as the old Player, so they do still.
If.

If it was permitted me to explain my
self thereupon, I cou'd——But one muſt
not tell certain Adventures, eſpecially
when Perſons of Rank are concern'd in
them.

Pray, Gentlemen, cries *Florimonda*, in-
terrupting them, don't brag of Ladies
Favours ; all the World knows what
Ladies they are---Let's talk of *Iſmenia* ;
'tis ſaid the Lord who ſpent ſo much
Money upon her, has left her at laſt.
Yes, ſays *Conſtantia*, and ſhe has loſt a
Tradeſman too, whom ſhe had almoſt
ruin'd, I know the occaſion of it. Her
Mercury ſerv'd her *qui pro quo*. He carry'd to the Lord a Letter ſhe wrote to
the Tradeſman, and gave the Tradeſman
the Letter ſhe wrote to the Lord. Great
Loſſes theſe, my dear replies *Florimonda*. As for the Lord ſays *Conſtantia*, he
had run out his Eſtate, but the Tradeſman had ſtill ſomething left, and was
worth keeping.

Such were the Subjects they talk'd of
before Dinner ; and while they were at
Table, I ſhou'd never have done if I
went about to repeat all the Scandal I
heard. The Reader will excuſe me for
omitting it, to tell how a poor Devil of
an

an Author, who came to *Arsenia's* when they had almost Din'd, was receiv'd.

Our Foot-Boy came and told my Mistress out a-loud, That a Man with foul Linen, dirty Shoes, and who, saving her Presence, look'd like a Poet, demanded to speak with her. Shew him in, reply'd *Arsenia*. Don't stir, Gentlemen; 'tis only our Author. So it was indeed, and one that had a Play in the House. He brought my Mistress her Part. His Name was *Pedro de Moya*: When he enter'd the Room, he made five or six low Bows to the Company, who took no manner of notice of him ; only *Arsenia* nodded her Head a little, in return for the Compliments with which he overwhelm'd her. He drew nearer to them, trembling, and in the utmost confusion: He let fall his Hat and Gloves, took them up, and approach'd my Mistress, to whom he presented her Part, with more Respect than a Lawyer gives a Petition to a Judge. Be pleas'd to accept Madam, says he, the Part I presume to offer you. She took it after a cold and scornful manner, and did not condescend so much as to answer his Compliments. This did not discourage our Author, who took hold of the Occasion, to
give

give another Part to *Rosinairo*, and another
to *Florimonda*, who treated him no more
Civilly than *Arsenia* had done. On the
contrary; the Player, as obliging as
these Gentlemen naturally are, insulted
him with the most picquant Rallery. *Pedro de Moya* was sensible of it, but durst
not retort, for fear his Play shou'd suffer.
He retir'd without saying a Word to
them in answer, but I cou'd perceive,
was mightily concern'd at the Reception
he met with. I doubt not but he pass'd his
Censures on the Players according to
their Deserts; and the Players, on the
other hand, began, as soon as he was gone,
to talk of the Author with as much
Courtesie. Methinks, says *Florimonda*;
Signor *Pedro de Moya* did not go away
very well satisfy'd.

Don't let that trouble you Madam,
cries *Rosinairo*. Are Authors worth minding ? If we suffered them to be equal
with us, it would spoil them. I know
those poor Creatures ; I know them full
well : They will presently forget themselves on the least Encouragement. Use
them like Slaves, and don't be afraid of
tiring out their Patience. It they leave
you sometimes in Anger, their Itch of
Writing will bring 'em back again, and
'tis

'tis enough for them that we will deign
to Act their Plays. Right. Says *Arsenia*; We never lose our Author, unless
he has made his Fortune ; and as soon as
that is done by our Merit only, he grows
lazy and Writes no more. True, the
Company can do without them, and the
Publick does not miss them.

This Discourse was applauded by them
all. As ill as the Actors treat the Authors, the latter have no help for it; and
the Players, by putting themselves above
them, shew what a contemptible Opinion they have of them.

CHAP. XII.

*Gil Blas took a Fancy to the Thea-
tre. He gives himself up to the Pleasures of the Stage, and in a little
while grows weary of them.*

OUR Guests sat at Table till it was
Time to go to the Theatre. I attended them thither, and saw the Play
again. I was so pleas'd with it, that I
resolv'd

resolv'd not to miss a Night. I never fail'd being there, and insensibly accustom'd my self to the Ways of the Actors. How wonderful is the Force of Habit ! I was particularly Charm'd with those that us'd most Rants and Gesticulations. I was not singular in it. The Beauty of the Pieces touch'd me as much as the manner of representing them; some of them put me into Transports; and I lik'd those best, where all the Cardinals, or the Twelve Peers of *France*, were introduced. I got some Parts of those incomparable Poems by Heart : I remembred I learn'd one entire Play, call'd the *Queen of Flowers*, in Two Days. The *Rose*, who was the Queen, had for her Confident the Violet, and for her Esquire the Jessamin. I thought nothing finer than such Works; as that, which, in my Opinion, did a great deal of Honour to the Wit of our Nation.

I was not contented with adorning my Mind with the fine Strokes of these Master-pieces of the *Drama*. I Labour'd to perfect my Joys, and in order to it, hearkened eagerly to whatever the Players said ; if they commended a Play, I esteem'd it; if they discommended, I despis'd it. I took it for granted, that

they

they underftood Plays, as Jewellers do Diamonds. Neverthelefs, *Don Pedro de Moya's* Play had a great Run, tho' they did not think it would have taken. However, I could not fufpect their Judgments; I had rather conclude that the Publick wanted common Senfe, than queftion the Infallibility of the Compa+ ny. But I was affur'd by every one, that the Plays, which the Players thought beft of, had generally the worft Succefs; and on the contrary, thofe that they dif, lik'd, were almoft always received with Applaufe. They told me they hardly ever hit right, and gave me Inftances of a thoufand Plays which fucceeded quite contrary to their Decifions. I had need of thefe, and many more Proofs, to give me an ill Opinion of the Excellence of their Tafte.

I fhall never forget what happen'd one Day at the Acting of a New Play. The Players thought it dull and tedious, nay, they imagin'd the Audience wou'd not hear it out : But they would venture, and Play'd the Firft Act, which was clap'd, and the Second more than the Firft. What a Devil, fays *Rofinairo*, this Play takes ! They then Play'd the Third Act, which pleas'd more than the Two former.

former. I can't comprehend it, says *Ricarda*, we concluded this Play would be damn'd---And see how'tis lik'd, Gentlemen, cries a Player that was by, with great plainnefs, there are a thoufand witty Strokes in it, which we did not obferve, and that's the Reafon of its Taking.

I ever after look'd upon the Actors to be wretched Judges, and gave them their Due, in my Sentiments of their Merit. They make good all the ridiculous Things the World fays of them. I have known Actors and Actreffes fpoil'd by being Clap'd; and looking on themfelves as Objects of Admiration, they have thought they did a Favour to the Publick when they Play'd. I was fhock'd with their Defects, but 'twas my Misfortune to take Delight in this way of Living, and to plunge myfelf in Debauchery. How could I help it? All their Difcourfe was pernicious to Youth, and I faw nothing but what contributed to corrupt me. If I had known nothing of what paft at *Cafilda's*, *Conftantia's*, and the other Actreffes, our own Houfe was enough to ruin all the Young Men in *Madrid*. 'Twas frequented not only
R   by

by old Lords, but by young Rakes, by Heirs juſt come to their Eſtates, by Citizens and Lawyers. The Grave and the Gay were confounded there, and every one welcome for his Money.

Florimonda, who liv'd in a Houſe in our Neighbourhood, Din'd and Supp'd every Day with *Arſenia*. There was ſuch a Friendſhip between 'em, that abundance of People were ſurpriz'd at it. They wonder'd Two Coquets could live ſo lovingly together, and doubted not but they would Quarrel one time or other about a Spark. In which they were miſtaken; they were hearty Friends: Inſtead of being jealous of each other, as the reſt of the Sex are, they liv'd in Common. They choſe to divide the Spoils of Men, rather than diſpute their Sighs.

Laura following the Example of thoſe two Illuſtrious Aſſociates, made the moſt of her Young Days. She had Reaſon to tell me I ſhou'd ſee fine Doings there. However, I was not jealous. I promis'd to imitate the Company in that Point ; I diſſembled my Sentiments for ſome time, and was ſatisfy'd with asking the Names of the Men whom I ſaw ſhe entertain'd in private. She always
told.

told me 'twas an Uncle, or a Coufin. She had, I found, a very numerous Family, exceeding that of King *Priam*. She did not content herfelf with Uncles and Coufins, fhe Convers'd alfo with Strangers, and Acted the Widow of Quality at the old Woman's I have fpoken of. In fine, *Laura*, to give a juft and exact Idea of her, was as young, as pretty, and as much a Coquet as her Miftrefs, who had no other Advantage of her, than that fhe publickly diverted the Publick.

I was borne down by the Torrent, for three Weeks ; I gave myfelf up to all manner of Pleafures ; but I muft own, that in the midft of them, I often felt that Remorfe which came from my Education, and imbitter'd all my Sweets : Debauchery, could not triumph over that Remorfe; on the contrary, it encreas'd in proportion with it, and by an effect of my natural Difpofition, I began to conceive a Horror for the Diforder of the Players Lives. Ah, Wretch ! cry'd I to myfelf, Is it thus that thou anfwereft the Expectation of thy Relations ? Is it not enough to have deceived them in chufing another Profeffion than that of a Preceptor ? Does thy fervile Condition hin-

der

der thy living like an honeſt Man ? Does
it become thee to live with ſuch wicked
people ? Envy, Choler and Avárice
reigns every-where among them. Mo-
deſty is baniſh'd by theſe : By thoſe,
Temperance and Induſtry : All of them
are Proud and Inſolent. In a Word, I
was reſolv'd to dwell no longer with
ſuch abandon'd Sinners.

End of the Firſt Volume.